Hope you enjoy the story —

Best,

For Renata *BRIAN*

a novel

B. Robert Sharry

ISBN:978-0615956817

For family and friends

1

Cape Ann, Massachusetts

Branca was giving advice about love and marriage to Renie, and it had Mamãe squirming in her seat.

"There are more tides than sailors," Branca said. "Take your mamãe, for instance. When she was a young girl, she was convinced that there was only one boy for her."

Branca shifted her gaze to Mamãe, hunched her shoulders, and teasingly made kissing noises. "His name was Mateus…"

"Enough, Branca," Mamãe said, "When your mouth is open, either a fly gets in or something silly gets out."

Branca was not deterred. She let her wrist fall limp and winked at Renie, but addressed Mamãe. "All I'm saying is that Mateus was obviously not the right man for you. Not to mention that, if your puppy love had not been interrupted, Renie would never have been born."

Mamãe looked for Renie's reaction and fretted about what might come out of Branca's mouth next. "The tourists will be here soon," she said, hoping to change the subject.

Memorial Day was approaching and soon throngs of pale-limbed tourists would descend upon Cape Ann—spreading themselves across the beaches by day, elbowing for space at lobster shacks in the evening. But for now the only sounds that could be heard inside the little cottage at Rose Hip Point were the loud calls of backyard chickadees mixed with the distant shrieks of gulls and the muffled explosions of ocean waves battering the cliff below.

The three women sat around the kitchen table with teacups nestled in their hands. These cups of tea were ritual—the pretext for an afternoon spent sharing, listening, and commiserating. For centuries this simple ceremony had conveyed a message: *Sit down, dear, have a cup of tea, and tell me all about it.*

The youngest of the women had unexpectedly appeared at her mother's door at 11:30 that morning. It was a two and a half hour drive from her home in the Berkshire Hills of Massachusetts. Mamãe could not remember Renie showing up without calling first since she was a college student with a laundry bag in tow, certainly not since her wedding fifteen years ago. And while Renie smiled amiably enough and made conversation, Mamãe detected strain behind the smile, indifference in the small talk. Her daughter's mind was far away and troubled.

Their conversation had been restricted to talk of gardening and recipes, even the weather. But when Renie's eyes welled up during a discussion of starting vegetable plants indoors from seeds, Mamãe could wait no longer.

"What is it, meu coração? What is the matter?" Mamãe asked in Portuguese-accented English.

Renie answered her mother but kept her gaze locked on her teacup. "Things at home are not...right. We've been fighting with each other for some time now."

"Fighting over what?"

"Oh, I don't know. Nothing, and everything."

"Will money solve your problem?"

"No, Mamãe, it's nothing like that, nothing so simple. I guess we've just grown apart."

"Grown apart?" said Branca in an accent identical to Mamãe's. "How does this happen? How does a woman let this happen?"

"Branca, please..." Mamãe said calmly.

"Auntie Branca, it's...more complicated than that," said Renie. She swept her black hair behind her ear, her eyes focusing on the rings on her left hand.

"This is not complicated," said Branca, a stubborn look on her face. "This is *marriage*. When I..."

Mamãe interrupted, "Has he hurt you, meu coração?"

"Not physically, although sometimes he gets so angry that it feels like he could easily lose control.

No, somehow he has a way of making me feel small."

"Ah—" Mamãe nodded knowingly, "—he beats you with his words."

"I've tried, Mamãe. I've tried so hard, for so long. But now I'm tired of trying, and I'm tired of feeling like I'm not good enough. I just don't care anymore. I've decided to leave him."

Mamãe reached over and placed her hand on Renie's. "Then it is good that you have come home. You are safe here."

"Well, I am not surprised," said Branca, "You waited too long to marry. You were almost *forty*. When you wait so long, the good ones are all taken, and you're left with the ones no one wanted in the first place or the ones who have been grown apart by the first wife, just like your Gerry.

"And why are you always attracted to older men? You've been that way for as long as I can remember. Always the man is much older. No wonder you grow apart.

"When my Fabio was alive, he didn't grow anywhere, I saw to *that*."

Tears flowed down Renie's cheeks. "Oh, Mamãe," she cried as she leaned in toward her mother. Mamãe leaned in too, and they met in a sitting embrace.

"I know, I know," said Mamãe.

Watching her sister and niece hold each other, Branca's face softened, as did her words. "Well, the important thing is that you're home with your family now. And as your mamãe has said, you are safe with us."

"Thank you, Titia Branca," said Renie as she rose from the table and leaned down to hug her.

"Besides," Branca said, returning her hug, "he is not even Portuguese. What were you thinking?"

In response to an astonished look from Renie and an icy stare from Mamãe, Branca added, "Well?"

Mamãe stood. "Branca and I will go with you to collect the things that are yours. We will go when he is at work."

"What about my studio, my students?"

"Your students will find a new teacher, and you will start a new studio here on Cape Ann."

"Mamãe, I don't have to come here. I'm fifty-five years old. I shouldn't be running home to my mother."

"Do not talk this way, meu coração. This is your home too, and it always will be. You are welcome to stay for as long as you'd like. We have been through worse than this together, you and I, and together we will survive this too. This house belongs to all of us—me, you, and your sister. And someday, when I am gone, it will be yours and hers to do with as you please."

"My friend, Rinaldo, he is a real estate man," Branca said. "He says you sit on a fortune here. Things are different from fifty years ago when you first arrived. Rinaldo says rich people will pay big bucks to be on the water, even if they only come for a few weeks in summer. Imagine that. But I suppose it is the same back home now. The sea will always have its allure."

"Let the rich people have it then," said Mamãe. "Perhaps we should have sold it long ago, right after…"

Renie leaned over and squeezed her mother's hand. "Don't, Mamãe, don't think about that now."

But it was too late. Mamãe was already thinking about it. Indeed, she thought about it every day of her life whether she wanted to or not. She closed her eyes and breathed deeply.

And Branca was mistaken: It had been more than fifty years since Mamãe's arrival in America. It was on August 12, 1957 when a frightened teen-aged girl came ashore at the Port of Boston.

FOR RENATA

2

City of Horta, Island of Faial, Azores

August 7, 1956

The girl ran along the dark, volcanic sands of Praia da Conceição with the uninhibited joy of a child and the grace and coordination of her fifteen years. A boy of equal age with an unruly mop of black curls followed close on her heels, but not too close—he'd learned the hard way about the sand the girl's feet kicked up as she ran.

Her swiftness raised a breeze that made her long, shiny hair float behind her like a bride's mantilla. The hem of her calf-length peasant dress hung heavy with saltwater from the times she had sprinted in and out of the surf.

God, she loved to run. And the longer she ran the more bliss she felt.

The setting sun caused her skin to glow the same copper color as the clear eyes that she now focused on the three beached dories that lay ahead. She knew the colorful boats and their owners, just as she knew everyone who worked and played on this beach.Running faster now, she aligned her long legs and sand-coated feet to meet the first of the boats at its broadest point. Three meters away now, each stride bringing her a meter closer. At last, with a grand jeté, she leaped over the first dory's mid-section and landed gracefully on the sand on the opposite side. She repeated this twice more until she had cleared all three with nimble hurdles.

Her exhilaration was at its peak, and she wondered if it could be possible to feel any happier or freer: *Perhaps in Heaven, perhaps dancing in Heaven.*

In the midst of her euphoria, she realized that her pet name had been called.

"Lindhina."

She stopped short and caused the boy trailing behind her to almost collide with her. The ends of her black hair fell to the small of her back, and they swayed as she turned toward the sound of her mother's voice.

Her mother called again in a tone that suggested it was the third or fourth time she'd had to say it. "Venha me ajudar com o jantar." *Come and help me with dinner.*

The girl smiled, perfect teeth gleaming. She was famished. She waved and called back, "Vindo." *Coming.*

Then she added, "Posso convidar Mateus para o jantar?" *Can Mateus come for dinner?*

"Não esta noite, Lindhina," her mother said. *Not tonight, my pretty little one.*

She turned round to face the boy and shrugged her shoulders. "Você vem para a minha janela mais tarde?" *Come to my window later?*

FOR RENATA

"Certamente." *Sure.*

She kissed him on the cheek, turned round again, and ran across the stone-covered square with its communal fountain.

Later, whenever Mamãe recalled that day she thought it would have been more apt if her mother had said, *Come and help me with dinner…and I will tell you the news that will kill your dreams.*

Gloucester, Massachusetts

There was a battle taking place in the Raposo kitchen on Portagee Hill. A battle Inacio Raposo knew he had already lost. A passerby might have thought that the argument /between mother and son was similar to that in millions of kitchens across America. But in this house, Elvis Presley was merely a convenient surrogate for an angry, frustrated young man who dared not challenge his mother over the true, underlying issue.

Inacio had turned up the radio volume.

SINCE MY BABY LEFT ME…

"Turn off that jungle noise," Angelina Raposo screamed in Portuguese.

Though Inacio could hear her perfectly well, he cupped his hand over his ear and said, "O quê?" *What?*

"Do you want the whole neighborhood to think a cartload of macacos has moved in here? What is wrong with you?"

"O quê?" Inacio said, louder this time.

10

The old woman charged at him with a wooden spoon. "Turn it off."

"Okay, okay. I didn't hear you." Inacio turned the radio off and slouched down at the kitchen table.

Angelina Raposo had worn only black since her husband and two older sons were lost at sea thirteen years ago. In her grief, the widow had taken to cooking and eating. Inacio regarded her as she moved back to the kitchen stove in a huff. Short and squat, a study in black with a perpetually stern expression, she reminded him of a photo of Queen Victoria he had seen in his junior high school history book.

She brought the conversation back to the real issue. "It's no use arguing," Angelina said in Portuguese. Wagging her wooden spoon, she added, "I gave you plenty of chances to find a wife on your own. Now, it's too late. Everything is settled. She will arrive in one year and you *will* marry her."

Inacio Raposo's mother had been hinting that it was time for him to settle down since his twentieth birthday. By then, he had already been working for six years. He paid his mother generous room and board and was in possession of a healthy savings account and a 1950 Oldsmobile Rocket 88.

On days off he always drove to the high school parking lot just as school was letting out. He had learned that nothing was more exhilarating to certain high school girls than a handsome older boy with money in his pocket and his own sports car.

FOR RENATA

Inacio would deftly sidestep his mother's coaxing with a "Yes, Mama," but as time went by Angelina became more insistent, finally saying, "You've been a playboy long enough. I want grandchildren, and you're my only hope."

By the time Inacio was twenty-four and still unmarried, Angelina Raposo had tired of his excuses and made it her business to find him a wife.

"Well, don't expect us to live *here*." And by "here," Inacio meant "*with you.*"

"Well, I know *that*," Angelina said. "You'll stay here only for a little while, until I can find a suitable place for you."

Though little taller than when he had begun the life of a fisherman at age fourteen, Inacio's appearance had been changed by time and weather. The smooth skin of youth had become a little coarser with each passing season. His deep brown eyes had lost the eagerness of adolescence.

Inacio stroked the black stubble on his tanned, angular face, eyed the letter and accompanying black and white photo on the kitchen table, and grunted.

"Besides," Angelina said, "she's healthy as a mule and has a very pleasant personality."

Inacio picked up the photo and studied it. He could tell by her squint that the sun had been in her eyes when the photo was taken. Her smile appeared forced. Her tits were practically nonexistent. And since the photo was from the waist up, he had no idea what her hips looked like.

B. ROBERT SHARRY

A mule with a pleasant personality — just what every man dreams of.

Horta, Azores

The girl sat at the long, wooden kitchen table, peeling potatoes with furious scrapes. "If I must marry, why can't I marry Mateus?" she cried out in Portuguese.

Her mother got very cross, and her eyes narrowed in suspicion. "Have you *been* with that boy?"

She knew what her mother meant. "No."

Her mother looked into her eyes for a long moment, judging whether or not she was telling the truth. Finally, looking relieved, she said, "Good. Now get this silliness out of your head. You are promised to Inacio Raposo. Your father and I have worked very hard for this. Do not be ungrateful, and do not sabotage all we have planned for your own good.

"And no more play. You are a woman now, and you will have to start acting like one. You will learn English, and do all the housework for the next year. I won't have the Raposos think I have sent them a child."

The girl began to weep. Her mother embraced her. "Don't cry, Lindhina. In one year you will leave the Azores for a better life in America.

"Why do you think I kept you in school with the priest for all these years? I want something better

FOR RENATA

for you. You can *read*, meu coração, something very few children or even adults can do here. Someday, when you have children of your own, you will know what it means to want the best for them, even if they do not see it.

"Look. The Raposos have sent a photo of Inacio. He is very handsome, no?"

3

August 1, 1957

The year had passed as her mother had promised. The girl had been taken out of school and become an apprentice dona de casa—*housewife*. She had cooked and scrubbed, laundered and mended, all under the supervising eyes of her mother. Thoughts of dance and Mateus seemed the faraway daydreams of a child now, surfacing only in the sad poetry she wrote late at night.

Most evenings, when the housework was done, she walked lackadaisically across town to the home of Senhorita Araújo to study the English language. During these walks she dwelled on her fate and the unfairness of it, the way no one—not her family or friends, not even Mateus—seemed to care that she would be leaving the island of Faial forever. And why must she leave? To be given like property to a man she had never met. *How can they love me if they're allowing this to happen? How can Mateus stand for it after all we have been to each other?*

FOR RENATA

The very idea made her angry and sad, and she contemplated the ways in which she might end her life in the name of love. Perhaps she would plunge a dagger into her heart, as Juliet had done, or make a lover's leap from a cliff, like an American Indian princess. *Then they'll be sorry.*

She had seen Mateus rarely over the past year. He didn't seem nearly as distraught as she'd thought he would be. She tried to hate him, but she couldn't. That morning she had entrusted a note to her sister, Branca, to give to Mateus at school.

At 11:00 p.m., barefoot and wearing a light cotton nightgown, the girl slipped out of her bedroom window and into the waiting arms of Mateus. Holding hands, they stole through the narrow stone pathways of the town. When they reached the southern end of the village, they left the road and hiked toward their Lugar Secreto—*Secret Place* – the flat top of an enormous boulder that overlooked a tiny cove. They had been coming there since they were ten years old. In daylight, they swam, sunbathed, and daydreamed. At night, they listened to the surf, talked about their dreams for the future, and wished upon the stars.

Their Secret Place could only be reached by climbing down a steep incline through thick brush. To see it, one needed to be directly above it. The flat-topped boulder had a black circle in the middle, the charred remains of their occasional fires. Tonight, the cove water below was black with a shimmering band of moonlight across it, but in sunlight it was as blue as the hydrangea blossoms that gave the island of Faial its nickname—Ilha Azul, *Blue Island.*

Eyeing the place from above caused the girl to remember: It had been a year ago, a carefree summer day. She was supposed to go to a neighboring village for a cousin's birthday party. But the cousin came down with the flu at the last minute, and the party was postponed.

She searched all over town for Mateus, and by early afternoon had decided to look for him at their Secret Place. She climbed down to this very spot and spied him from above. He was lying there on his back, naked, his head resting on his neatly folded clothing. She had last seen his penis when the two of them were five years old. Things had changed.

His bronze skin glowed in the afternoon sun except for the thick, black crop of hair at the base of his hardness. She squatted behind a low bush and surveyed his long, lean body as he slowly stroked himself.

She knew that Mateus was committing a sin and wondered if watching him was sinful too. But while she closed her eyes and turned her head, she found herself peering at him again after a few moments. He had cupped his scrotum with his left hand and was rubbing faster with his right.

Then he took a deep breath, held it, and pumped feverishly.

The girl stared, eyes wide and mouth agape.

FOR RENATA

Mateus let out a loud groan as the first of his seed shot out in a great arc. There came more spurts until a glistening stream ran from the hollow of his neck, down his breastbone and stomach, to his navel. His feet curled back, and his ribs and chest heaved as he started to breathe again.

The girl was jostled from the memory. "Hmm?" she said.

"Eu disse, 'Você está bem?'" Mateus said. *I said, Are you all right?*

The girl blushed at the realization that she herself was breathing heavily now. "Eu estou bem. Vamos continuar, estamos quase lá," *I'm fine. Let's keep going, we're almost there.*

She took his hand. "E eu tenho um presente para ti." *And I have a gift for you.*

Inacio Raposo stood before the bathroom mirror, coated his hands with Brylcreem and ran his fingers through his curly black hair. He'd had a sore throat for weeks now, but he wasn't about to let that hold him back. The *mule* with the *pleasant personality* would arrive in Gloucester on August 12th, and on the 16th he would be a married man. He only had two more weeks to sow his wild oats as far and wide as he could.

Tonight it would be with Rowena, a forty-year-old divorcee from New York City who came to her Cape Ann seaside cottage each July and August to escape the city heat. She would make dinner for them and serve it on an open porch that overlooked

Good Harbor Beach and the Atlantic. Then they would have each other for dessert.

The two lay on their backs on the flat-topped boulder, as they had hundreds of times before, and gazed at the night sky. Mateus put his hands behind his head and interlaced his fingers. The girl's hands rested primly on her stomach. They built no fire tonight. It was too warm for that. Despite the warmth of the still night air, the coolness of the stone beneath the girl penetrated her nightgown, and she shivered.   With eyes welling, she whispered, "I'm going to miss you so much."

"Me too," Mateus sighed.

"My heart hurts," she said, her voice breaking.

Mateus unlocked his fingers and stretched his left arm out. The girl instinctively raised her head. When she lowered it again, it came to rest on Mateus's solid bicep. His long, smooth fingers cupped her shoulder, and he drew her closer to him. They stayed that way in silence for a time before she garnered the courage to roll onto her side and place her left hand on his chest. She felt the beating of his heart against her fingers, and she rested her head on his chest so that she could hear it too.

Several times she took a full breath as if she were about to speak, and then sighed when courage deserted her. Finally, Mateus noticed. "O quê?" *What is it?*

After a moment, she closed her eyes tight and blurted out, "I want you to make love to me."

She felt his body tense.

FOR RENATA

"But your husband…" he said.

She pursed her lips and narrowed her eyes. "He's not my husband yet." She raised her head and looked into his eyes. Her face softened. "And I want to give myself to you. I love you."

She kissed him the way she had seen Sophia Loren kiss Marcello Mastroianni, the way she had practiced on her mirror and on her pillow.

But their love-making was not tragically beautiful, as she had imagined it would be. It was awkward, painful, and mercifully brief. Mateus had stayed dressed, lowering his pants to his knees, and she had hiked up her nightgown just enough for him to enter her.

Mateus did not gaze longingly into her eyes. He did not kiss her passionately or say, *I love you.* She winced with every painful thrust until he finished and collapsed atop her, panting.

She held him fast in her arms, stared up at a million stars, and wondered if Inacio Raposo would be able to tell that she was not a virgin.

On the porch overlooking the Atlantic, a wicker table held a flickering tea light, two dinner plates of half-eaten food, and two empty wine bottles. The wicker chairs were empty.

Rowena was bent over the porch railing, facing the rolling whitecaps that showed through the darkness. Inacio stood behind her, thrusting into her while balancing his wine glass on the small of her back. A cooling ocean breeze glided over his skin.

"That's it. That's the spot," she cried. "God, you know how to fuck me, don't you."

Inacio burned with fever. His body glistened with sweat, and his sore throat hurt like hell. For the first time in his life, fucking felt like a chore, and he slowed his pace.

"Don't stop *now*, baby, I'm gonna come," Rowena pleaded. She grabbed the porch railing tightly in her hands and rhythmically moved with him, smacking her bottom against his pelvis.

Inacio moved faster, pounding her until he felt her gush and heard her release a sound that was half scream, half laughter.

He withdrew from her slowly. Rowena made a guttural moan, and her upper body sagged limply over the railing, her legs and buttocks shuddering involuntarily.

Inacio hadn't climaxed, and he didn't care. He just wanted to get home and go to bed. He staggered a few feet to where their clothing lay in a crumpled heap. He bent to pick up his pants but was overcome with dizziness.

Rowena giggled. "I just might have to take you back to Manhattan with me."

The Portuguese fisherman tilted his head back and stared at a blur of stars. His body swayed, and then he collapsed.

FOR RENATA

4

August 7, 1957

The girl sat on the ferry, tightly clutching her suitcase and travel documents, and looked out the window at the pier. Her mother, father, and younger sister, Branca, stood on the dock. Her mother dabbed at tears with a handkerchief, her father smiled stoically, and ten-year-old Branca pouted down at the water. She looked around in vain for Mateus, and then cursed him.

The boat eased away from its mooring and began its run from Horta to the island of San Jorge, the first leg of the journey that would take her to Inacio Raposo in America. As the ferry gained speed, she finally caught sight of Mateus in the distance, leaning against a cedar tree. He stared at her but did not wave. *He's not waving because he's not going to say good-bye. He'll dive in and swim to me, and then together we'll go to Lisbon or maybe Rio de Janeiro.*

But Mateus didn't move from the cedar tree. The girl placed the fingertips of her right hand against the window and watched her childhood sweetheart and her hope shrink as the boat moved farther from shore. Eventually it turned, and Mateus and her entire family vanished from sight. She let her forehead fall against the window and wept.

Angelina Raposo climbed the stairs carrying a tray with a bowl of Portuguese fish soup, some homemade bread, and a cup of tea. Inacio had taken to bed the week before complaining of a sore throat, fever, and achiness. Mother and son had argued because Inacio would not eat.

"How can you get better if you don't eat?" Angelina had shouted.

"How can I eat when my throat is on fire and everything makes me queasy?" Inacio had rasped back.

But the black-clad widow was determined. Inacio would eat, even if she had to force him. At the top of the stairs she turned to the right, walked the few steps to Inacio's bedroom, and crossed the threshold."I don't want any argument from ..."

The old woman's eyes grew wide. She dropped the tray and ran for the telephone.

Angelina paced the floor by her front door and peered out the window every few seconds, willing the doctor to hurry. When he finally arrived, she threw open the front door and rushed out to meet him. She grabbed the doctor by the wrist and pulled him quickly up the stairs and into Inacio's bedroom.

Inacio was shivering and soaked with sweat. Angelina explained to the physician—in a mix of broken English and Portuguese—that she had earlier found her son delirious and violently twitching, as if in the throes of a seizure.

The doctor began his examination, but Angelina's incessant questions were so distracting that he finally escorted her from the room, told her to be quiet, and shut the door in her face. The old lady paced the hallway outside the bedroom and said the rosary in Portuguese until the doctor emerged from the room a few minutes later. Angelina glared at him.

He cleared his throat and delivered his diagnosis.

5

Mark Valente stood hunched over a laptop computer on the Cape Ann Oceanographic Institute's research vessel, *Ved-ava*, as the ship bobbed on the calm Atlantic. He was looking at a nautical chart, but his thoughts had turned to Jill, as they so often did.

They had met while undergraduates at Boston University. His major was biology, hers, political science. They had fallen in love and made the beginnings of a life together in a tiny hovel at the north end of Boston.

When Mark received his Ph.D., the Oceanographic Institute offered him a job. That night they celebrated at a small Italian restaurant. Later, after making love, they held each other in bed, kissing. Jill's eyes closed and her breathing became deeper with the beginnings of slumber.

Mark studied her face and stroked her blond hair. His heart joyful, he put his lips to hers and whispered, "Marry me?"

Jill's blue eyes opened wide, and she smiled. "I thought we didn't need that whole *marriage* thing."

"I need you, and I want to marry you."

"Then, yes."

But that had been twenty years ago, and Jill had been gone for ten years, now.

An intern entered the bridge, interrupting his thoughts. "Excuse me, Dr. Valente," he said, "but there's a call for you on the satellite phone."

"Do you know who it is?" Mark asked without taking his eyes from the computer.

"Somebody from a Veterans Affairs hospital. They said it's personal."

"Veterans Affairs? Hospital? Hmm." Mark stood up straight and made eye-contact with the young man. "Thank you, ah…"

"Carl."

"Thank you, Carl."

Mark took the phone and put it to his ear. "This is Mark Valente."

As he listened to the voice at the other end of the call, Mark's face turned ashen and his jaw slackened.

"Dr. Valente, are you still there?" the voice on the other end of the line asked when Mark let silence hang between them for a moment too long.

"Yes, yes, I'm here," he said. "Sorry, it's just a bit of a shock. Are you certain it's *him*?"

"Yes, we're certain. I take it you weren't aware of his condition."

Mark shook his head in disbelief. "I don't see how I could be. My uncle disappeared more than thirty-five years ago, and hasn't been heard from since."

Mark drove from his house on Cape Ann to the Soldiers' Home on the outskirts of Boston in less than an hour. He locked his pick-up truck with a click of the remote and walked across the parking lot.

This responsibility for Uncle Pete had been thrust upon him for no better reason than that he happened to be the man's next of kin. He just wanted to do his part and be done with it. He shook his head and took the marble steps of the large brick building two at a time.

He was torn by the prospect of coming face to face with his uncle. Mark's mother, Marybeth, had always spoken affectionately of her troubled brother, but Mark knew that Pete's disappearance had caused her a heartache that had stayed with her for the rest of her life.

Mark had never really known his uncle. He had met him a few times as a child, but he'd been too young to remember much. His mother had described Pete as "broken." The war had broken his body, she'd said, but a girl named Cindy had broken his heart and spirit. Mark's father just thought Pete was nuts.

Now, after decades of silence, Pete had turned up here. The Director of Social Services had tracked Mark down and asked if he'd be willing to become his uncle's court-appointed guardian. Because he knew it was what his mother would have wanted, Mark had agreed.

The clerk at the information desk directed Mark to the office of Dr. Patel, who explained that Peter

FOR RENATA

Ahearn suffered from a form of dementia, possibly early-onset Alzheimer's. "There's no way to know the cause for certain in a man so relatively young," she said. "But during his service in Vietnam, your uncle was exposed to Agent Orange.

"Peter spends most of his time sleeping or staring at the television. He seldom speaks anymore. And on the rare occasions when he does, it's usually incomprehensible, a kind of gibberish that sounds like *mee-nall-may-soo-ah*.

"If they mean anything at all, they might be Vietnamese words he learned long ago. Victims of dementia often remember the distant past with crystal clarity. But to be perfectly candid, we're somewhat baffled. When he was brought to us three months ago, his impairment seemed pretty moderate, and he was functioning and communicating rather well. He was diagnosed with MCI, or mild cognitive impairment, and I prescribed a daily dose of Aricept to help alleviate his symptoms.

"We completed a CT scan and an MRI, which showed some signs of plaque on his brain, as might be expected, but no indication of a tumor. Then he just stopped talking overnight — well, except for those sounds he makes..." the doctor paused for a moment. "The thing is: When he does that, he does it in a way that sounds as if he's practicing, like for a spelling test, like it's something he's afraid he'll forget. There is no medical reason for it that I can see. It's as if he just made a conscious decision to shut down."

B. ROBERT SHARRY

Mark nodded. "Doctor, you said someone brought him here: Who? And where did they bring him *from*?"

"Good questions, Mr. Valente. But I don't have the answers. I was hoping that *you* might know."

What Mark knew of Peter Ahearn would fit in a thimble: He only had a few blurry childhood memories of his own, and the recollections his mother had passed on to him over the years.

FOR RENATA

6

Hollistown Harbor,
Massachusetts

December 24, 1969

Seventeen-year-old Peter Ahearn sat on the mahogany piano bench and bowed his head over the old upright's keyboard. His smooth, long fingers skimmed across its keys.

Of the ten people in the room that evening, nine sang "Jingle Bells" to Peter's accompaniment. The lone abstainer was Cindy Everhart, Peter's girlfriend of eleven months and three days.

Peter's grandparents, Thomas and Elizabeth Ahearn, sang the loudest. They stood at opposite sides of the piano, waving their punch glasses from side to side like sloshing metronomes.

Peter's four-year-old nephew, Mark Valente, doe-eyed with a mop of dark brown hair, sat beside him on the piano bench. Peter's left arm was woven around Mark's tiny back and under his arm, so that Peter could play bass chords with his left hand while blocking the boy from banging on the piano keys.

B. ROBERT SHARRY

Mark's mother, Marybeth Ahearn Valente, carried silverware and napkins to the dining table. As she passed behind Peter and Mark, she bent down, kissed Mark on the cheek, and tousled Peter's long, wavy blond hair.

The oak pedestal dining table was usually round, but that night it was oval because two of its leaves had been added to accommodate grandparents and guests.

Tommy Ahearn sat at the table with Marybeth's husband, Chris Valente, and Cindy. Though Tommy wore civilian clothes, his unfashionably short hair gave away his military status.

The Ahearns' kitchen was enormous for the times. In addition to the oak table and eight matching chairs, there were two sofas, a wing chair, a built-in knotty-pine bookcase, and the late-nineteenth-century upright piano that Katherine had learned to play as a child. All three Ahearn children had taken lessons, but only Peter had practiced diligently and developed a passion for music.

Marybeth finished placing the silverware just as "Jingle Bells" ended.

Grandma said, "Peter, dear, play "Silent Night.""

"No," cried Grandpa, "That's too downbeat. How about "Deck The Halls"?"

"How about neither," Cindy murmured with a roll of her eyes.

Marybeth pretended not to hear.

"Deck the halls with boughs of holly…"

FOR RENATA

Marybeth looked at Cindy, smiled through gritted teeth, and sat down next to her. "Isn't it exciting that Pete's applied to Berklee Music School? I just know he'll get in."

"I guess," said Cindy.

"Don't you want him to, Cindy? It's not like he'd have to go away, he could just commute to Boston."

"It's not that. It's just stupid. It's not like he's going to come out of a music school and then get some great job, or anything. He'll just end up playing at bars here and maybe in Boston on weekends. In the end he'll be working at the fish processing plant anyway, so why waste the time and money?"

"Oh, but Cindy, he's dreamed about this for so long. And who knows? He might just surprise you and become a big success, or at least have fun trying. He's a really good musician, you know. He can listen to anything and play it by ear. And look how happy he is when he plays music."

"Yeah, maybe he can teach band." Cindy rose from the table, walked the few steps to the sideboard, and refilled her punch glass.

Marybeth slid her chair to the right, sidling up to Tommy, and fumed, "She is such a drag. What does Pete *see* in her, anyway?"

Tommy looked over at Cindy, made a show of glancing up and down her perfectly proportioned body, and then gave Marybeth a deadpan stare.

"Really?" she said, shaking her head. "Why do I even bother?"

Tommy grinned, put his arm around his sister, and pulled her in close. "Mother hen."

"I'm serious, Tommy. Look at her. She's just going to break his heart one day."

Tommy chuckled, and then stood up and kissed the top of his sister's head. Peter was playing a rock 'n' roll tune. Tommy walked toward their mother, his arms spread wide. "C'mon, Ma, let's show 'em how it's done."

"Tommy, stop," Katherine said. "You know I can't dance to this." When he stood his ground, she smiled. "Well, at least let me take off my apron," she said as she untied it and placed it on the counter.

Tommy swept her into the air and danced around with her in his arms.

Katherine giggled. "Tommy Ahearn, you put me down this instant." Then she called out to her husband. "John, tell your son to put me down."

"Put your mother down, son," John Ahearn said without looking up from his newspaper.

7

August 12, 1957

The ship sailed from The Azores to Bermuda, and then on to the Port of Boston. The girl followed the other passengers and eventually passed through customs.

A lanky, elderly man in a dark wool suit and red silk tie twirled a fedora in his hands as he approached her. He had a full head of thick, wiry salt-and-pepper hair and a matching mustache. The old man, who clearly recognized her from the photograph her mother had sent to Inacio's family, introduced himself as Pio Alpande, her fiancé's uncle.

She grasped his weathered hand, kissed it, and asked for his blessing. Pio smiled, gave his blessing, and donned his hat. He took the girl's scruffy suitcase in one hand, her arm in the other, and led her to a black 1950 Oldsmobile.

Uncle Pio smelled of tobacco and bay rum lotion, scents the girl found familiar and comforting. Once they were in the car, she had the opportunity to study his face and hands. They were tanned, creased, and rough. *The face and hands of a fisherman,* she thought.

During the hour-and-fifteen-minute drive through foggy mist, Pio told her of Inacio's illness: Rheumatic fever brought on by untreated strep throat. The doctor had prescribed antibiotics just in time to save Inacio's life. There was a chance of heart damage, but Inacio was young and strong, and would most likely have a full recovery.

The wedding, of course, would have to be postponed until Inacio was well enough.

Outwardly, the girl's face registered concern. But as she looked out the car window and watched the strange-looking houses of Massachusetts pass by, she felt a sense of relief, like a prisoner who had received a stay of execution.

Then she sat up straight. *The wedding would have to be postponed.* Her brow furrowed and she thought hard. *I should have had my monthly visit by now.*

Uncle Pio led the girl up three steps to the porch of the two-and-a-half story tan Victorian in the section of Gloucester known as Portagee Hill. The dark oak front door loomed before her like the mouth of a terrifying monster. What she had known in the back of her mind for the past year struck her with force: There was no going back. She froze in mid-step.

Uncle Pio turned to look at her, his weathered face a tableau of questions. The girl returned his gaze, her eyes fearful. After a moment, the old man's face broke into a comforting smile, and he held out one large, calloused hand. She hesitated before placing her delicate gloved hand in his. Pio gave a reassuring nod. The girl nodded back and swallowed hard, and then they went through the door together.

The two stood in the front hall. The house was much darker inside than she was used to, and it smelled of cooking spices and wood polish.

"Look what I have found," Pio Alpande announced in Portuguese, "the newest and most beautiful member of the family."

There was silence. The girl looked past the hall to the neatly furnished living and dining rooms. The house was much larger than most anything in Horta. So much shiny wood everywhere. *They must be very wealthy.*

She caught movement at the top of the stairs. A dark figure appeared.

"Ah, there you are," Pio called up the stairs to Angelina. Then he turned to the girl. "This is my sister, Senhora Raposo."

The girl's eyes had adjusted to the dimness. She saw Angelina's stern, shadowy face, and a slight gasp escaped her lips. "Bom dia, Senhora, prazer em conhecê-lo," the girl said, her voice shaking. *Hello, Senhora, it's nice to meet you.*

After a moment Angelina spoke. "Bom dia," she said without a hint of warmth. She continued in Portuguese, "Pio, take her to the kitchen and give her something to eat. I'll come down soon."

"How is Inacio?" Pio called up the stairs.

"No better, no worse. He sleeps now."

The girl wanted to scream at the old woman, *How long until I am married?*

She knew what happened to girls who became pregnant and did not marry soon. Her girlfriends at school had discussed it. The lucky ones went to convents for the rest of their lives. The others went to live in a *bordel*. Every girl in town had heard about Maria, who had been used by a rich boy from a banking family. He had told her he loved her and wanted to marry her, but only to trick her into giving him her flower. It was said that Maria now worked in a brothel in Spain where she was forced to service up to one hundred men a week.

I need to know: Will I be a married woman soon, or will I be exposed a whore and shipped back to Horta in disgrace?

FOR RENATA

8

August 22, 1957

She had been at the house of Angelina Raposo for one week now, and had yet to lay eyes on her fiancé. And this *was* the house of Angelina Raposo. The girl had learned that Angelina's brother, sweet Uncle Pio, had injured his back a few years prior, and was no longer able to perform the grueling work of a fisherman. He lived here at Angelina's pleasure, and helped his sister keep house.

She had tried to make herself useful by asking after chores that needed doing. But Angelina and Pio had developed their own routine, and the house was always spotless.

Pio had taken her to mass several times. Our Lady of Good Voyage was just a few blocks away. Sometimes, after church, they would take a different route home, past a Portuguese bakery. Pio had treated her to a *cavacas*—sweet popover—which the girl thought was scrumptious, and a *galão*—a café latte—which she thought tasted like mud compared to the one back home. Most importantly, though, he always offered cheery, reassuring conversation.

She spent the majority of her time in the house, reading and praying. And, as often as she dared, she asked Angelina when she would meet the man with whom she would be spending the rest of her life.

She was reading at the kitchen table one day when Pio and Angelina descended from the upstairs. Pio entered the kitchen first. He smiled at the girl, nodded his head, and gave a surreptitious thumbs-up sign. Angelina followed within seconds. She motioned to the girl, and said, "Come."

She followed Angelina, and as they climbed the stairs, she smoothed her dress and fixed her hair. She was about to meet her future.

Inacio sat up in bed, his skinny frame supported by two pillows. His bed sheets, pillowcases, and pajamas had been laundered and ironed by Angelina. Inacio's hair had grown long during his illness, but he was otherwise well-groomed, having shaved this morning for the first time in weeks. He fidgeted with his brown cotton bedspread.

Angelina knocked on the bedroom door, and then opened it without waiting for a response. She stepped into the room and looked Inacio up and down before motioning for the girl to enter.

Inacio held his breath and watched as her figure slowly filled the doorway. He stared for a moment, then exhaled and smiled. "Hi," he said.

It was her turn to exhale. "Hello," she said in English.

"I'm Inacio."

"I know," she said, and they both released a nervous chuckle.

"Come closer?" he asked.

Angelina gave a look that said *Not too close.*

Inacio looked at Angelina but addressed the girl. "My mother is a little old-fashioned."

"Some things never go out of fashion," the widow said.

But to Inacio's surprise, Angelina stepped aside just a bit. The girl took a few hesitant steps and stopped at the foot of the bed. Inacio stared at her for a moment. The photo her family had sent of the squinty-eyed girl with the forced smile had not done her justice. He sensed a shyness in her that indicated that she didn't know how attractive she was. It gave her an appealing air of virtuousness.

"So, how do you like America?" he asked.

"I do not see very much. But what I see—and the people I meet—is very... gentle?"

"I think you mean 'nice'"

"Nice," the girl repeated.

"O seu Inglês é muito bom," Inacio said. *Your English is very good.*

"Obrigado. Thank you. I study and practice for the year."

"That's enough for today," Angelina said.

"Mama..." Inacio protested.

But Angelina was resolute. "More tomorrow. Now, you rest," she said, and motioned for the girl to leave the room. The girl turned around.

"Wait," Inacio said.

She turned back to face him.

"You're very pretty, muito bela."

She blushed.

"You remind me of Natalie Wood."

The girl furrowed her brow.

"*Rebel Without a Cause*?" he asked.

"I am sorry," she said, shaking her head.

"Never mind, it doesn't matter. See you tomorrow."

"See you tomorrow," she parroted, and then left the room.

Can you tell that I'm not a virgin? Can you tell that I am pregnant? How beautiful will you think I am if you find out?

Her mind was racing. As Angelina closed the bedroom door, the girl excused herself and slipped into the bathroom. She let the water run in the sink to cover the sound of her search of the medicine cabinet. She didn't know the English word for what she sought, but she recognized the illustration of a razor blade on its cardboard packet.

FOR RENATA

9

June 14, 1970

Peter Ahearn and Cindy Everhart, accompanied by their respective best friends, Chip O'Connell and Linda Gonsalves, maneuvered through dozens of family and friends in the back yard of the Ahearn home at Hollistown Harbor. The party was in celebration of Peter's graduation from Gloucester High School.

Most of the guests had been received at the Ahearn home barely three months before, following the funeral of Tommy Ahearn, who had been killed in action in Vietnam. Some of the somberness of that day seemed to have carried over.

Marybeth Valente asked her husband to keep an eye on their son, Mark, and then wove through the crowd to find her brother. Peter and Cindy had stopped to chat with next door neighbors, Frank and Irma Schmidt.

"That new car's a beauty," Frank was saying.

"Thanks, Mr. Schmidt. It's a '66 Dodge Dart GT. It's not exactly new, but it's new to me," said Peter, "It's a graduation gift from my parents."

Marybeth joined the group. "Hi, Mr. and Mrs. Schmidt, thanks so much for coming," she said.

"Little Mark is so precious," Irma said, "I could just eat him up."

"Hmm, precious is not the word that comes to mind when I'm chasing after him."

"Well, that's to be expected: snips and snails, and puppy dogs' tails, you know," Irma said.

Cindy smiled. "I think you're just so good with him, Marybeth. I hope someday I'm half the mother you are."

"Oh, I'm sure you will be," Marybeth smiled coolly. She hadn't forgotten the way that Cindy had insinuated herself into the family during their time of grief, even going so far as to stand beside Peter while the family received mourners at Tommy's wake.

Marybeth turned to Peter. "Have you seen Ma?"

"No," he said, his brow furrowing. He quickly scanned the crowd. "I see Dad over there by the barbecue, but I don't see Ma anywhere."

"She went into the house a while ago," said Cindy. "Do you want me to help you find her?"

"No," Marybeth said. "You stay here and enjoy yourself with the other *guests*, I'll find my mother."

Marybeth went inside and instinctively headed to her parents' second-floor bedroom. The door was closed. Marybeth knocked and, after pausing for a moment, opened it. Katherine Ahearn sat in a Victorian ladies' chair, a framed portrait of Tommy in her lap. She was stroking the glass-covered image of her son's face with the fingers of her right hand.

"Ma?" said Marybeth.

"May-bet," Katherine answered. It was a nickname Marybeth had given herself because she hadn't been able to pronounce her name when she first started speaking. It had stuck because John and Katherine thought it was cute, and the entire Ahearn family had called her *May-bet* until she'd entered the sixth grade and announced that she would no longer answer to *that baby name*.

"Are you all right, Mother?"

"I'm fine, Darling. Do you need me for something?"

"No, I just didn't see you outside and wanted to make sure you were okay."

Marybeth crossed the room and knelt on the floor beside her mother. She rested her head on Katherine's shoulder and looked down at the photo of Tommy.

"I'm going to miss him so much," Marybeth said, "for as long as I live."

Katherine stroked her daughter's hair and smiled. "You know, I was just thinking about the way Tommy used to follow me around when I vacuumed. Do you remember that old Electrolux canister vac? Tommy was just a little tyke, maybe two or three years old, and he loved the feel of the warm air that blew out the back of it. Wherever that vacuum was, he'd lie down behind it. He used to put his elbows on the floor and prop up his head in his hands, close his eyes, and let that warm air blow on his sweet little face."

Katherine's smile disappeared. "God, it makes me so angry, foolish wars. Now Peter will go too, and there's nothing I can do to stop him. He didn't discuss it with me or your father, of course. He just marched right down on his eighteenth birthday and enlisted. I know what he's thinking: He has a misguided notion that he'll somehow avenge Tommy's death. And how? By killing some Vietnamese mother's son.

"He'll leave for boot camp in a few weeks, and soon after he'll be in Vietnam. And I won't sleep a wink. Your father will worry, but he won't be kept up nights like I will.

"You see that worn spot on our headboard?" Katherine turned her head and nodded in the direction of the full-sized bed she shared with her husband. A faded softball sized spot on the maple headboard was lighter in color than the finished maple surrounding it.

"That's where I would rest my head while I sat up waiting for all three of you to come home at night. Your father would snore away, but I could never sleep until I'd heard the front door closing behind the last of you."

Mother and daughter were quiet for a long time. When Katherine Ahearn spoke again, her voice quavered. "It's true what they say: It's an awful thing to outlive a child. I don't know what I'll do if we lose Peter too. I just don't think I could bear it.

"I should have seen this coming. I should have known how Peter would react. He's always been very loyal and *very* impulsive. I was so lost in grief that I didn't pay attention. I might have been able to stop him."

Marybeth had moved from her mother's side to the bedroom window and absent-mindedly surveyed the crowd in the backyard. Her father was cooking hot dogs and hamburgers on the brick fireplace grill that he had built years ago. A few feet away, Peter was emptying bags of ice into a large metal cooler. On the other side of the yard, Cindy, Chip, and Linda were huddled in the shade of a maple tree. Chip must have said something funny because both girls were laughing hysterically. Marybeth bristled as she watched Cindy lean her forehead against Chip's chest and place her hand on his bicep. She had heard stories about Cindy's promiscuity. Rumor had it than she had been seen entering a Rockport motel room with her high school English teacher, a thirty-seven-year-old married father of three. Marybeth believed it.

"Don't worry, Ma, Pete will be fine, I just know it," Marybeth said absently.

10

August 23, 1957

The girl stood naked. She had folded her clothes and laid them on an oak, marble-topped commode. She plugged the bathtub drain with its rubber stopper and opened the spigots. As the claw-foot tub slowly filled with water, she opened the medicine cabinet and removed one razor blade. She sat on the edge of the tub and brought the blade to her left arm. Shutting her eyes tight, she drew the blade across her flesh. But when she looked at the cut, she realized it was only a scratch. Though hurting herself went against every instinct, she would have to cut deeper. She didn't close her eyes this time. She aligned the blade on the scratch, pursed her lips, and sliced.

Her blood began to trickle. She grabbed one of three sanitary napkins she had packed in Horta and dabbed at the self-inflicted wound on her upper arm. After wrapping the blood-stained napkin in toilet paper, she planted it in the wastebasket. She used a styptic pencil from the medicine cabinet to stanch the bleeding, and then bandaged her arm with a strip of cloth. She would reopen and rebind the same wound a dozen times over the coming days.

After she had bathed and dressed, she turned the skeleton key to unlock the bathroom door and went downstairs. Angelina stood at the stove and gave the girl only a passing glance as she entered the room and sat at the kitchen table.

"Senhora?" she said. The widow turned and looked at her. The girl started to say something, but Uncle Pio appeared in the doorway before she could get the words out.

"What is it?" Angelina asked. Now Uncle Pio was waiting to hear what she had to say too. Tears formed in her eyes.

"Well?" Angelina demanded.

The girl rose from her seat, approached Angelina, and whispered in her ear.

"Oh," said Angelina. "Don't worry." She turned to her brother and said, "Pio, go to the store and get a box of Kotex."

The girl turned away and covered her eyes with her hands. Uncle Pio groaned.

Over the following days the girl took every opportunity to ingratiate herself with her future sogra—*mother-in-law*. It was vital that she have time alone with Inacio. She pleaded with Angelina to let her help care for him. Angelina was reluctant, but the girl had recruited Uncle Pio's support, and together they convinced the widow to relent.

She served Inacio his meals, convincing the emaciated fisherman to take a few more bites each time he ate, and sat at his bedside and read aloud to him from Portuguese novels. And when he became stronger, she accompanied him on short morning walks outside. At first Inacio tread as shakily as an old man. Once, after he nearly tripped on the sidewalk, she took his hand in hers. And from that day onward, they held hands during their strolls, which they started to take twice daily, in the morning and afternoon. She used these opportunities to entice him. She flattered him, laughed at his jokes—even though she seldom understood them—and caressed his forearm with her fingertips.

One picture-perfect summer day she became more daring.

Though Inacio's bedroom door was always left open, Angelina's approach was always announced by the creaking of the stairs.

The couple had just come back from their morning walk, and Inacio was sitting on the edge of his bed. The girl turned her back to him and undid the top two buttons of her simple, collared blouse, confident that she'd have ample time to redo them should Senhora Raposo decide to perform a surprise inspection. She then walked over to his bookcase with an exaggerated sway in her hips and retrieved the latest novel she'd been reading to him.

Under her clothes she was wearing delicate new undergarments, a matching white brassiere and briefs bordered with lace and embroidered with tiny pink roses. They were a gift her favorite aunt, Sofia, had given her to wear on her wedding day.

She held the book against her chest with her left hand and turned around. With her right hand, she grabbed a straight-back wooden chair from its place against the wall and pulled it closer to the bed, as she customarily did when she was about to read to Inacio. She sat up straight in the chair, clutching the book to her chest to keep her hands from shaking.

She closed her eyes for a long moment, and when she opened them again, she did not look at Inacio. Holding the book out straight to block his view of her blouse, she began to read, her voice shaking with each syllable.

Inacio was accustomed to looking at her face as she read. They would often let their eyes meet over the top of the book, locking gazes for long moments.

In her peripheral vision, she saw that Inacio was leaning his head to the left to look around the book, and she drew it closer to her. He leaned forward even more, straining to see her.

After reading a few paragraphs, the girl took a deep breath, leaned forward, and rested her elbows on her knees. She continued to read aloud while she pretended to be oblivious to Inacio's view of her lingerie and the swell of her breasts.

Nerves compelled her to read louder and faster than usual. At one point she glanced beneath the book and caught sight of Inacio's crotch. The shape of his arousal strained against the inseam of his pants. She pictured Mateus stroking himself at their

B. ROBERT SHARRY

Secret Place, and she was certain her face went crimson.

In the next moment, Inacio's fingers appeared at the top of the page as he grasped the book by its spine and tore it away from her. Their eyes locked together, and she tensed. Something in Inacio's glare frightened her. She rose from the chair and took a step back.

Her effort to play temptress had backfired. In her haste to legitimize her pregnancy, she had acted too boldly, and now Inacio saw her as wanton.

Inacio stood up and stalked toward her until he was just inches away. She trembled and gripped the fronts of her blouse together. She felt her face flush and cast her eyes downward.

Inacio flung the book onto the bed and grabbed a fistful of raven hair at the back of her head. She brought her eyes back up to meet his. He looked furious.

He tightened his grip on her hair and pulled her in close. She recoiled and brought her hands up to cover her face.

"You are so beautiful," he whispered in Portuguese.

It took a moment, but she finally realized that what she had seen in those dark eyes, what had frightened her so, was not anger at all. It was raw desire.

She slowly lowered her trembling hands, and the two stood face to face, both of them gasping for breath.

FOR RENATA

"I want you," he rasped. He kissed her and cupped her small breast so roughly it made her flinch.

Far from failing, her plan was working too well. She had to think quickly. She needed to cool his passion for the moment but keep his desire simmering.

She would have submitted to him that instant, had she thought it was safe. But she knew it wasn't. It was not only possible that Senhora Raposo would catch them in the act, it was likely. Inacio's bedroom was located just a few feet from the top of the stairs, and Angelina always stood in the same spot on the first floor when the girl was in Inacio's room — a place midway along the stairwell where she thought she was invisible to anyone on the second floor. Each time the girl left her fiancé's bedroom, she could see the tip of Angelina's black-clad right shoulder before the woman silently slipped from sight. *Gato escondido com o rabo de fora,* she thought. *A cat hiding with its tail showing.*

But Angelina Raposo could send her packing just as easily as Inacio could. There was only one sure route to legitimacy: She needed to marry, and soon.

"I want you too," she breathed in her native tongue, "but not now, not like this. From the moment we met, I've yearned to share the closeness of man and woman. But we can't until we are husband and wife."

Inacio shook his head almost imperceptibly. "I don't think I can wait. I want you now."

"And I want you to have me, Inacio, but as your wife. Do you want our life together to begin with a sin against God? I don't. I can't."

She turned away from him and walked to the open window, swaying her hips as she went. She fixed her gaze on a sun-dappled, leafy oak whose branches spread out so far and wide she could almost touch them. "We'll just have to wait until you're well enough to marry."

Inacio's glance darted about the room, and then came back to rest on her body. He stole up behind her, cupped her shoulders in his hands, and pressed himself against her. "I am well enough."

The girl allowed herself a quiet sigh of relief. She felt certain that Inacio would have married her there, on the spot, if he could. But there was one more formidable obstacle left to breech. She would point out the barrier to Inacio, and then pray that his ego would become the battering ram.

"You may *think* you're well enough, Inacio, but isn't that for your *mother* to decide?"

FOR RENATA

11

September 14, 1957

One month after her arrival in America, the sixteen-year-old girl became a married woman. The bride wore a white dress she and her mother had sewn for the occasion. The groom wore a black suit, white shirt, and black tie.

They exchanged their vows before Father Abade. The new young priest towered over the bride and groom, who stood 5'4" and 5'7" respectively. Father Henrique "Rick" Abade, at 6'2", was a bear of a young man who had wrestled and played football at Holy Cross. He was hairy and sweated a lot—one of those men who needed to shave twice a day if he wanted to look well groomed in the evening. His paternal grandparents, a fisherman and his wife, had emigrated from The Azores at the turn of the century along with their four children.

After the couple placed their wedding bands on each other's hands, Padre Abade wrapped his stole around them. Since this was the young priest's first wedding ceremony, he was sweating even more than usual, and the stole was damp with perspiration.

When Mr. and Mrs. Inacio Raposo exited the Our Lady of Good Voyage church, cheering friends and family showered them with flowers and candies.

Afterwards, the couple received guests at the home of Angelina Raposo. In the days before the ceremony, Angelina had made all the food herself, with Uncle Pio and the bride-to-be acting as her sous chefs. The kitchen aromas had been heavenly, but they were the smells of home, and had caused awful pangs of homesickness in the girl.

A barrel of Portuguese red wine was tapped and, soon after, most of the guests were dancing. The bride's shoe was passed around. Every man and boy stuffed cash into it and eagerly waited his turn for a dance with the beautiful newlywed.

The men at Portuguese weddings were fond of playing good-natured pranks, like hiding the newlyweds' luggage, or stealing the groom's car. Early that morning Inacio had loaded their suitcases into the trunk of his 1958 Oldsmobile 98 and parked it three blocks away.

At 10:00 p.m. Inacio took his wife by the hand and led her into the kitchen. The couple said their goodbyes to a beaming Uncle Pio and a tearful Angelina before sneaking out the back door.

They arrived at the Parker House Hotel in Boston less than forty-five minutes after leaving Gloucester. They would spend their wedding night there, and then head out the next morning for a week at Niagara Falls. When Inacio gave his name at the front desk, he felt certain the clerk was looking down his nose at him.

"Yes, I see the reservation here," the clerk said in a nasal tone that suggested he was sorry he'd found it. "Mr. and Mrs. Raposo for one night," he said, and then let the key drop into Inacio's hand as if it were lint he had picked from his lapel.

Inacio picked up their suitcases and the couple headed for the elevator bank. An elevator door opened and two smartly dressed businessmen emerged. One of them ogled Inacio's wife before smirking at Inacio. *What are you going to do about it?* the businessman seemed to say as he passed them.

Inacio put the suitcases down and turned. His face was screwed up in jealous anger, and his fists were clenched. He started after the man but stopped when he felt his wife's gloved hand take his arm. Inacio turned to look at her. She smiled and shook her head. Inacio gave a slight nod to her, unclenched his fists, and picked up the suitcases.

It was her first ride in an elevator, and she clung tightly to her husband's arm. When they reached the hotel room, Inacio used one suitcase as a doorstop. She felt herself being hoisted into the air, and then her husband carried her across the threshold, kissed her passionately, and lowered her onto the bed.

While Inacio was busy collecting the suitcases, she slipped into the bathroom and locked the door. She turned on the faucet, stared at herself in the mirror, and wept. *I want my mamãe. I want my papai. I want Mateus. I want to go home.*

She imagined her father coming for her, breaking down the hotel room door. Her papai would scoop her up in his arms, like he used to do when she was a child, and carry her back to their home in Horta.

Then she pictured Mateus. She wanted Mateus to have the same passionate jealousy in his eyes that she had seen in Inacio's in the hotel lobby. She wanted him to storm in and knock Inacio out cold. Then Mateus would take her by the hand and spirit her away to Rio de Janeiro, where they would live the lives they had dreamed of—he as an artist and she, a dancer. And, together with their beautiful baby, they would live happily ever after.

A muffled sound startled her. Inacio was knocking on the bathroom door. *How long have I been in here?*

She wiped her tears away and cracked open the door. Inacio looked worried. "Are you all right?"

No, I want to go home. "Yes," she said, "I am sorry."

"You've been crying."

"Tears of joy," she said.

He held up her suitcase. "I thought you might want this."

She opened the door wider and gave a half-smile and a nod. "Thank you."

She closed the door gently, and cringed at what she knew was to come.

12

June 14, 1970

After the graduation party Peter Ahearn drove his red Dodge Dart through the darkening back roads of Cape Ann. Cindy sat next to him, and Chip and Linda shared the backseat. The quartet passed a joint around and took chugs from a bottle of Thunderbird wine that Chip had procured with the help of an older cousin.

Peter was on the way to the O'Connell house to drop off Chip when he glanced in the rearview mirror and saw his two friends kissing. He grinned, tapped Cindy on the shoulder, and motioned for her to look behind. She swiveled around in silence, and watched as Chip's right hand traveled a path from Linda's right knee up to her left, blouse-covered breast. Linda tolerated the grope for a few seconds before she took Chip's hand in hers, guided it back down to her knee, and patted it gently. Lips never parting and eyes never opening, the couple repeated the process so many times that it caused Cindy to giggle.

"This can't go on forever," Cindy said. "One of you has to give in."

The couple practically leaped away from each other.

"Well, it's not going to be me," Linda said, her face crimson.

Chip didn't say a word. He just looked at Cindy, raised his eyebrows, and grinned. This made Linda sigh with indignation and Cindy laugh.

Peter held the steering wheel with his left hand while he reached into the back seat with his right and playfully swatted at Chip's knees. "Don't make me stop this car young man. You behave yourself back there."

Laughter erupted in the car. Even Linda, try as she might, couldn't suppress a smile.

After he dropped off Chip and Linda at their homes, Peter drove Cindy to the house her mother rented in East Gloucester. An old screened pie safe sat on the front porch. Cindy's mother worked as a waitress at a local seafood restaurant, but she and Cindy supplemented her income by baking pies at home. They stored them in the pie safe, and sold them on the honor system. Cindy's mother was named Eleanor, but to many she was known as *The Pie Lady*. Peter knew that Cindy was embarrassed by her mother's moniker.

"Where did you say your mom went?" Peter asked as they walked into the darkened kitchen.

Mr. Chips, the family cat, purred as he weaved in and out of Cindy's ankles. She bent down and scratched his head. "New York City," Cindy answered, and straightened herself. "She went with her new boyfriend. They're going to see a musical starring Lauren Bacall."

"It's too bad she had to miss graduation."

"Yeah, but it's no big deal. She thinks this guy could really be *the one,* so…"

Cindy grasped a lock of her long hair and twirled it around her finger. "And she felt really bad about not being here. She asked me if I minded and everything. Besides, it's not like I was on the honor roll or anything."

"What about your dad?"

"He's got a whole brand new family," Cindy said. "He doesn't exactly have time for his old one."

Peter felt sorry for her and a little guilty that he had brought up a subject that dampened Cindy's mood. "Hey, you've still got me," he said, and caressed her arm with one hand.

"Not for long. In another couple of weeks you'll be gone too."

"Yeah, but I'll be back."

"Right, in three years. And that's *if* you come back. What if you end up like…Oh, Pete, why? Why did you have to go and do it?"

Peter tried to take her in his arms, but she pushed him away. "I can't explain it, Cin. It's just something I needed to do."

"You didn't even tell me…*me.*"

"I'm sorry. I should have told you, but I was afraid you'd get upset and try to talk me out of it. I didn't even tell my family. Chip was the only one who knew."

"Chip? You told Chip O'Connell, but not me. That's just great. I'm supposed to be your girlfriend, remember?"

Cindy folded her arms and turned her back to him. Peter put his hands on her shoulders, but Cindy shrugged him off and stepped away.

"I was thinking maybe you could be more than that," Peter said.

"More than what?"

"More than my girlfriend. I was thinking maybe we could get married when I come back."

Cindy turned around to face him but kept her arms folded. "You expect me to sit around in this shit hole and wait for you while you're in Vietnam for three years?"

"No. Listen, it won't even be half that. I'm going to be training in Georgia for a few months before I ship out. I'm sure I'll get some time off. I can be home in less than twenty-four hours by bus, or you could even take a bus down there. And then when I go to 'Nam? It'll only be for twelve months. That's it. We could be married in less than eighteen months, and then wherever I'm posted after that, we'll go together. It'll be an adventure."

Cindy unfolded her arms. "What happens then?"

"Well, after that we could live in Boston. I could go to Berklee on the GI Bill and play music on the side. Maybe you could go to Beauty School while I'm away, just like you talked about. And then you could get a job as a hairdresser in Boston."

"And what about after that?"

FOR RENATA

"After that? I don't know, Cin. After that we can do anything you want, live anywhere you want."

Cindy looked down, raised her right foot onto its tip-toes and watched her knee as she shifted it from side to side. "California?"

"California? Sure, if that's where you want to be."

Cindy looked thoughtful, and then a coquettish smile lit up her face. "Did you just propose to me, Peter Ahearn?"

Peter chuckled. "Yeah, I guess I did."

He furrowed his brow. "Don't worry, Cin, everything's going to be fine, and we're going to be really happy."

"I haven't said *yes* yet. Let's do another joint while I think about it. Pot either makes me really horny or really paranoid. Tonight it's making me really horny."

That night they would be able to make love on a bed for the first time. Before, sex had taken place mostly in the back seat of the Ahearn Buick, a few times in the backstage area of the high school auditorium, and once, at dusk, in the woods near the Hollistown Harbor reservoir where dozens of mosquitoes had feasted on Peter's back while he thrust to satisfaction.

They began on the couch and had removed each other's clothing when Mr. Chips leaped onto Peter's lap and pierced his thigh with an errant claw. Peter cried out. He instinctively withdrew his hands from Cindy's body and cupped his shrinking erection.

"Jesus."

"Chips," Cindy scolded. She tried to lift the cat, but his claw was still imbedded in Peter's thigh.

"Ow, ow, ow," Peter cried.

"Be nice, Chips. Time for you to go outside, anyway."

Cindy cradled the cat's body with one hand after she had detached it from Peter. "You love me, don't you, Chips?" She asked as she carried the animal through the kitchen and gently released him on the back stoop.

When Cindy returned Peter was massaging his thigh with his fingers. She knelt between his knees. "Oh, poor baby, did that bad kitty hurt you? Let me kiss it and make it better."

She bent forward and kissed his upper thigh. Peter felt her warm, heavy breasts brush against his legs, and he sighed as he leaned his head back on the couch and closed his eyes.

"I think he clawed my dick." Peter grinned.

"He did?" Cindy asked with mock concern.

"I'm pretty sure."

"Well, I guess I better kiss that all better too."

She took him in her mouth and moved her head up and down his length. Peter hardened more and his whole body shook. Soon he tensed, and exploded in a series of spasms. Cindy remained motionless, and kept him in her mouth until he had softened and his breathing had returned to normal.

Peter pulled her to him and wrapped his arms around her.

"Thank you, thank you," he murmured.

"Come to bed," she whispered.

FOR RENATA

Moments later they were kissing on her mother's double bed, their limbs entwined. Peter felt her slick wetness on his thigh, and before long, he was hard again.

"Tell me you love me," she said.

"Of course I do."

"Say it."

Peter had learned early on how important this was to Cindy. They'd been "going out" for barely a week when she had first whispered *Tell me you love me, even if you don't* while they made out at the rear of the Bijoux Theatre. Peter had sensed yearning in her request and, feeling sorry for her, he had complied. But a lot had changed since then. Cindy had captivated him. She was the most exciting person he'd ever known.

"I love you," he whispered, meaning it.

Cindy smiled. "Be right back," she whispered as she tiptoed from the bed. She opened the top drawer of her mother's dresser, rummaged beneath the underwear, and came up with a condom. She ripped it from its foil envelope as she walked back to the bed, and then unrolled it over his hard length. Peter raised himself up on one elbow.

"No. Lie down. I want to be on top of you," she said. She sat astride him and guided him inside her. Peter held her hips and began to thrust, but Cindy leaned in and whispered to him. "Just stay still, and let me do the moving, okay?"

"Okay," he breathed.

Cindy rested her hands on Peter's shoulders and hung her head. Her blond hair brushed against his chest and ribs as she moved — not up and down as he'd expected, but slowly back and forth.

After a time, he grasped her hips and had to restrain himself from an almost overpowering urge to pound into her with all his might.

She leaned in, gently nibbled his earlobe, and started to move again, faster this time.

And she ground on him with more pressure now, rubbing herself against him faster and faster. Her heavy breasts bounced in time with her movement. Her breathing became quicker. She began to emit a tiny moan with each breath, barely audible until their volume and tempo grew with the rhythm and intensity of her movement on him.

And she rubbed against him —

And she rubbed —

And she rubbed until —

Her whole body trembled —

She whimpered…and collapsed onto his chest, her body limp. He held her tightly and felt the pounding of her heart. From time to time she quivered, and moaned softly as she did.

After several minutes, she lifted her head, laced her fingers together on his smooth chest, and rested her chin on her knuckles.

"Maybe," she said, peering at his face.

"Maybe?" Peter cocked his head.

"Maybe, I'll marry you."

FOR RENATA

13

September 14, 1957

The new bride trembled as she made her way from the bathroom to the bedside. The nightgown her mother had made for the wedding night was stiff and a little scratchy. Inacio had turned down the bed. He stood looking out the window and was smoking a Pall Mall cigarette. He turned to face her, but she avoided eye-contact.

"You look very beautiful," he said.

"Thank you."

"I'm going to take a bath. I'll just be a little while."

She nodded.

When he disappeared into the bathroom, she began to pace. She sat on the bed for a moment, and then stood up and paced some more. She repeated this process several times until she heard the bathtub drain gurgling. She jumped into bed, pulled the covers up high, and stared wide-eyed at the ceiling. Her papai was not coming to save her.

Mateus was not coming either. She pursed her lips and narrowed her eyes. *I will think of this as something like a vaccination, painful but necessary.*

The bathroom door opened. Her eyes grew wide again. She popped up, turned off the bedside lamp, and lay back down in the dark.

Inacio started across the darkened room and stubbed his toe. "Shit." he said, hopping on one foot. He quickly added, "I'm sorry, I didn't mean to curse in front of you."

He stood by the window again, and she knew from his silhouette that he was naked. He was larger than Mateus, and she wondered if it would hurt more than it had her first time. *Oh, Mateus.*

Inacio approached the bed.

And now he is getting in beside me.

She tensed. She made fists and crossed her wrists over her chest, like a corpse. And then she felt his warm body pressed against hers, and she realized she was shivering.

"Darling," he whispered, "I know this is your first time and you're nervous. But I'm going to be very gentle with you. And if it hurts you, just tell me, and I'll stop. I don't ever want to hurt you."

He kissed her lips tenderly for a long time. The warmth of his body and the gentleness of his whispered words eased her tension. And after a while she began to respond with soft kisses of her own. He removed his hand from her shoulder and traced the outline of her figure until he reached the bottom of her nightgown. She felt the roughness of his fingers as they probed beneath her nightdress and traveled the length of her body, from calf to outer thigh and hip, to the curve of her waist, her ribs, and on to her breast. He rolled her nipple lightly between his thumb and forefinger for a time before easing her nightgown up and over her head and tossing it to the floor.

Inacio gently parted her legs and knelt between her thighs. She closed her eyes and tensed her body in anticipation of the pain to come. But he did not enter her. He leaned down and took her left nipple in his mouth, teasing it with his tongue. She felt his hardness hot against her thigh. Before long his mouth was moving down her body, exploring and planting wet kisses until he reached… *My God, what is he doing? He's kissing me down there.*

She had never heard of this. She and her girlfriends had talked about sex, but no one had ever described anything like this. She closed her eyes even tighter and turned her head, burying it in the pillow. She remembered herself as a young girl in the bathtub. Her mother had told her it was "dirty" down there, that she was always to wash quickly. To touch herself in that place would be sinful.

But it's not me, it's him. It's him… What are you doing to me? It feels…think about something else. But the something else was Mateus lying naked on the rock, stroking himself as she watched.

Inacio continued to kiss and lick. She felt a strange pressure build up inside her, and it was frightening and pleasurable at the same time. She could still see Mateus stroking himself, faster now, and she began to move with him. She longed for Mateus to be inside her, to fill her.

Inacio's tongue moved faster. Mateus pumped wildly...he was close now, so close. She felt tingling and warmth throughout her body as she moved herself up and down, up and down until...

Mateus's seed shot high in the air, and then there were no more illusions, just waves of pleasure. She had gone someplace else, someplace outside of herself, someplace devoid even of thought.

When she came back, she realized that she still tingled everywhere, that she was pulsing down there.

And that Inacio was deep inside her

14

May 2, 1958

Angelina and Pio sat calmly while Inacio paced the perimeter of the waiting room at Cape Ann Women's Hospital.

"Mr. Raposo." the doctor called out as he entered the room. He extended his hand to Inacio. "Congratulations. You have a healthy baby girl. You can go in now."

"And my wife?" Inacio asked.

"She's doing just fine. Follow me."

As the doctor led Inacio, Angelina, and Pio down the hallway, he asked, "Have you chosen a name yet?"

"Well, I was hoping for a boy, of course, but we decided on Renata Angelina, for a girl," Inacio answered. [He pronounced it Ray-*nah*-tah]

Renata Angelina Raposo was wrapped tightly and lie sleeping in her mother's arms. Inacio beamed as he kissed his wife's lips and then the baby's tiny forehead.

"Oh, I almost forgot," said Inacio. He fumbled through his jacket pockets, and pulled out two cigars. He gave one to the doctor, and one to Uncle Pio.

Angelina regarded the new mother with suspicion. She turned to the doctor. "This child does not look so small for having come before its time."

"Hmm?" the doctor looked at Angelina and then turned his attention to the pleading eyes of the new mother.

"Oh," the doctor said, "well, it's not unusual for this size in a premature delivery."

"Is that so?" Angelina asked in a tone that suggested that her real question was *What kind of fool do you take me for?*

"Absolutely, I've seen bigger. I could tell you some stories…"

Uncle Pio broke in. "Parabéns Avó." *Congratulations, Grandma.* Pio threw his arms around his sister.

Angelina tried to break the embrace. "Doctor…"

But Pio held her fast and talked over her. "Doctor, thank you for bringing this beautiful, healthy baby into the world. We know you're a busy man, so we'll let you get back to your other patients now."

Pio turned to his sister. "And we have a baptism and celebration to plan. Come along, Angelina. Let's let this young family have some time alone. I'll take you home so you can start cooking."

Angelina whispered angrily to Pio as he led her from the room. "That baby is no more premature than…"

Pio fixed Angelina with a grave expression and whispered back. "Be careful, sister. You have no proof of what you imply. I remember you, yourself, sending me to the store for feminine napkins, and I don't think they were for *you*…" Angelina looked back over her shoulder. A nurse had taken the baby from its mother and was handing it to Inacio. Angelina Raposo glared at her daughter-in-law.

"Don't look at her, Angelina," Pio said, "look at *him*."

Angelina's focused her eyes on Inacio. He cradled tiny Renata Angelina in his arms and was cooing at the baby through a broad smile. The old woman's expression softened.

"Isn't that the important thing?" asked Pio. "See how proud and happy he his. And that's what you want, isn't it? Remember how angry was the boy who lost his father and brothers at twelve years old, and was doing a man's work at fourteen? I tell you: This girl is good for him. Let it be, sister."

The young mother watched as her husband held the baby. Silently, she thanked God for giving her a second chance. She vowed to Him that she would always be a loving wife and mother. And she thanked Him for Uncle Pio.

The young family would have to spend a few more tense weeks at the home of Angelina Raposo. But then they would move to their new home.

B. ROBERT SHARRY

Inacio's savings, together with the wedding gifts they'd received, had been enough for a down-payment on a tiny cottage on Rose Hip Point, a mile-long peninsula that poked out from the village of Hollistown Harbor into the sea like a bony, accusatory finger.

FOR RENATA

15

April 3, 1971

At Logan Airport in Boston, a large group of Peter's family and friends gathered at the arrival gate.

Cindy stood front-and-center, and wore her engagement ring. Her face displayed practiced expressions that Marybeth attributed to the viewing of too many soap operas: lip-biting apprehension, eye-squinting concern, and head-tilting adoration.

The only authentic emotion to register on Cindy's face was one of wide-eyed revulsion that flitted across her features when Peter first walked into view.

Peter wore his dress green uniform. The empty bottom of his left coat sleeve was folded up and pinned to its inseam, and his left eye was covered with a thick bandage.

The contingent of family and friends clapped and cheered, and some held up homemade signs that said *Welcome Home* and *Our Hero*.

Cindy quickly recovered and reverted to her soap opera repertoire. She ran to meet Peter — Marybeth was certain that she would have run in slow motion if she could have managed it—and they fell into an awkward embrace. Peter held her as best as his injury would allow him and leaned in to kiss her. But his gauze-covered, protective metal eye-shield poked her cheekbone, startling them both and causing the botched kiss to end in nervous laughter.

A lmost everyone agreed that Peter wasn't the same after returning from the war. He was quieter, more withdrawn. But Marybeth felt differently. She thought that Peter was adapting to his injuries and responding to therapy rather well, and that his spirits were about as high as could be expected, under the circumstances. His low points seemed to come, she noticed, after those times he'd spent alone with Cindy. And then, almost two months after he came home, insult and injury collaborated to take an even greater toll on him.

The members of John Ahearn's local Veterans of Foreign Wars (VFW) Post were very supportive of Peter. They had insisted that he lead their contingent in the Gloucester Memorial Day Parade. Peter's family were hopeful that it would give him the boost he needed to break out of his funk.

Clad in a black eye patch and dress greens with the left sleeve pinned up, Peter sat atop the rear seatback of a forest green 1970 Cadillac Convertible Deville. As the open car rolled down Main Street, which was colorfully decorated for the occasion, Peter smiled self-consciously and waved to the crowd.

FOR RENATA

Though the procession started out peacefully, 1971 was the height of the anti-war movement, and halfway through the parade, a cry of "Tin Soldiers. How many more?" was heard above the cheers. A barrage of tomatoes flew from the sidelines. One found its way onto Peter's lapel.

Like Secret Service agents, the VFW marchers — most from World War II, some from World War I, the Korean conflict, and the Vietnam War — closed ranks around Peter and scanned the crowd for the tomato-wielding assailants. Peter searched the crowd too, but not for his attacker. This was the part of the procession route where Cindy had said she'd be watching the parade.

A middle-aged spectator sprinted from the sidewalk and removed her cardigan. She used it to blot tomato from Peter's face and uniform, and then smacked a kiss on his cheek and rejoined her cheering friends. Peter wished it had been Cindy.

Then he saw her or, rather, the back of her as she turned and snaked her way through the crowd of spectators, and then vanished.

That evening Cindy reappeared at the VFW picnic. Peter was huddled with a half-dozen other veterans. He had just taken a sip of draft beer from a large paper cup when Cindy tapped him on the shoulder. He turned and smiled at her.

Cindy placed her engagement ring in Peter's coat pocket, said "I just can't deal," and walked away.

B. ROBERT SHARRY

After several months of trying to help his troubled son, John Ahearn had wearied of the inevitable snapping and snide remarks that came from Peter's mouth whenever a suggestion about work or school was made. So, it was warily that he had approached Peter one morning.

"Pete?"

"Yeah?" Peter answered without taking his eyes off the television.

"You remember my friend, Ed Boino?"

"No."

"Sure you do. He's the light keeper up at Rose Hip Point. Remember, we used to go up there sometimes when you were little?"

"No."

"Well, he remembers you. And, as it happens, he's getting ready to retire. It's a civilian job that comes under the Coast Guard. Ed says he'd be happy to arrange for you to be his replacement.

"It's kind of isolated up there, but it's good-paying government work, and your mom and I would come up and visit you a lot. I know Marybeth would too."

John Ahearn pursed his lips and awaited the tirade.

Peter stood, took one step toward his father, and then stopped.

FOR RENATA

16

January 14, 1959

Inacio stood in darkness and peered through the window at the woman inside with the pixie haircut. He could hear the music she danced to as she made her way about the kitchen and gathered ingredients for the evening meal. Then she stopped dancing and stared straight at him, and his heart stopped. But then she started to dance again, and he realized she hadn't seen him. She had seen only her own reflection in the window pane. He was invisible to her. He felt a tingling move from his spine to the back of his neck and ears.

Inacio leered at her body. As she swayed between the refrigerator and stove, spice rack and stove, sink and stove, her ass jiggled. She'd never have that kind of shake if she wore a girdle. Inacio hated girdles.

She walked out of the kitchen and into the living room. Inacio knew it would be only moments before she returned. He scurried to the kitchen door, turned the doorknob ever-so-quietly, and slipped inside. She was coming back. He could hear her

78

humming along with the record playing in the living room. He quickly knelt behind the table and chairs in the dining area and prayed that she wouldn't see him.

She was in the kitchen now. He could hear the *click* of her shoes on the linoleum. Her footsteps caused tiny vibrations in the floor that he felt through his knees, and he tingled again.

Her humming became less audible, and the sizzling sound from the stove became irregular. She must be facing the stove.

He rose up without a sound as she continued to hum, dancing in place.

But she wasn't alone: She balanced a smiling baby on her left hip while she poked at the contents of the cast iron skillet with a wooden spatula.

Inacio stole up behind her and spoke in a menacing rasp. "Você tem uma bunda bonita, Senhora." *You have a pretty ass, lady.*

The woman shrieked. She dropped the spatula and clutched the baby with both arms. Sensing its mother's distress, the baby's smile dissolved into a look of alarm. The woman spun around, wide-eyed with fear. Her expression changed when she saw her handsome husband beaming manically at her, his teeth gleaming and the dark tendrils of his hair bouncing with his laughter.

"Inacio, você está louco. Assustou-me quase até a morte." *Inacio, you are insane. You scared me almost to death.*

"I'm sorry," he continued in Portuguese, putting his arms around his wife and daughter. "I'll never do it again."

"That is what you said the last time."

"This time I mean it," he kissed his wife tenderly. "It's your own fault, though. You do have such a pretty ass."

"Shh, don't talk that way in front of the baby."

The Portuguese fisherman took the infant girl from her mother. His voice became higher-pitched and tender. "You don't know what your papai is saying, do you, meu coração?" he cooed.

"You know only that I love you and that you are a beautiful princesa. Yes, you are."

"And she knows that she will have her papai around her little finger, and that he will spoil her," Mamãe smiled.

"Don't listen to your mamãe, my love. She is just jealous because you have surpassed her as the most beautiful woman in the world.

"You are Renata Raposo, RR. The most beautiful women in the world have initials that are the same, Marilyn Monroe, Brigitte Bardot, and now, Renata Raposo."

"You are right about that, my darling. She is the most beautiful child, no?" Mamãe said.

"She is the most beautiful child, yes. And do you know why? It's because she has the magic of Raposo blood flowing through her veins."

Mamãe blushed and turned to face the stove. "

B. ROBERT SHARRY

But tell me, my love," her husband said to her back, "It's not so bad to be the second most beautiful in the world, is it?"

"No, not if our daughter is the first," Mamãe called over her shoulder.

Inacio sniffed the air, the aroma of fresh fish simmering in olive oil with garlic, onions, tomatoes, and wine. "What is that heavenly smell, my little Renie-bird? [he pronounced it "Rainy-bird"] Your mamãe is cooking something wonderful for me. A bacalhãu fresco, I think, if my nose does not betray me."

Mamãe smiled. "Yes, and I want you to eat all of it. You are still too skinny, Inacio. You can't get completely well if you don't eat more."

Inacio came up behind her and kissed her neck. "Can I help it if I have more of an appetite for you than for food?" His gaze moved to the frying pan. "The fish looks wonderful. How can such a beautiful woman also be such an incredible cook? What is your secret?"

"Well, I get the freshest cod because my handsome husband is the best fisherman in all of Cape Ann."

"Only Cape Ann?" he asked with mock sadness.

"I meant in all of Massachusetts."

Inacio again feigned dejection.

"I meant in all the world," she said.

"Your husband is a lucky man to have a wife who is such a good cook, and has such a pretty ass."

"Inacio…"

FOR RENATA

"What?" he laughed, "I'll stop saying it before she's old enough to understand."

"I don't want you to *ever* stop saying it. I just don't want you to say it in front of our daughter."

"Ahh, did you hear that, minha menina *(my little girl)*? Do you know what that means? It means you'll be going to bed early tonight so that your papai can say a lot of things to your mamãe that you're not allowed to hear."

Inacio held the baby girl high above his head, brought her face down to meet his, and then rubbed noses with her. She laughed with delight, so Inacio did it again and again.

"You are all right for now, Renata Angelina," he said with a loving tease, "but next your mamãe must give me a boy."

After dinner, while his wife did the dishes and tidied the kitchen, Inacio bathed the little girl. He powdered her, and then diapered her and dressed her in a soft, pale-pink sleeper sack. As Inacio bent over and lowered his smiling daughter into her crib, his wife approached from behind, put her hand on his broad back, and rubbed it lovingly.

"You are a wonderful papai," Mamãe said.

"Look at her—" Inacio beamed "—and tell me: How could I not be?"

17

July 19, 1962

The sands of Good Harbor Beach, Gloucester, glowed in the fiery afternoon sun like a bed of hot coals. Barefoot bathers tended to prance rather than walk to minimize the scorching of their soles.

Little Renata made a game of hopping from foot to foot. "Ouch...ouch... ouch...ouch..." she cried in rhythm. "Mamãe, olhe para mim. Ouch...ouch ...ouch...ouch..."

Mamãe looked up from her book and answered in Portuguese. "I see you, meu coração, it's like you are dancing."

"No, Mamãe, I'm *hopping*."

"Well, hopping is a kind of dancing."

"Olhe para mim, Papai. Ouch...ouch... ouch...ouch. Papai, olhe para mim."

"English, Renata, speak English."

"Look at me, Daddy."

"Yes, I see you, my Renie-bird. But, if it hurts you, why not come on the blanket, under the umbrella?"

83

FOR RENATA

"No. I have to *hop* so my piggies don't burn. Ouch...ouch...ouch...ouch."

"Ohhh, well maybe you could hop down to the water then, like a bunny-rabbit."

"No, Papai. Bunny-rabbits hop with two feet at a time. I'm only hopping with *one* foot at a time."

"Of course. How foolish of me," he laughed.

Renie hopped from foot to foot down to the water and then ran along the ridges of the surf.

Keeping an eye on his daughter, Inacio turned his head toward his wife. "I wonder where she gets that stubborn streak from."

Mamãe leaned in close and wrapped her arms around his bicep. "When have you ever known me to be stubborn, my love?"

"Well, have you made an appointment with the doctor yet?"

"Oh, don't start."

"Start what?"

"You know very well what."

"My darling, it *has* been more than four years."

She smiled and kissed him. "Yes, my love, four years of trying *vigorously*. Has it been so horrible for you?"

Inacio grinned and shook his head. "That's not the point. I'd like to have a son before I'm too old."

"You are barely thirty, my love. We have plenty of time."

"What could it hurt just to talk to a doctor?"

Mamãe drew apart from him and sighed. "I hear your voice, Inacio, but I think the words, they are your mother's."

"She is just concerned for us."

"I wish she would concentrate on concerns of her own."

Inacio fixed her with a solemn gaze. "I love you more than life, my darling, but be careful how you speak about my mother."

"I am sorry. It's just that…"

"Papai, Papai. Save me!" Renie screamed as she ran from the water, "A giant shark is after me."

The little girl was soaked with seawater. She leaped into Inacio's arms and hugged him tightly around the neck.

"A shark?" Inacio played along. "Where is it? I'll kill it with my bare hands."

Renie squinted and pointed to the sea.

Inacio shaded his eyes with his hand and surveyed the beach. He made a fist and shook it in the air. "Don't you dare come near my Renie-bird, Mr. Shark, or I'll grab you by the tail and throw you so far out to sea that you'll be lost forever. Then you'll be sorry."

Renie giggled. Inacio cradled her in his arms and kissed her. "He's gone, meu coração. He's swimming away as fast as he can. Don't you worry: Your papai will never let anything bad happen to you."

FOR RENATA

18

September 14, 1963

On their sixth wedding anniversary, Mr. and Mrs. Inacio Raposo had dropped off their daughter, Renata Angelina, at her elementary school. Uncle Pio would pick up Renie at the end of the school day, and take her to Angelina's to spend the night. After their appointment the couple planned to celebrate their anniversary in the elegant dining room of The Clipper Inn, a wooden, oceanfront hotel with a colonial motif.

They sat across from the doctor at his large, walnut desk. Inacio twiddled his thumbs nervously. He already regretted buckling to his mother's pressure to have fertility tests and decided that, no matter what was wrong with his wife, he did not want her to carry a burden of guilt. He was already thinking about the ways in which he might console her when the doctor delivered his diagnosis.

"Well, the news is not good, I'm afraid," the doctor said in a businesslike yet compassionate voice.

Inacio took her hand in his and gave it a little squeeze.

B. ROBERT SHARRY

"Our tests show that Mrs. Raposo is fine but you, Mr. Raposo, are another story. Your sperm count is just too low for you to become a father again."

The Raposos were silent. Inacio, at first, looked shocked, and then embarrassed. The doctor had experienced this pause hundreds of times in his career, and had learned early on to let the couple take a moment to absorb the disappointment.

Inacio shook his head. "I don't understand. Is it because I'm too old?"

The doctor chuckled. "No, no, nothing like that. The reason is right here in your medical history: You had a severe case of rheumatic fever. I'm afraid it damaged you to the point where it would take a miracle now. You should consider yourselves very lucky to have conceived a child before you got sick."

Inacio frowned and his eyes darted about. After a moment, he turned his head slowly to stare at his wife, drawing his hand from hers as he did. His lip curled and he fixed her with an icy stare. She kept her eyes trained on her lap.

"There's always adoption..." the doctor had started to say.

But Inacio was already on his feet and leaving the office. Mamãe sat in silence, her head bowed, for a long while. Finally, she let her eyes meet the doctor's for just a moment. Then she slowly rose and walked out.

FOR RENATA

Inacio Raposo knew how to handle a whore. He remembered the first time he'd had to put one in her place. It was 1945, and he was only fourteen.

He had just returned to port at Gloucester's inner harbor following his first run on a fishing trawler. His father and two older brothers had been claimed by the sea during a Nor'easter two years before. Inacio had suffered some hazing at the hands of his new crewmates, but it was good-natured, partly out of the crew's respect for his father's and brothers' memories, and partly because his uncle, Pio, was on board.

Dozens of laughing gulls circled and hovered about the ship as Inacio walked the metal gangplank to the wooden dock below. The dark green water of the harbor shimmered in the bright sun and lapped at the ship's hull.

Raymundo, the crewmate who had played the most practical jokes on the boy, grinned at him. "You know, when I first saw you, I thought the Captain had brought you along as *bait*," he teased. He threw his arm around Inacio and pulled him in close. "Not bad for your first time out."

Uncle Pio patted Inacio's back. "You did well, Inacio. Your papai would be proud."

"Obrigado, Tio Pio," *Thank you, Uncle Pio*.

While Raymundo, Pio and the rest of the crew lounged patiently, chatted and smoked cigarettes, Inacio paced the dock, seeking his land legs. He strode back and forth edgily while the *Pincesa's* five-thousand pound fish hold was unloaded and weighed. When, at last, the captain was paid for his haul and, in turn, had paid his men in cash, Inacio told Uncle Pio that he was meeting friends to play baseball when school let out at three o'clock.

Pio nodded his head. "Go on, you've earned it. Just don't be late for supper. You know how your mother gets."

"Do I ever," Inacio smiled and headed in the direction of a nearby park. As soon as he was out of sight of the wharf, he changed direction and hustled determinedly toward his true destination.

His pubescent heart pounded, and he trembled like the shaky wooden stairway he climbed to the second-story apartment.

Jody opened the door wearing a pink floral housecoat. Sad, cornflower blue eyes peered out from behind strings of orange hair. She was overweight, but not grossly so, as legend had it. She was quite pretty but looked much older than her 20 years.

"Yeah?" she said.

Inacio deepened his voice. "You Jody?"

Jody folded her arms and gave him a once-over. "Depends. What do you want?"

"If you're Jody, you know what I want."

He looked around impatiently while Jody scrutinized him. He wanted to get inside quickly so as not to be seen by people who would recognize him, especially his crewmates, who might already be seated at the bar on the first floor.

Jody the Irish whore lived above *The Sou'wester*, a fisherman's tavern. The story around town was that she had dated a fisherman who had knocked her up, sailed off to the Second World War, and never came back. The punch-line, often told in a drunken wheeze, was that the fisherman had jumped overboard from a Navy destroyer rather than return to marry the fat sow. Jody's devout Irish Catholic parents had disowned her and would long suffer the shame of her promiscuity.

The thing of which he was most afraid played on the teenager's mind: Other boys had warned him that if a woman "froze up" during sex, the man would be unable to remove his cock no matter what, and the two would be "locked" together. An ambulance or fire truck would be summoned and a special, harness-type device—kept secret from the general public—would be employed to detach the couple. Eventually the man and woman would be separated but only after lengthy, excruciating pain was exerted on the man's still-erect penis.

Jody unfolded her arms and put her hands on her hips. "How old are you?" she demanded.

The boy scowled and answered defiantly. "Old enough to fuck a woman and young enough to do it about ten times."

"Really," Jody chuckled and shook her head, "Well, c'mon in."

Inacio stepped inside and saw Jody's toddler sitting at the kitchen table, nibbling at what aroma told him was cinnamon toast.

Jody said, "Stella, you stay right there. Mommy's going in the bedroom for a little while, okay?"

Stella nodded her head.

Inacio followed Jody down the short hallway and into the bedroom. She closed the door gently. The young prostitute sighed as she turned around to face the boy, and robotically unbuttoned and removed her housecoat.

Jody watched Inacio's face as his eyes surveyed her pear-shaped body. Then she turned her head and looked away. Self-consciousness mixed with shame gave a rosy hue to her delicate face.

Stretched, pendulous breasts peaked with wide, bumpy, pink areolae hung almost to her narrow waist. Shallow, ruddy stretch marks showed harshly against the pale, wilting pleats of her belly. A wispy triangle of orange hair was flanked by heavy inner thighs that pressed together and flattened each other.

Inacio hardened instantly. He rushed forward and began to knead her breasts.

"Steady there, Slick," she said, "You got a pro?"

Inacio's expression changed from awe to confusion.

"A prophylactic, do you have a rubber?"

Inacio stared at her with his mouth agape.

"Never mind," Jody said, "I have one."

She walked to a scarred mahogany dresser. As she opened a top drawer, she smirked and added, "I don't think I have *ten*, though."

After separating Inacio from a five-dollar bill and stuffing it in the pocket of her housecoat, Jody undid his pants and pulled them down. She knelt and sucked him for a minute and then slipped a prophylactic on him with expert efficiency. She climbed on the bed and lay on her back with knees raised, feet flat, and thighs spread wide. Her breasts compressed and slumped to her sides.

Inacio kept his clothes on in case she froze up. With pants around his ankles, he climbed on top of her. He grabbed her breasts and squeezed them hard, and alternately sucked them ravenously.

"Ooo, that feels so good," she cried.

She guided him inside her and said, "Now, show me how you can fuck. A big, strong guy like you, I bet you can move hard and fast, can't you?"

Immediately, Jody began to moan, "Faster, faster."

Moments later, Inacio had finished and crawled crablike off the side of the bed. He pulled his pants up, leaving the condom in place. Jody giggled and shook her head as she slowly eased herself to the edge of the bed.

As she stood up Inacio's right fist slammed into her jaw and sent her reeling back onto the bed. Dazed for a moment, she now grew red-faced with fury and began to climb off the bed. "Why you little…"

Inacio extended the index finger from his fist and pointed it at her. "That's for laughing at me," he said, and then shook his fist and added the warning, "Don't get up. I'll just put you back down again."

Inacio watched the young mother's facial expression change from primal ferocity to uncertainty and fear. This gave the boy a feeling of satisfaction, and brought a smirk to his lips.

"What're you gonna do, call a cop?" he chuckled as he backed up and opened the bedroom door.

He rushed down the hallway and glimpsed 3-year-old Stella sitting obediently in the same kitchen chair. He turned and gave the little girl a smile and a wave as he passed by.

Through eavesdropping on his mother, he would later learn that Jody had met some unsuspecting accountant in Boston who knew nothing of her work, only that she was a war widow with a toddler. *Once a whore, always a whore*, Angelina Raposo half-whispered to a friend when she didn't know Inacio was sitting in the next room.

Once a whore, always a whore.

Mamãe gingerly opened the passenger car door and slid onto the bench seat beside her husband. They sat in silence for a moment. Then Inacio shot her a glare so contemptuous that she could feel it. She stared straight ahead and swallowed hard.

Inacio snarled, and then exploded. He punched the side of her face full-force as he screamed, "Whore!" The vicious blow sent her flying. Her momentum abruptly halted when the opposite side of her head smashed against the passenger window. Her body instinctively jerked into a defensive curl, and she struggled to stay conscious.

"I don't understand," she cried, "it must be a mistake."

"*Lying* whore." Inacio struck again and hit the hand she had raised to protect her face.

FOR RENATA

Inacio slipped the transmission into Drive and raced home like a madman. Along the way he alternated shrieked obscenities with brutal back-handed blows. The car skidded to a halt in the dirt driveway of their cottage on Rose Hip Point. Inacio, his face contorted, flung open his car door, grabbed her by the hair, and dragged her across the car's front seat and onto the ground. She clung desperately to his forearm and flailed her legs in a futile attempt to stand up. He pulled her along the driveway, across the lawn, and over the backdoor threshold to the kitchen. He hurled her headlong across the linoleum floor and into the refrigerator with such force that she blacked out. Moments later, she shook the daze from her head and opened her eyes. Inacio stood over her holding a knife.

She began to weep, pleading quickly in her native Portuguese tongue. "Please, Inacio, please don't do this."

Inacio did not respond, and his silence and murderous stare were somehow more menacing than his screams and punches. Panic engulfed her, and she blurted out the truth.

"Inacio, please listen to me. It's true. Yes, yes, yes, it is true. It was just once, a few days before I left home. I was young and foolish. I was angry because I was being sent to a strange place to marry a man I didn't even know.

"And then when I came here and you were sick, and I was... I panicked. I was afraid. I'm sorry."

Inacio was unmoved.

"But that was before I got to know you...and love you," she whimpered.

Inacio kicked her in the stomach. "Don't you dare talk about love, you fucking whore. You tricked me. You made me love you and your bastard kid. And it was all a lie."

His eyes watered. "You were *everything* to me." He shook his head and turned away. "And now it's all gone," he said, more to himself than to her.

"Inacio, it doesn't have to be," she cried desperately, "Look at all we've built together, all we've been to each other. We can get past this. We don't have to lose it."

Inacio grabbed her hair, pulled her face close to his, and put the knife to her throat. "It's already gone, you fucking whore, because of you and your lies."

She feared for her very life now and began to sob. "Inacio, please, please. I'm sorry, so sorry. Please forgive me. Please don't do this to me. Don't do this to *us*."

She was astonished to see a slight smile come to Inacio's lips. Then the smile faded and his eyes grew colder. And she begged for her life. "Please, Inacio, don't. I'll do anything, anything."

Inacio raised the knife.

"No, Inacio... Nooo!"

FOR RENATA

19

After Mark had signed documents confirming the guardianship, an administrative assistant in the Social Services department of Veterans' Affairs showed him to the room his uncle shared with a ninety-year-old World War II vet named Horace.

Mark studied Peter's left profile from the doorway of the room. A distant, unfocused memory emerged from his childhood. He and Uncle Pete sat together somewhere...at a piano, that was it. Mark was looking up to him—a child's view—as his uncle sang some silly lyric. They both laughed, and then touched foreheads. The memory fluttered from Mark's mind and left him smiling for an instant.

Peter sat in a chair next to his bed while a black-and-white rerun of *Bonanza* played on a flat screen television that hung on the wall. Since Mark was standing to his uncle's left, and Peter's left eye was concealed beneath a black eye-patch, he couldn't tell whether the man was watching TV or sleeping.

When Mark walked around the back of the chair, he saw that Peter's right eye was wide open. He studied his uncle's rugged features for a moment. A thin scar ran from just beneath his right ear to almost the corner of his mouth. His longish, graying hair was combed back and the ends flipped up at the back of his neck.

"Uncle Pete," Mark said. "I'm your nephew, Mark — Marybeth's son? Do you recognize me?"

Peter turned his head and stared at him for a moment. Mark thought he saw a flash of recognition in the old man's eye. But then Peter brought his attention back to the television. *Dumb question*, Mark thought, *he hasn't seen you since you were a toddler.*

Mark sat on the edge of the bed, watched muted Hoss and Little Joe Cartwright, and made one-sided small-talk. He checked the time on his iPhone every few minutes. When he thought he'd stayed a polite amount of time, he stood, put his hand on Peter's shoulder, and said, "I've got to go now, Uncle Pete, but it was nice to see you. I'll come back and visit some more when I can."

Mark started for the door, but Peter blocked his way with the stump of his left arm. The older man rose from his chair, crossed the room and opened the closet door. He reached for something on the top shelf.

With his right and only hand, Peter Ahearn retrieved a thick, leather-bound book and pushed it into his nephew's hands. When he released his grasp, he let out an audible sigh, as if he'd been relieved of a heavier weight than that of the book alone.

FOR RENATA

Mark stared at his uncle and wondered how a man so young, just sixty, could be so broken. He turned the book over in his hands. Its rich brown leather cover was gold-embossed with the words *Keeper's Log.*

Mark was about to ask, "You want me to have this, Uncle Pete?" But he realized it would be another dumb question. Instead he nodded and repeated, "I'll come back," this time with more sincerity.

20

October 9, 1963

Inacio became incensed as he rapidly opened and shut cabinet doors in the tiny kitchen. "Where is it?" he muttered.

"Where's what, Papai?" Renie followed on his heels. "I can find it for you."

Inacio pushed her aside.

The little girl shrank. "I just wanted to help you," she murmured.

"I don't need your help," he said. "Where is it?" he repeated, glaring at Mamãe.

Mamãe's shoulders sagged. She bent down and opened the oven door. She took the whiskey bottle out and placed it on the countertop. Inacio grabbed her throat with one hand and lifted her onto her tiptoes. "Don't ever do that again," he spat.

He took the bottle and a water glass to the living room and set them on the side table next to his easy chair. He turned the television on and poured four fingers of whiskey while he waited for the TV set to warm up. He sank into the chair, propped his feet up on a footstool, and took a sip.

FOR RENATA

Renie watched her papai for a few minutes. When he seemed more relaxed, she slunk over to the easy chair and crawled onto his lap.

"Get off," he said brusquely.

Renie scampered from the chair and across the room.

"Come, meu coração," Mamãe said, "Let me give you a nice warm bath."

Afterwards, when she was nice and clean, Renie knelt at her bedside and finished her prayers with "…and please make papai not be mad anymore." Then Mamãe tucked her into the blankets, and sat on the edge of the bed and read to her.

"In the great green room…"

"Why is Papai mad at me? Am I naughty?"

"No, meu curacao, he is just tired."

Mamãe read three and a half storybooks before Renie lost the battle with her eyelids.

Later that night a noise stirred Renie from her sleep. She listened, but the house was quiet once more. She closed her eyes and rolled over. Then there it was again—a sound she didn't recognize.

Frightened, she slipped out of bed and hurried across the hall to her parents' bedroom. The door was closed. She reached for the doorknob and heard the sound a third time: *WHAP*. It came *from* her parents' room.

She gathered all her courage, turned the doorknob, and pushed inward. The door swung open.

Though they faced her, they did not see her. Mamãe was naked and knelt on the far edge of the bed, her bottom high in the air. Her welt-covered back curved downward, and her shoulders and face were buried in the bedspread. Her black hair splayed out around her. Her hands clutched the bedspread in tight fists.

Papai was naked too. Eyes closed, he stood behind Mamãe and thrust his pelvis against her bottom. Papai's right hand held a thick leather belt. He raised it high in the air and then brought it down hard on the small of Mamãe's back: *WHAP*. Mamãe's body twitched and her cry was muffled by the bedding.

Little Renie gasped.

Mamãe's face came up, and Papai's eyes flew open at the same time. Mamãe's eyes were teary and swollen.

"Get out!" Inacio screamed, "Get out!" He launched the belt across the room. It struck Renie on the cheek.

The little girl recoiled in horror and her lower lip quivered.

Mamãe implored, "Go, meu coração, quickly. Get into bed, and I'll come to you soon."

Renie turned and ran back to her room, crying "I'm sorry, Papai, I'll be good," as she went. She flung the door shut, ran, and jumped into bed. She pulled the covers up over her head. Her little body trembled as she sobbed.

Soon, her mother came to her, wearing a bathrobe. She settled in next to Renie and held her close. Renie found reassurance and comfort in the warmth and scent of her mother.

FOR RENATA

"You were naughty, Mamãe?"

"Yes," she answered. "Mamãe made a mistake."

"That's okay, you won't do it again." Renie's tone sounded very adult.

Mamãe stroked her daughter's hair. "No, I won't."

Later that night Renie dreamed that she was floating in the ocean while a giant shark circled her. She saw Papai on the beach. She screamed to him and swam toward him, but the harder she stroked, the farther away he became.

The shark was upon her now. It opened its huge mouth wide and bared its enormous razor-sharp teeth. Renie felt herself being sucked in to its mouth along with volumes of sea water. The shark's jaws began to close as if in slow motion and Renie knew that she about to be bitten in half.

She sat up in bed, screamed and flailed, and called for her papai. Mamãe held her, whispering, "Shh, meu coração, it is just a pesadelo, a bad dream."

21

December 19, 1969

Renie sat at her desk in the back of her sixth-grade classroom. She rested her chin on the palm of her hand and stared gloomily through a row of large windows with mustard-colored frames. Snowflakes swirled among the bare trees beyond. The din of twenty-five classmates chattering, giggling, and squabbling was nothing more than white noise to her.

The bell rang and the clamor subsided as Mr. Alvarez smiled and said, "Good morning, class."

"Good morning, Mr. Alvarez," the class replied in unison, and the clamor began to rise again.

"Settle down, settle down. Time to take attendance," the teacher said.

He was darkly handsome, just like Renie's papai. But, unlike Papai, he was tall, and his smooth hands were always clean. He dressed neatly in one of three suits that he rotated. Charcoal gray today. And he was never drunk or angry.

FOR RENATA

He had a daughter, Nancy Alvarez. She was in the fourth grade and had beautiful blonde hair. Renie wished that she had blonde hair. And she wished that Papai and Mrs. Alvarez would go away so that Mamãe could marry Mr. Alvarez, and Nancy Alvarez could be her little sister, and Mr. Alvarez could be her papai. That way she could be Renie Alvarez and Mamãe could be Mrs. Alvarez, and they could be smiling and happy like Mr. Alvarez, and Mrs. Alvarez, and Nancy Alvarez always were.

"Renata Raposo," Mr. Alvarez said. She had become lost in daydream while he was doing the roll call.

"Present," she answered.

"Antonio Teixeira."

"Present," the boy said.

"Good, everyone's here today. Pass your homework assignments to the front of the class, and then we can get started."

Mr. Alvarez collected the papers from the front row and placed them on his desk. "Now, we're going to start with a history lesson."

There was a mass shuffle as the children all dug out their history books.

"No, no," Mr. Alvarez said, "you won't find this lesson in your books. This is a special lesson, especially for those of you—maybe even most of you—who are of Portuguese descent.

"Has anyone heard of a man called Pedro Francisco? You might also know him as Peter Francisco."

Branca Neves's face lit up and she raised her hand high in the air.

Branca Neves was Renie's best friend...or the closest thing to a best friend Renie had ever known. They had met on the school bus on the first day of first grade.

Renie had loved kindergarten and was excited to be going back to school. She was wearing a pretty new dress her papai had bought for the occasion. When she sat next to Branca on the bus, she immediately introduced herself. "Hi, I'm Renata Raposo. I live on Rose Hip Point Lane, Hollistown Harbor, Massachusetts. You can call me Renie. What's your name?"

"Branca Neves," she said, and Renie giggled.

"What's so funny?" Branca asked.

"Your name; it's *Snow White*."

"In English, I know," Branca said as if she were saying it for the hundredth time. "I have two brothers, so far, that my daddy says are my dwarfs. He says my mommy might get five more so I'll have seven. But my mommy told him *Keep dreaming,* so I might not."

"My auntie's name is Branca too," said Renie.

"What's her other name?"

"I don't know, I forget. I just call her Titia Branca."

Branca came to play at Renie's house after school one day, and then stayed for supper. But it was after Papai had gotten mad and stopped liking Renie, and Renie got that awful feeling in her chest. But when she was with Branca and having fun, her chest forgot to hurt for a while.

They got off the school bus at Renie's stop and Mamãe was there waiting for them. She held their hands and they skipped the whole way home.

Renie and Branca had so much fun playing in the backyard. But then Papai came home and drank whisky, and the fun stopped. And when Mr. Neves came to pick up Branca, Papai talked really loud and couldn't say all his words right, so he sounded silly, except when he said some bad words. And then everyone was sad, and Mr. Neves took Branca home, and the next day at school Branca said she couldn't come to Renie's house anymore. Branca said Renie could come to her house, but Papai wouldn't let her. And now they were only friends at school and sometimes after church. And now Branca had other girlfriends and they could go to each other's houses, so they were more fun than Renie.

Mr. Alverez said, "All right, Branca, what can you tell us about Pedro Francisco?"

"He was the Giant of the Revolution," Branca said.

"Very good, Branca, I'm impressed," the teacher said. "How did you hear about him?"

"My father told us. Pedro was a patriot and a friend of George Washington's."

"That's right," Mr. Alvarez said, addressing the entire class, "In fact, George Washington, the Father of our Country, said that if not for Pedro

Francisco, a Portuguese immigrant, we might never have won the Revolutionary War. And Pedro was just a teenager at the time, not much older than you.

"He had come to America all alone on a ship when he was just five years old. He was kidnapped from the Azores. And the cruel captain of that very same ship abandoned the little boy on the docks in Virginia.

"Well, eventually he was adopted by the uncle of Patrick Henry, remember him? *Give me liberty, or give me death!*

"Peter grew so tall and so strong that he became a blacksmith. And when he was sixteen, he joined the Continental Army and became their strongest and bravest soldier.

"He was so big and so tall that General Washington had a special five-foot-long sword made especially for him.

"Though you won't find him in your history book, he *should* be in it. Peter Francisco, the Giant of the Revolution. The Portuguese immigrant patriot who saved our country..."

Renie sat up straight and smiled. She listened with rapt attention as Mr. Alvarez became increasingly animated and enthusiastic. Renie thought she might not want to be a nurse when she grew up, after all. She might want to be a teacher instead

22

June 3, 1972

Renie Raposo held her Admiral portable radio in one hand and tucked a sketchpad, with two charcoal pencils inside, under her arm. "American Pie" had been popular for months, and even Mamãe was not immune to humming along.

"If you're going to the lighthouse, will you take this fish stew to Mrs. Gallagher and return her pie plate?" asked Mamãe. "And don't forget to tell her how much we enjoyed her rhubarb pie."

Renie rolled her eyes.

"Don't be that way, Renie. Look, I've put everything in a bag for you, and there's room for your sketchbook too."

Renie took the bag and headed for the back door. Mamãe tapped her own cheek with her forefinger. "Aren't you forgetting something?"

Renie plodded back and pecked her mother on the cheek. She left the house and headed for the road that ran past their cottage and ended at the lighthouse. Rose Hip Point Lane consisted of two parallel dirt tracks with a wide strip of crabgrass growing between them. Renie walked along the left track.

She would graduate from junior high school the following week, but she'd already decided to be "out sick" that day. Mamãe had made her a new dress to wear for graduation, but the hem was hopelessly low and out of style. Most of the girls she knew would be wearing mini-dresses, and a few would even don hotpants outfits. Besides, no one would notice she wasn't there until she didn't come forward to receive her diploma. Even then they would just shrug and move on to the next graduate. She told herself she didn't care.

Except that she would like to think that Mr. Alvarez would miss her. Once, when she was young, she had fantasized that he and her mamãe would get married and that Nancy Alvarez would be her little sister. But things had changed. Mr. Alvarez had let his hair grow longer, and his style had evolved from suits into hipper double-knit sport coats and slacks. And as Renie's body and mind matured, she began to see him differently.

While once she had dreamed of sitting on his knee while Mr. Alvarez smiled and read to her, she now imagined that she herself might one day be Mrs. Alvarez. And why not? In less than two years she'd be the same age as Mamãe had been when she married Papai.

One lazy afternoon, in the privacy of her bedroom, she had pictured Mr. Alvarez naked. In her mind, the handsome teacher had posed like

Michelangelo's statue of David. And then she had broken into tears and sobbed into her bedspread.

She had started to write her thoughts and feelings in a composition book, which, when not in use, was rolled up and hidden behind a baseboard she had pried loose at the back of her closet.

Mamãe was sympathetic to her mood swings and always tried to talk to her about any manner of things. But Mamãe was over thirty. If she didn't even know what girls were wearing these days, how could she possibly understand what her daughter was going through?

Renie was shaken from her thoughts by a sound she seldom heard on Rose Hip Point — a car motor. When she looked back, she saw a sporty red car coming up fast from behind her. She jumped from the lane and watched as it whizzed by.

The driver's window was all the way down. The car radio and her portable one were tuned to the same station and, for the split second it took for the car to pass, she heard "A Horse with No Name" in stereo. The driver was a young man with wavy blond hair, a cinnamon beard, and aviator sunglasses, and he was steering with his right hand. He didn't seem to notice her. His left arm hung out the window and Renie realized that it ended at the elbow.

Peter Ahearn drove his 1966 Dodge Dart the one-mile furrowed length of the dirt road that was Rose Hip Point Lane. He arrived at the lighthouse more than an hour late.

Ed Boino stood outside the light keeper's quarters, impatiently shifting his portly frame. A patch of thermal underwear showed through on his paunch where a button was missing from his plaid flannel shirt. Peter parked his car on the dewy grass and then sat in it for two full minutes while "A Horse with No Name" finished playing on the car radio.

Finally, Peter turned the engine off and reached for the car door handle with his left hand. But his left hand wasn't there anymore, and neither was his forearm. He cursed and lit a Marlboro, and then reached across his body with his right hand and opened the car door. He climbed out, slammed the door shut with his hip, and dragged on his cigarette.

"Mornin', Pete, good to see you," the old light keeper called out. As he walked closer to Peter, he said, "I remember when your Dad would bring you and May-bet and Tommy up here and we'd play Wiffle ball right here on the grass. Gosh, I guess you've grown a bit since those days. Your dad still brags about you all the time."

Peter's silence caused a look of concern to cross Ed's face. "What kept you, son? Did you have a flat on the way over or something?"

"Nope."

Ed waited for Peter to elaborate. When he didn't, Ed shook his head a few times. "All right, then. Let's not waste any more time. Come on, we'll start in the tower."

Ed walked briskly across the lawn to the tower door. As he put his hand on the doorknob, he turned his head back, expecting Peter to be right behind him. Peter was a good twenty yards away, ambling along as he gazed out at the vast, rolling sea.

When Peter finally caught up to him, Ed let out an exasperated sigh. "You know, Pete, I'm all done here, so I don't much care about your attitude. I'm happy to do your father a favor. But the Coast Guard won't be so forgiving. They'll expect you to be conscientious about your duties. A lot of people will be counting on it."

Peter stared at him through his Ray Ban Aviator sunglasses. Ed shook his head again and entered the tower. Peter flicked his cigarette onto the grass and removed his sunglasses, revealing the black eye patch that covered his left eye. He slipped the sunglasses into his shirt pocket next to his cigarettes and followed the old man into the semi-darkness of the tower. He waited for his good eye to adjust to the dimness, and tucked his long, blond hair behind his ears.

"There are eighty-nine steps to the lantern room, and believe me, before long you'll get to know each one of them personally," the old light keeper said.

When they reached the seventy-ninth step, they entered a circular room with a control panel and workbench.

"This is called the Watch Room. This is where we keep all the tools of the trade. Anything you'll ever need to service the lamp and Fresnel lens can be found right here.

"Another ten steps and we'll be in the lamp room."

Most of the round lamp room was taken up by an enormous glass prism — the Fresnel lens.

"She's a first-order Fresnel, almost ten feet high and weighs about a ton," Ed said with pride. He waited for a reaction, but Peter seemed unimpressed. He was staring at the lens with the same disinterested gaze that seemed to be his standard look.

"She can be seen from twenty miles out," Ed continued. Then he added, "That is, *if* she's cared for properly.

"We'll get into that tomorrow. Let's head down and take the cliff path to the dock. I'll go over the basics of the skiff engine, and then I'll show you the generators and give you a tour of your new home."

As the two walked around the lighthouse property, Ed Boino became animated in his descriptions of all of the equipment. Except for an occasional "Uh huh," Peter appeared detached and uninspired, even bored.

The tour ended at the white clapboard house that was the light keeper's quarters. Built in 1800, the small house was older than the current lighthouse, which had been built in 1915 to replace the dilapidated original. Dwarfed by the adjacent tower, the two-story home appeared even smaller than its eight hundred square feet.

Ed and Peter crossed over the worn granite slab doorstep to the wide pine floorboards of the light keeper's quarters. Peter's eye was drawn to a spinet in the living room, and he grimaced. The piano was backed up against the common wall shared by the living room and kitchen.

"Not a whole heck of a lot to see," said Ed. "Just two up and two down. You got your kitchen and living area down here, and upstairs there are two small bedrooms and a bath. I've always used the second bedroom as an office and a storage space.

"The place is small all right, but you'll have everything you need. I'm leaving most of this stuff. Heck, most of it was here when I moved in thirty years ago."

"Uh huh," said Peter as he turned and walked back outside into the bright sunshine.

Ed took a deep breath in and blew it out. Then he followed Peter and caught up with him on the lawn as he neared his car. "Pete," Ed called.

Peter stopped and turned to face the old man.

"Pete, your father's been a good friend to me, otherwise you wouldn't be here. So I'm gonna give you a word of advice."

Noting Peter's reaction, the old light keeper continued. "You can roll that eye all you want, son, but if you never listen to another word I say, listen to this: I wasn't much older than you are now when I took this job. I came here to get away from a world I didn't much like for reasons I don't know you well enough to go into."

Peter pulled his aviator sunglasses from his shirt pocket and put them on.

"The point is this, Pete: If you think you're gonna escape something or someone by coming here, you'd better think again. Whatever your troubles are, they'll follow you here. They'll follow you wherever you go.

"So, my advice is this: Think of this as a time in your life, not the rest of your life. I'm going back to Gloucester now because my sister's got a cancer and she's all alone, and for the first time that I can remember, I'm needed.

"While you're here, do the job and do it well. But don't stay too long, son, or one day you'll wake up an old man and discover that life has passed you by."

Peter turned and walked toward his car. The old light keeper called after him. "Do you know I haven't been sick in over thirty years, not even so much as a cold?"

"Good for you," Peter tossed over his shoulder.

"That's what I used to think. I thought it was because I was such a hardy breed."

Peter had reached his car and was opening the door.

"But then I realized the real reason why," Ed said. Peter stood behind the open car door and faced him. The old man had his attention.

"The reason why I never get sick is that I'm never close enough to another living soul to catch anything."

After a moment, Peter Ahearn folded himself into his car seat. A few seconds later he was speeding down Rose Hip Point Lane.

23

Mark sat on his living room sofa and flipped through the mint green, maroon-lined pages of the Keeper's Log. A sealed, yellowing envelope marked *For Renata* dropped from the book and onto his lap. He picked it up, contemplated it for a moment, and then set it aside and began to read.

July 2, 1972
 The therapist down at the V.A. said it would help if I wrote down my "feelings." Well, most of the time I don't feel anything, and the rest of the time I feel like shit. Oh yeah – that's much better.

July 3, 1972
 Same shit, different day.

July 4, 1972
SSDD. Except that today I heard that Cindy got married to Chip O'Connell. Some friend he turned out to be. They didn't wait very long. Marybeth thinks they might even have been fooling around while I was gone.

B. ROBERT SHARRY

Peter Ahearn tossed the pen onto the Keeper's Log and flung down the roll top of the old oak desk before standing and staggering to the front door. As he crossed the living room, he passed the piano, and then swiveled around to glare at it. His face became contorted. He raised his only hand, made a tight fist, and hammered the keys with all of his might. The discordant sound still echoed through the room as he stepped out of the light keeper's living quarters and walked to the edge of the cliff at Rose Hip Point.

The corners of his mouth fell and his lower lip quivered. He whispered into the warm, humid evening air. "Oh, Tommy, I failed you. I didn't even kill a one of 'em. And when I came home, Ma and Dad and everyone in town pretended I was a hero. But I know the truth: I was just a scared fuck-up who got himself blown up."

Peter pictured his older brother as he had last seen him. Christmas of 1969. Peter had been seventeen and a high school senior. Twenty-two-year-old Tommy had been home on leave. The two spent a lot of time together that Christmas, passing a football back and forth, smoking pot, eating McDonalds, and cruising around Gloucester in Tommy's tan '63 Belair.

It seemed like just yesterday.

Peter's thoughts left the past and he found himself staring with one eye at the stump of his left arm, the stark reality of the present.

FOR RENATA

"You should see me now, Tommy. I'm broken and ugly, and kids are afraid of me. And I can't do the one thing I was really good at any more."

He looked across the water at Gloucester's inner harbor. In the distance, Independence Day revelers milled about the waterfront, and he wondered if Cindy and Chip were among them. He seethed as he pictured the two of them together, naked, doing the same things that he and Cindy had done to each other at every opportunity.

The first flashes of fireworks appeared at Stage Fort Park, followed quickly by the faint cracks of the explosions.

I hate this life.

B. ROBERT SHARRY

24

July 6, 1972
    Met one of my neighbors today. Mr. Raposo is a fisherman who lives about half a mile down the point. Ed Boino warned me about him – said he's a fast-talking drunk who likes to borrow tools, but doesn't always remember to return them...

Inacio Raposo was not a tall man, but if the people who knew him were asked, they would have said that he was. It was the way he carried himself that caused the illusion. Thin and muscular, Inacio stood as erect as if he wore a back brace. When he walked, he strutted, rooster-like. His entire upper body, from narrow waist to puffed-out chest and rigid shoulders, appeared fused, and twisted a little left or right with each step he took.

Peter looked on impassively as Inacio, wearing jeans, work boots, and a faded navy-blue T-shirt, swaggered up the lane. When the fisherman came close enough for a handshake, Peter was surprised to discover that the man was a head shorter than he.

"I'm Raposo," he smiled, exposing a mouth full of perfectly straight teeth. He took Peter's hand in both of his and pumped it vigorously. "I live in the second house down on the right."

Peter made the connection with Ed Boino's caution and gave a simple answer. "Uh huh."

Inacio's smile dimmed only slightly. He reached back and pulled two brown bottles of beer, slippery with condensation, from his back pockets.

"Here you go," he offered, holding one out to Peter.

Peter eyed the fisherman warily. "No thanks."

After giving a quick *suit yourself* shrug, Inacio returned the bottle intended for Peter to his pocket. He dug deep into his front pocket and produced a switchblade, which he deftly opened with a flick of his wrist.

Peter's eye widened, and he took a half-step back.

In a few quick motions, Inacio flicked the bottle-cap off with the blade, closed the knife, and shoved it back in his pocket. He took a short swig of beer. "You gotta lighten up, man," he said with a smirk. "You're way too uptight."

Peter's body relaxed. He felt the blush of embarrassment, but his face maintained a stern expression. "How can I help you, sir?" he asked in an official tone.

"Help me? You think I want something? I just came by to say hello. We're neighbors, man.

120

B. ROBERT SHARRY

"My wife wanted me to bring you a cake, but I said *Fuck that. A man don't want a cake on a hot July day. He wants a beer.*

"And don't call me *sir*. Call me Inacio or Raposo. I may be old enough to be your father, but that doesn't mean you have to remind me of it."

Peter's expression softened, but he didn't smile. "Sorry," he said, "I'm Pete... Pete Ahearn."

The other man's gleaming smile returned. "That's more like it. Now, how about that beer?"

Peter gave a slight smile. "Thanks, but no. I'm on duty."

"Man, you really do need to lighten up. I know what you need...You need to get laid. Maybe you think you can't because of...you know —" he gave a slight nod toward Peter's stump "—but there are girls that hang out down by the docks that would take good care of you.

"I could get one of them to come up here, if you want. They're whores, of course, so you'd have to pay her, but as long as you know how to handle her—no problem. You just gotta be the boss. They'll try to take advantage of you, but you just can't let that happen, that's all."

Peter nodded his head as if he understood. Clearly he wasn't convincing, though, because Inacio said, "You think I'm kidding, Pete? I'm not. I learned a long time ago how to handle a whore. Had my first one when I was fourteen. She was a fat Irish bitch who lived above the Sou'wester. She tried to give me some shit, and BAM." Inacio shook his fist as punctuation. "I laid her out right then and there. She never gave me shit again."

Inacio finished his beer, hurled the empty bottle and watched with satisfaction as it sailed over the edge of the cliff and out of sight. He reached behind himself and pulled the other bottle out.

"Last chance…" he said, holding it out to Peter once more.

"No, thanks," Peter said, "I gotta get back to work now."

The two men shook hands again and Inacio walked across the lawn. When he reached the dirt lane, he stopped and turned back.

"Hey, Pete," he called, "I'm doing some plumbing at my house. You got one of those big pipe wrenches I can borrow?"

25

At 10:00 a.m. Mark stepped out of the chilly wind and into the calm, warm interior of Açores, a tiny Portuguese bakery and café in downtown Gloucester.

The smell of warm pastries and strong coffee rose and mingled with a soft instrumental sound of guitarra Portuguesa. Each confection in the lighted display case shone like an individual work of honey-glazed art.

Mark looked around and spotted his father at one of the round bistro tables in the back of the café. Chris Valente waved him over, and stood to give him a hug.

"My, how you've grown," Chris said.

"Good one, Dad. I'm forty-seven years old and I just saw you last Sunday."

"That's what old men do. We make silly jokes. It's all we have left," Chris folded his newspaper and set it down on the table.

"Thanks for coming downtown, Dad."

"I had to anyway. My tax return has to be postmarked by midnight. You get yours done?"

"I'm on extension. I just scan and email everything to the accountant, and she takes care of it for me."

"Oh, Mr. big-shot Ph.D. has *people* to do his taxes. Coffee's on you today, then."

"You got it."

"And pastries," Chris said, rubbing his hands together. He went up to the counter, and motioned to the woman behind it. "Two bica dupla, please, and one of your luscious sweet breads."

"Yes, sir, duas bica dupla e um pão doce," the woman answered.

"So," Chris returned to the table and sat across from his son, "tell me. What's going on?"

"Oh, I've been trying to deal with this business of the V.A. and Uncle Pete."

Chris nodded. "Yeah, I was afraid that might be what was eating you."

"You ever hear of a woman named Renata, Dad?"

Chris thought for a moment. "I've heard the name, but I can't think of anyone I know by that name, why?"

"It's the weirdest thing. Uncle Pete kept a journal while he was at the lighthouse, and inside there is a sealed envelope marked "For Renata". I haven't opened it so I have no idea what's inside.

"But I read a little of the journal, and so far, it seems like Pete was pretty messed up.

B. ROBERT SHARRY

"What the hell *happened* to him, Dad? Why didn't he ever contact any of us?"

"Who knows, Mark? I mean, he had some bad breaks for sure, but I think Pete was his own worst enemy in a lot of ways.

"Yes, he was wounded, and yes, that shallow girl jilted him, but you know what? A lot of guys were wounded and a lot of guys were jilted. The difference is that they didn't cut themselves off from everyone who cared about them, everyone who wanted to help. Pete did, and he made things worse for himself and everyone around him."

Chris looked around the café, and then leaned toward Mark, lowering his voice. "That was an awful night after the Memorial Day parade and picnic. You know what that self-absorbed ninny, Cindy, did to Pete? In front of a whole bunch of people, she just returned the ring and said *I just can't deal*. Can you even imagine anyone being that callous?"

Chris stirred raw sugar into his coffee and shook his head. "Pete just stood there like he was frozen and watched her walk away.

"And, then—get this—she hops into Pete's best friend's waiting car and drives off with him.

"Pete came to our house late that night. You were upstairs, fast asleep, thank God, and I was upstairs too, but I could hear Pete and your mom talking in the kitchen. I felt so bad for him. He was really hurting, I remember him asking your mom *Am I that repulsive?*

"He lived with your grandparents for about a year after that. He didn't leave the house much, except to take an occasional walk to the liquor store after dark. Mostly he sat and watched television while he drank himself numb and felt sorry for himself.

"Grandma and Grandpa repeatedly tried to convince Pete to do something with his life. Grandpa suggested job after job that could be done with one arm and one eye, and Grandma pushed for him to go to college. No matter what their approach, Pete would just hiss *Leave me alone,* and tune them out.

"You know, I shouldn't say this, but sometimes I think it might have been better if Pete hadn't made it home at all. Seems to me he died anyway."

Later that night Mark Valente lifted the Keeper's Log from his coffee table, leaned back on the sofa, and started reading where he had left off the night before.

While the other inhabitants of Cape Ann slept, he read through the night. Shortly before dawn broke, as the fishermen and lobstermen rose from their beds, Mark read the final journal entry, dated May 4, 1975. He sat bolt upright in astonishment and whispered, "My God, Pete, what did you do?"

26

July 8, 1972
Met my closest neighbor today, Mrs. Gallagher is a busybody who lives a quarter-mile down the point and looks like she's a hundred...

It was 6:00 a.m. The sun had been up for forty-five minutes and Peter had darkened the Fresnel lens for the day. He was pouring his second cup of coffee when he heard a gentle knock on the front door. He peered out the kitchen window and took in the profile of the old woman on the stoop. Her long, grey hair was piled on top of her head in thick braids. She had a short, upturned nose and thin lips that were curled into a slight, friendly smile. Her navy, floral dress had a lace collar and half-sleeves, and its hem fell below her knees, revealing stockings and maple loafers with thick heels. She was apple shaped and slightly plump, with no discernible contrast between her waistline and her torso and hips.

FOR RENATA

Figuring that she was either peddling religion or soliciting for a charity, Peter decided not to answer the door. Then he changed his mind. He thought it might be amusing to see the look on the old lady's face when a freak with an eye-patch opened the door. He grinned to himself, opened his good eye as wide as he could, and flung the door open.

But it was Peter who was startled. The old woman didn't even flinch. In fact, as if joining in his game, she opened her eyes wide to mimic Peter's expression and broadened her smile. Peter was struck by the surprising warmth and depth of her pale blue eyes.

"Good Morning, Peter."

Peter cleared his throat. "Hi," he answered, red-faced.

"I'm Mrs. Gallagher."

Peter's confusion was obvious.

"I'm your *neighbor*, dear," she said, and held up a small basket covered by a white linen napkin.

"Mr. Boino told me you were taking his place. I brought you a small housewarming token to say *Welcome to the neighborhood*." She breezed past the young man and led him into his own kitchen.

"These scones are just out of the oven," she said, unveiling the basket. "Smell," she said, and lifted the treats to Peter's nose.

Peter felt the warmth rise to his face as he took in the pleasant aroma. "Mmm," he said, because he thought it was the polite thing to do. It had been a while since he'd done anything out of politeness.

Mrs. Gallagher lowered the basket onto the kitchen table, retrieved a jar that was nestled among the scones, and then re-covered them so as to preserve their heat. She held up the jar and pointed to its amber contents. "And this is my homemade rose hip jelly. Hopefully you have butter and tea, dear?"

Peter hadn't yet issued an invitation. "Um, butter, yeah," he said, flustered. "But I don't think I have any tea."

"Oh," Mrs. Gallagher sounded dubious. "Have you checked the top shelf of the cabinet to the left of the sink?"

Peter regarded her with suspicion.

"Edward always kept a box of Bigelow up there."

"Edward?"

"Mr. Boino, dear."

Peter opened the cabinet door and, sure enough, there was a box of Bigelow "Constant Comment" tea on the top shelf.

Mrs. Gallagher beamed with the satisfaction of one who's been proved correct. She took the old copper kettle from the stovetop, added water from the kitchen faucet, and put it on the burner to boil. "Why don't you get the butter out of the fridge, Peter? We'll place it near the kettle so that it softens a bit."

While Mrs. Gallagher's tea steeped she broke open a still-warm scone, slathered the halves with butter, and spread them with a thin layer of rose hip

FOR RENATA

jelly. She handed one to Peter and watched with obvious anticipation as he took the first bite.

"Mmm," he repeated, meaning it this time. Peter had been eating cornflakes every morning, and sometimes cornflakes served as lunch and dinner too. The blend of the warm, crumbly scone, the creamy butter, and the cool sweet jelly was a welcome change for his palate.

"Really good," Peter declared as he took another, larger bite.

The old woman's face lit up with pride. "I'm so happy you approve, Peter," she said, and took a dainty bite of her own.

"What kind of jelly did you say this is?"

"Rose hip, dear, just like the name here. Rose Hip Point is riddled with wild rose bushes. And the hips, you see, are the seed pods."

"Oh." Peter nodded his head while he subdued a yawn.

"I collect them every year after the first frost, usually at the beginning of November. The frost helps sweeten them a bit. Perhaps you'd like to help me gather them this fall?"

Not in a million years. "Maybe."

"Oh, that'll be lovely, Peter."

"Ah...Of course it'll depend on how busy I am."

"You won't be busy then, dear. Spring and summer are your busiest times, Edward told me. You may even have time to help me make the jelly."

"Oh, I couldn't. I don't know anything about..."

"It's simple, really. We clean out the seeds, cook the hips, and then strain them for the juice. Then we just add a little pectin, a little butter and lemon juice, *lots* of sugar, and voila.

"Ooo, and we can make a little jam while we're at it. I like to add lemon zest to the jam, it makes it sort of marmalade-y. I wish it was fall right now — I'm so excited, I can hardly wait."

Peter nodded his head but didn't speak. There was a brief but uncomfortable period of silence that was broken by Mrs. Gallagher.

"Tell me about yourself, dear."

Peter rose from his seat at the kitchen table. As he strode across the kitchen and opened the door that led outside, he said, "I'd love to, Mrs. Gallagher. Like you said, though, this is my busy time of year. Thanks so much for stopping by, and for the scones and jelly."

Mrs. Gallagher was nonplussed, but she stood and followed him.

"Of course, dear. I understand."

When the old woman left, it felt like all the air in the room went out with her. Peter was happy she was gone, but he felt more alone than ever.

FOR RENATA

27

July 15, 1972
*   Marybeth and Ma keep calling, wanting to come over. I tell them no. I don't feel like having company...*

Katherine Ahearn, at the wheel of her husband's 1970 Stratomist Blue Buick Riviera, arrived at Rose Hip Point at 10:00 a.m. The temperature had already risen to 85 degrees and was predicted to be near 100 by 3:00 p.m.

She got out of the car and pulled at her yellow and white sundress where perspiration had sealed it to her body. She smoothed the front as best as she could with the palms of her hands. The kitchen door of the house swung open and Peter appeared. Katherine was shocked by the gaunt and disheveled soul standing before her.

"Oh, dear God," she said, tears welling in her eyes. She hurried to him and took his face in her hands. "My dear boy," she whimpered, "what are you doing to yourself?"

Peter backed away from his mother. "Ma, what are you doing here?" It came out as a statement of irritation rather than a question.

Katherine looked wounded. "Can't a mother bring a few things to her son?" she asked, defensively. She opened the car trunk and pointed to a cardboard box.

Peter riffled through the box. "These are my old ski clothes, Ma."

"And some summer things too."

"Ma, I told you I don't want *anybody* coming here."

Katherine Ahearn stood very erect. "Well, I. Am. Not. Any. Body," she said, enunciating each syllable.

Peter looked like a little boy who had just been scolded. "That's not the point. I just need some time alone right now," he said, his eye darting every which way except at his mother.

"No, you need to be around the people who love you."

"What do *you* know?"

"I know you better than you know yourself, Peter Ahearn. I know why you came up here, and I know it's not good for you."

"You and Dad are the ones who kept telling me to get a job."

"Or go to school," Katherine said.

Peter began to pace. "Oh, right, Ma, maybe I should have gone to Berklee just like I planned. How many one-armed musicians do you know?"

FOR RENATA

"You don't have to study music, Peter. You have many talents, and there are any number of careers for you to choose from. But if your heart's still set on music, well, you could study composition. You've always liked writing songs…"

"Oh, please," said Peter.

"Peter, you need to be around people. I understand that you might not want to confide in your father and me about…things, but surely you have friends you could talk to."

"Who, Ma, Chip O'Connell?"

"I know how that must have hurt you, and I'm truly sorry for it. But Peter, you're just twenty. You have your whole life ahead of you. Don't let this setback ruin your entire life."

Katherine sighed and began to tear up. "You know what I've always said about you? *When Peter has a problem, he solves it. You may not always like the way he solves it, but he solves it.*

"Now, I'm worried because you're not yourself, and you're not solving your problems, you're making them worse.

"You're mad at the world, and I don't blame you. Lord knows you've had more than your share of tragedy and disappointment, and at such a tender age. I don't know how to make you understand that there's much more to life than you think there is right now."

The anger on Peter's face faded and was replaced by concern. "Don't cry, Ma, I'll be all right."

"You don't have to confide in me, but please promise me you'll find somebody to talk to."

"I will, Ma…"

"And that you'll eat more."

"I will, Ma, but I have to get back to work right now."

Katherine smiled through her tears. She cupped Peter's face in her hands once more. "I wonder: How are you going to solve this one, Peter?"

28

July 17, 1972
I'm tired. There's more to this lighthouse gig than I thought there would be, and I never get enough sleep. Even little things piss me off...

Peter awoke at 4:00 a.m., his body and bed sheets drenched with sweat. As usual, Cindy was on his mind. She was there every morning when he awoke, and she was there every night when he closed his book, switched off the bedside lamp, and shut his eyes.

The air had been still and thick with humidity for three days. The temperature had reached 97 the day before and hadn't dropped below 78 throughout the night.

At 4:30 a.m. Peter sat at the picnic table near the cliff's edge, and clutched a ceramic mug with his only hand. The pre-dawn blackness was all that cloaked his naked body.

He stared eastward over the ocean, and could scarcely distinguish the horizon. Faint birdsong became lost in the thunderous battle-cry of a bullying sea as it pummeled the cliff's already battered face. Then waves hissed in retreat and gathered strength for the next assault.

The black of a moonless night faded, and the horizon revealed itself, a line of demarcation between a charcoal sea and a slate sky—a pale opening act for the rising sun.

The sky above the water was clear, but a narrow band of low clouds hung over the land. An oily drop of rain splattered upon Peter's shoulder. A few seconds later, he felt another, followed by several more. The raindrops felt oddly warm to him, but when enough had fallen that his body was covered completely, Peter's skin cooled, and he shivered.

The very tip of the sun peeked above the border between sea and sky and everything changed. The sky above the Atlantic turned light blue and was streaked with a few wispy, brushstroke clouds. The ocean a few moments before had been dark, now it shimmered as though coated with gold leaf. The sun rose to three-quarters and sat on the edge of the world like a terracotta dome on a glass cathedral.

And still rain fell on Peter.

A distant memory surfaced in his mind: His beloved maternal grandfather, who had come to live with the family shortly before Peter was born, had succumbed to a heart attack at the breakfast table when Peter was eight.

FOR RENATA

At Grandpa's wake Peter was overcome with sorrow and began to sob uncontrollably. Tommy, then thirteen, had flung his arm over Peter's shoulder and pulled him close. Peter buried his face in Tommy's chest, his small body convulsing with grief, his tears wetting Tommy's white dress shirt. Marybeth joined the huddle and rubbed Peter's back. When young Peter at last stopped trembling, Tommy leaned down and said, "It can't be sunshine and birds singing every day, you know, Pete."

"Tommy," Peter said softly, and then shook himself from the memory and turned his attention back to the sunrise.

It began to rain harder on him. Peter stood with arms and legs spread wide, like a Vitruvian Man missing half a spoke.

After a time, the shower became a sprinkle, and then stopped. Peter picked up his mug, drained the last of the rain-thinned whiskey it held, and walked back to the lighthouse to begin his workday. Today, as every day, he would trudge through, zombie-like, waiting only for the moment he would find the courage to do what he knew he must. And each night when that courage eluded him again, he would crawl back into bed and read until sleep came and brought with it a transitory escape. Sleep was seldom restful and often fraught with nightmares. But in dreams, he could at least touch the horror with two hands and see it with two eyes.

29

A *ugust 1, 1972*
    Ed Boino has been teaching me how to maintain the generators and the Fresnel lens. He's kind of a stickler for doing things by the book. I like it better when he's not looking over my shoulder. The tower is sixty feet tall and has exactly eighty-nine spiral steps (take my word for it). By the time I raise the flag at 8:00 a.m., I've already been working for a couple of hours. And by the time I turn the tower light on for the night, I'm dead tired.

October 29, 1972
    Old Lady Gallagher came over this morning and tried to get me to pick her rose hips for her. I told her I wasn't feeling well. It wasn't really a lie.

October 31, 1972
    I feel like a one-armed, one-eyed circus freak. No more shopping. I'll have Vasconcelos's Market deliver everything from now on…

Peter exited the A&P through its newly installed Horton automatic sliding door. He carried a brown paper bag brimming with groceries. He walked to the passenger side of his car and hoisted the grocery bag onto the roof. Using the stump of his left arm to hold the bag in place, he opened the passenger door with his right hand. He was reaching for the bag when he heard the taunting refrain: *"He's a one-eyed, one-armed, flying purple lighthouse keeper."*

Peter spun around in time to see three boys — he guessed they were about twelve or thirteen years old from their size and the pitch of their laughter. They sprinted toward the safety of the opposite side of the A&P.

He could run after them, but what would that accomplish? And what would he do if he caught them? Besides, when he'd swung around to look at the boys, he had knocked the grocery bag to the ground. Half of its contents were strewn around the pavement, and a couple of the canned goods had rolled under the car.

Peter fell to one knee, righted the half-empty bag, and refilled it one item at a time before hefting it onto the passenger seat. Then he slammed the passenger door shut with enough force to make the entire car rock side to side for a moment.

Peter rounded the car, hopped into the driver's seat, and sped away. The tires seemed to shriek in anger and frustration. Two cans were left on the ground where the car had been parked. A teenage girl with long, black hair and a sad expression picked them up.

The next morning Peter found the cans on his granite doorstep.

B. ROBERT SHARRY

30

November 15, 1972
    Today the sea is like me: dark, cold, and restless,
like it's pacing back and forth outside my door. And I am
tempted. I'd like to stand on the edge of the cliff and just
let myself fall forward. Maybe the icy seawater would
freeze my brain and stop the endless stream of thoughts
that races through it. I wouldn't shiver. I'd just fall
asleep in the sea and never wake up. And all of this pain
would be gone.

Christmas, 1972
    Ma, Dad, Marybeth, and her husband and kid came
over this morning. Ma and Dad said they didn't know
what to get me so they just gave me cash. Marybeth gave
me a new album – The Concert for Bangla Desh – and
she told me it was sad that I didn't have any Christmas
decorations. Give me a break…

On Christmas Eve, Peter was watching the local
six o'clock news on the couch when he heard a soft
knock at the door. *Cindy.* He rose, crossed the

room, and turned off the television. He had fantasized about the day when she would show up to tell him what a terrible mistake she'd made by marrying Chip.

Peter opened the door. His smiled faded when he saw Mrs. Gallagher standing on the stoop.

"I hope you haven't eaten yet, dear. I brought some chicken pot pie and Apple Betty."

Peter made no attempt to hide his disappointment. "This really isn't a good time, Mrs. Gallagher."

"Oh? Do you have company, Peter?"

"Well, no, but…"

"No one should be alone on Christmas Eve, dear," she said as she started to enter the living room.

You mean you *shouldn't be alone on Christmas Eve. Some people* want *to be left alone.*

Peter blocked her entrance by putting the stump of his left arm on the door frame.

"I'm really not in the mood for company, Mrs. Gallagher. I'm sorry."

The woman looked stung for a moment, but then a smile returned to her face as she held out the food. "Of course, dear, I understand."

Peter felt a sharp and unfamiliar twinge of shame as he accepted the homemade dinner.

Mrs. Gallagher added a cheerful "Merry Christmas, dear" before turning and stepping off the granite slab doorstep of the light keeper's quarters.

B. ROBERT SHARRY

Peter watched the old lady trudge through the snow. "Merry Christmas, Mrs. Gallagher, and thanks for the food," he called out meekly.

He closed the door and carried the food to the kitchen.

Bridey Gallagher leaned against the wall of the mud room and slipped out of her winter boots before entering her kitchen. She shuffled across the linoleum floor in her stocking feet. "Brigid McCarthy, you pick up your feet this instant," she said aloud, mimicking her mother's admonition of a lifetime ago.

She picked up a cookbook, balanced it on top of her head, and glided gracefully toward the cabinets. "Very good, Bridey," she said when she reached them. She bowed her head slightly and caught the book in her hands as it fell from her head, just as she'd done when she was a girl.

Her stomach growled. She had thought she would share the chicken pot pie and Apple Betty with Peter, but now she'd have to come up with something else to eat. Thoughts of Mother had given her an idea: She opened a cupboard door and spied them, the egg cup and timer Mother had bought for her at a church rummage sale in 1905. The egg cup was delft blue and decorated with the outline of a plump blue hen on the front. On the back, a fresh-laid blue egg rolled down a blue chute to a blue bed of straw.

"I'll have breakfast for supper," she said.

FOR RENATA

She put the teakettle and a small saucepan on to boil, then set a place for herself at the kitchen table. She brought out cinnamon bread for toast, butter, and rose hip jam. When the water around the egg came to a boil, she flipped the timer over and watched with childlike fascination as the sand drifted to the bottom. She scooped the egg up with a teaspoon and gently transferred it to the egg cup. With one good practiced tap of the spoon she broke through the shell and peeled off the dome. The egg was done perfectly, as all her eggs had been for nearly seventy-odd years.

But the egg was different from those of her youth. She had grown up on a small farm in upstate New York, so she was used to fresh eggs, which came in shells of different sizes and colors. Some shells were even light blue or light green. She remembered the day her older brother, Jim, had told her that those were "lucky eggs." To eat one would bring good fortune. She smiled and shook her head.

"And the yolks were different too in those days," she said aloud, "not this pallid, sickly yellow you see now, but a deep carroty-orange."

She buttered her toast, wagged the knife, and said, "And the toast was different too. We had thick slices from Mother's homemade bread, bread that I helped her make, no less. My word, there was no such thing as pre-sliced bread back then." The truth was, though, that she dearly loved this sliced cinnamon bread.

She remembered buying her first loaf of sliced Wonder Bread. She had been almost thirty years old. Henry had acted indignant, saying that it was a sign of the laziness of modern society and the beginning of the end of the American work ethic. But the twinkle in his eye had told her that he was speaking tongue in cheek.

But she wouldn't have cared even if he had been serious. She hadn't bought it for the convenience, she'd bought it because little Jack had pestered her to buy some after a visit to a friend's house.

Jack.

She wondered for the millionth time if she had done everything she could have. *Perhaps Jack would still be here if only…* Maybe he'd be married. Maybe he'd have a little boy and a little girl who called her "Grammy."

They have made our world dirty, Jack's note had said. *And I am weary of feeling unclean.*

Thoughts of Jack led to thoughts of the young light keeper, and her appetite deserted her. Bridey cleared the dishes. She poured a warm-up in her tea and placed the cup and saucer on her nightstand, next to Agatha Christie's *Murder at the Vicarage*.

She made the rounds of the house and shut off the Christmas lights before preparing for bed. Then she disrobed, washed her face, and put on a full-length, soft flannel nightgown. She brushed her hair one hundred times, re-braided it, and got into bed. The sheets were cold and her feet were frigid. She turned onto her left side, brought her knees up, and shivered.

Henry moved over from his side of the bed to the middle and pressed up against her. He smelled

FOR RENATA

of hair tonic and pipe tobacco. The warmth of his body passed through his pajamas and her nightgown to her back. He flopped his heavy, flannel-covered arm over her shoulder and interlaced the fingers of his right hand with hers. She snuggled back into the nest of his embrace and brought the bottoms of her cold feet to rest against his warm shins.

"You'd think that, after all this time, I wouldn't still miss you so much it hurts," she whispered. Then Bridey Gallagher did something she hadn't done in ages: She cried herself to sleep

31

Mark Valente felt burdened by his uncle's confession. A trip to the archives of the local newspaper had revealed that the cause of death had been determined "accidental". And records of the Hollistown Harbor tax assessor's office had shown property on Rose Hip Point Lane under the name "Raposo".

But even if the girl his uncle had written about did still live on Rose Hip Point, what could Mark do? He could go see her, certainly, but how would he tell her what he knew or how he knew it?

Six weeks after reading his uncle's Keeper's Log, Mark had finally made his decision. Now it was time for him to see it through. After a fifteen-minute drive, he sat fidgeting in his truck in front of the house on Rose Hip Point Lane. It was a quintessential New England seaside cottage complete with weathered, grey cedar siding, white trim, dark green shutters, and a white, wooden screen door that framed a scarlet front door. The name on the mailbox, Raposo, told him he had the right house. But was it the right time? Could it *ever* be the right time?

Mark was about to share his Uncle Pete's confession with the person whom it would affect the most. He gripped the Keeper's Log tightly under his arm and slowly approached the door. His eyes searched for a doorbell but found none. He slid behind the screen door, and lifted the small brass knocker, bringing it down three times — *rap, rap, rap.* After what seemed like an eternity but might, in fact, have been no more than ten seconds, he abandoned the decorative knocker in favor of the heel of his hand — *thump, thump, thump.*

Several more seconds passed before the door swung open. And there she stood. Mark knew her instantly. There was no mistaking her after reading the Keeper's Log. Her complexion was a flawless olive, her hair was coal black, and her eyes were the color of caramel. She would be in her fifties now, but looked at least a decade younger. And her beauty was striking.

"Oh, hello," she smiled. "I *thought* I heard the door. Can I help you?"

"Renata?"

She looked at Mark quizzically. "Do we know each other?"

"Not exactly. My name is Mark Valente. I think you knew my uncle, Peter Ahearn? He was the lighthouse keeper at Rose Hip Point during the early seventies."

"Oh, of course." With recognition came the sad smile that had been described in the Keeper's Log.

"How is he? *Where* is he? We always wondered what became of him, he left so suddenly."

Mark hesitated. A strange feeling came over him: Guilt. He had never seen such a beautiful woman. He understood now why Pete had fallen so hopelessly and completely in love. Though he had just met her, Mark felt like a schoolboy. He was mesmerized by her dusky, sparkling eyes and coral lips. She was the great love of his uncle's life and Mark couldn't take his eyes off of her. He felt himself blush.

"I'm sorry, what?" Mark asked.

"I was asking where Pete is now."

"Right. Sorry. Pete lives at the Soldiers' Home near Boston. I'm afraid he has a form of dementia, and he's really not able to live on his own anymore."

"Oh, I'm so sorry to hear that. And so young for dementia, he couldn't be more than sixty."

"Sixty, exactly. The doctors think it could be related to exposure to Agent Orange while he was in Vietnam," Mark said.

"My God, he was just a boy. But then, most of them were. You say Pete's your uncle?"

"Yes, he's my mother's brother. I'm his closest living relative, and the court has appointed me his guardian.

"I wanted to speak with you because, well, I think he was very…I think you were very important to him."

"Me? That's sweet, but it's been so many years. I mean, I remember him, of course. He was very kind to me at a difficult time in my life. I was in high school then, and...well, come in, come in," she said.

She led Mark through the living room, where several seascapes and landscapes—some sketches, some oils, some watercolors—hung on the walls. He noticed an oil painting of the Rose Hip Point Lighthouse in which a tall, slim man with an eye patch leaned against the lighthouse door. Uncle Pete.

They entered the kitchen where she offered refreshment. "Can I get you anything? Coffee? Water?"

"Well, if it's no trouble, I wouldn't mind a cup of coffee."

"No trouble at all. In fact, I could go for some too," she scooped ground coffee into the filter of a drip coffee maker. When she spoke again, she kept her eyes on the coffeepot. "Um, please don't misunderstand me. I'm very sorry to hear about Pete's condition, but...what is it that makes you think I was so important to him?"

Mark hesitated, then let out a sigh. "He kept a journal of sorts called a Keeper's Log during the three years he was at the lighthouse."

"Oh?"

"Yes, and he wrote quite a bit about you."

"About me? What did he write?"

"Ms. Raposo..."

"Actually, it's Bennett, at least for the time being. I've been living in the Berkshires, but I'm starting over, you might say. I'm staying here at my mother's house until I get resettled. And please call me Renie. Everyone does."

Mark noticed that she was wearing a wedding ring. He wanted to say *What kind of fool would ever let you go?* but he only managed a soft-spoken, "Sorry."

"You were saying?"

"Right, I was about to say that you might want to read the Keeper's Log, that you *should* read it."

"This is all very mysterious, Mr. Valente."

"Call me Mark, please. I know how strange this must sound, but it would be very difficult for me to explain everything if you don't read Pete's journal for context."

"Where's he been all this time?"

"I don't know. He just vanished thirty-seven years ago. I was pretty young at the time, and there's been no contact, even with family, since he left Rose Hip Point."

"Is that it?" Renie asked, nodding her head toward the book.

"Yes, but I should probably tell you a few things about Pete before you take a look at it."

"You mean, for *context*? My God, what does he say about me?"

"I'm sorry, I don't mean to be so cryptic, I just need you to understand how Pete got...the way he was."

"You mean physically, his arm and his eye?"

"Well, that, yes. But also his frame of mind when he became light keeper."

"I already know that he was injured in Vietnam."

"Right, his older brother, my Uncle Tommy, had gone there before him and was killed in action."

"I'm sorry."

"Thanks. Anyway, Pete enlisted as soon as he heard about Tommy. I think a lot of younger brothers are apt to do that.

"Pete wasn't over there very long before he was badly wounded in a booby trap, he lost part of his left arm and the sight in his left eye.

"Before he left for basic training he'd gotten engaged to his high school sweetheart, a girl named Cindy. But when he returned, Cindy broke off their engagement. Pete moped around his parents' — my grandparents' — house for about a year and nearly drove them crazy. He drank a lot, and acted sullen, nasty, and withdrawn. My mother described him as 'broken'.

"Anyway, one day a friend of my grandfather's, Ed Boino…"

"I remember Mr. Boino, he was the light keeper before Pete," Renie said.

"Exactly. Mr. Boino told my grandfather that he was retiring and that he could arrange for Pete to take his place at the lighthouse. I guess the thought of being in isolation appealed to Pete. I don't know, I think he was mad at the whole world, and he saw Rose Hip Point as a sort of refuge."

"But how do I fit into all of this?" Renie asked.

"Here," Mark answered by offering the Keeper's Log. "A lot of the entries have to do with weather and maintenance, but you can just skip over those."

B. ROBERT SHARRY

Once the coffee was brewed and poured, they settled into chairs around the kitchen table. Renie opened the Keeper's Log with a certain reverence. She smiled anxiously at Mark and began to read.

FOR RENATA

32

January 15, 1973
I should never have come here. It wasn't so bad in the warm weather. Then, at least, there was plenty of work to keep me busy. But now I just check the generators, clean the lens, and turn the light on and off. There's too much time to think. I wish I could turn my brain off as easily as I do the tower light. Ironically, for a "light" house, it's so fucking dark in here all the time. I leave the TV on day and night.

February ?, 1973
Don't know what day it is, don't care. Oh wait, I know. It's the day the Coast Guard decided to make a bullshit surprise inspection. The Chief Warrant Officer said that the brass and the Fresnel lens weren't clean enough, and the house smelled like a ship's head. He told me, "If you wanna live like a pig, that's your business." I

said, "What's the problem, then?" He said, "The problem is, if the light's not maintained, peoples' lives are at risk, so you better shape up."

Fuck you. So you can only see the light from fifteen miles instead of twenty — big fucking hairy deal. Fire me — you'd be doing me a favor, asshole.

February 14, 1973
The nighttime is the worst and nighttime starts at around four o'clock now. As evening falls, so do my spirits...

Peter Ahearn entered the tower at its base and began to climb. He reached out with his right and only hand, grabbed the iron railing, and lugged his gaunt body up the spiral of concrete steps with the weariness of a man four times his age.

He had carried an awful heaviness in his chest, day-in and day-out, for almost two years now. Like an insidious parasite, the weight had lodged itself in his heart and fed on his spirit. It had sapped his energy, made his head bow and shoulders droop, and infected his mind. And tonight it would become unbearable.

At the eighty-ninth step he reached the Lantern Room. Two thousand pounds of thick, rippled glass left scarcely enough room for the narrow catwalk that surrounded it. Peter opened the door to the balcony and shivered as he stepped into the frigid February air. He looked out over the angry Atlantic and then stared straight down, a hundred and twenty feet, to where the sea threw powerful

FOR RENATA

punches at the cliff's face. It would be dark soon. His thought was the same every evening: *Just let yourself fall and all this pain will be gone.*

Peter closed his eyes, stretched his one and a half arms out wide, and fell forward. After a few moments, he pushed his body up from its leaning position against the chest-high railing, walked back inside, and shut the door. He turned his face away from the glass behemoth and threw the switch that brought it to life. The light equivalent of half a million candles was concentrated into a pulsing beam that shot out twenty miles over the dimming ocean to guide the seafaring, as it had for more than two hundred years.

The young man started his second descent of the day. Each morning, shortly after dawn, he would trudge the same eighty-nine steps and throw the switch in the opposite direction, dousing the light for the day.

At step seventy-nine he stopped. From the corner of his good eye, among the tools in the Watch Room, something caught his attention, a twelve-foot length of thick rope that lay coiled on a bottom shelf.

He took the rope, looped it under the stump of his left arm and over his shoulder, and continued down the spiral staircase. At the base of the tower he followed a short passageway to the light keeper's quarters. He passed through the kitchen and settled himself on the living room couch.

It took considerably longer for Peter to make a noose than it would have for a man with two hands.

B. ROBERT SHARRY

Everything took longer. He looped the rope with his hand and used his teeth to pull the working end through, forming the knot that would rest against the back of his neck. By the time he had finished, another hour had gone by and darkness had enveloped the landscape of Rose Hip Point.

Peter went to the kitchen and fetched a straight-backed, wooden chair. He threw the working end of the rope up and over an exposed oak beam that ran the length of the small house. Standing on the pale-yellow, distressed chair that would be his gallows, he checked the length of the rope.

Satisfied that his feet would not reach the floor once he had kicked the chair out from under himself, he got down and scouted for a place to tie off the other end of the rope, known to sailors as the "bitter end". He needed to find something that would hold his body weight, something that weighed more than he did.

He chose the old, enormous roll top desk and tied the bitter end to its right front foot. He went back to the kitchen and returned a few moments later with a bottle of whiskey. He sat down at the desk and lit a cigarette. Alternately, Peter swigged from the bottle and drew on Marlboros as he stared up at the instrument of death he had fashioned. After a time, the bottle was empty and the ashtray, full.

He stepped up onto his gallows chair and slipped the noose over his head. *This is for you, Cindy. Am I that repulsive?*

FOR RENATA

Taking several deep breaths, Peter Ahearn closed his eyes and counted to himself, *one…two…three…*

He was startled by a loud pounding on the exterior door. Distraught and disoriented, he made to step from the gallows chair and was jerked back by the noose at his throat.

"Just a minute," he croaked as he loosened the knot and removed the rope from his neck.

He pulled the rope from the beam and stuffed it behind the couch.

The pounding continued.

He carried the gallows chair back to the kitchen.

Still the pounding came.

"Coming," he cried.

Peter stopped short of the door and took a moment to compose himself before unlocking the deadbolt and reaching for the doorknob. He had turned the knob only a fraction when the door opened inward with force enough to push him back.

Mrs. Gallagher and the freezing air that accompanied her blew past him. The old woman carried a pie and a box of tea, and immediately headed for the kitchen.

"Hello, dear, I hope I haven't come at a bad time. Oh, for crying out loud…it's so frigid out that the pie's gone cold. No matter, I'll pop it in the oven and it'll be nice and warm in a jiffy.

"Are you all right, Peter? You look a little peaked. You just have a seat in this chair while I put the kettle on. We'll have warm apple pie and some nice hot tea in no time at all. Won't that be nice? That'll take the chill off, I can tell you.

"Sit down, dear, sit."

A dumbfounded Peter sank down onto the chair that had almost served a very different purpose. He put his elbows on the table, rested his forehead on his only hand, and fought the urge to sob.

Mrs. Gallagher didn't seem to notice.

"Now where do you keep your cups and sauc…? Never mind, I remember from when I used to visit Mr. Boino. He's such a dear man, have you heard from him at all, Peter? I do hope he's well. And I wonder how his poor sister is coming along with her treatments.

"And I hope you won't think I've put too much cinnamon in the pie. My dear husband, Henry, would always say: *You went a little heavy on the cinnamon this time, didn't you lamby-kins?* That's what he called me, lamby-kins. Isn't that sweet?

"And I would call him 'Hanky' because, you know, Hank is a nickname for Henry. And it was my little joke that I was the girl who was never without a Hanky.

"I remember the very first time I made my apple pie for Henry, it was autumn and we had driven upstate to pick our own apples — McIntosh, I think. Yes, I'm certain they were McIntosh. They're the very best for pie, if you ask my opinion.

"Peter, be a dear and grab a knife and some forks, and some dessert plates for the pie, won't you?"

FOR RENATA

Peter stood up, lumbered to the kitchen counter and pulled open a drawer. Mrs. Gallagher continued to drone on, but her words had become just a buzz in the background to the young light keeper.

He looked through the doorway into the living room, and stared at the bitter end, still knotted around the foot of the desk. After a moment, he returned to the table carrying a knife and two forks in his hand.

Mrs. Gallagher placed teabags in the cups. "...and I said, *You don't mean it.* But she swore it was true and...Oh, Peter, you forgot the plates, dear.

"Well, you can just imagine my consternation..."

February 15, 1973

I almost did it. I was ready. I was standing on the chair and counting to three and I was ready. Then Old Lady Gallagher showed up. She brought apple pie and her own tea this time. She made me try the pie and I couldn't swallow. She talked and talked about nothing for hours. By the time she finally left, I had lost my nerve.

33

March 7, 1973
  I saved two lives today…

It was one o'clock in the afternoon and unusually warm for early March. Peter was performing routine maintenance and testing the foghorn when he heard what sounded like a scream. He looked out over the ocean, squinted, and shaded his eye from the sun's glare with his hand.

He scoured the seascape in the direction from which the sound had come. Then the scream came a second time, and he zeroed in on what was hardly more than a speck in the ocean, far off the point.

He marked the position in his mind and ran down the cliff path to the floating dock, untied the skiff and jumped on board. After four or five sturdy yanks on the pull cord, the outboard engine sputtered to life, and Peter headed out to sea at full throttle.

FOR RENATA

The engine's whine made it impossible for Peter to hear anything else, let alone the screams of a person in peril. He headed toward the place he had spotted from the tower. As he got closer, the speck grew larger. Eventually, he could make out a small, capsized rowboat, and when he was within fifty feet of the boat, he could see two people in the water, a man in his sixties and a boy of about ten. They wore life jackets and clung to the overturned boat.

Peter pulled in close and set his engine to idle. The old man cried out, "Get my grandson first. Please, hurry!"

Peter's eye met the boy's. The kid's teeth stopped chattering and his clear, grey eyes grew even wider as he took in the sight of the tall man with an eye patch and one arm.

Peter crouched and extended his hand. "Come on, kid. You want to freeze to death?"

The old man shouted, "Go, Billy, go!"

Billy hesitated a moment. Then he closed his eyes tight and lunged for Peter's outstretched hand. Peter hoisted the boy into the skiff with ease. The heftier grandfather proved more difficult but Peter still managed to get him on board quickly.

Peter shifted the boat back into full throttle and raced to the lighthouse. Carrying the boy, he prodded the old man up the cliff path and into the light keeper's living quarters, and then called for an ambulance. He turned the thermostat to its highest setting. He hurried upstairs and got blankets while the boy and the old man stripped out of their wet clothing. Peter lit a fire in the stone fireplace for good measure.

By the time the paramedics arrived, grandfather and grandson sat wrapped in blankets before a roaring fire, sipping hot cocoa from steaming mugs.

One of the volunteer paramedics had been Peter's football teammate in high school. "You done good, man," he said after pulling Peter aside. "In water that cold, every second counts. You saved two lives today, Pete."

March 8, 1973

I worked on the skiff's engine today. I had a little trouble starting it yesterday and the paramedic said that even seconds can make the difference between life and death in cold water. It starts on the first try now, every time.

FOR RENATA

34

*M*ay 15, 1973
Mrs. Gallagher drove up with a station wagon full of plants today. Some are vegetables and herbs, some are just flowers. She showed me where to plant them and how to take care of them.

And, of course, she brought a dessert. She's really a pretty nice lady. I kind of feel sorry for her because she's all alone.

June 8, 1973
Another surprise inspection by the Coast Guard today. This time was different though. It was the same Chief Warrant Officer (CWO) who royally chewed my ass out last time. But this time the Fresnel was spotless, the brass shiny, and everything shipshape. I know now that he was right: People's lives are at stake, and I'm responsible. I got an "outstanding" on the inspection.

June 9, 1973

The CWO came back today and brought some people with him...

At 11:00 a.m. the prickly sensation on Peter's back warned him that the sun was burning his skin. He dropped the thick whitewash brush into one of the pails hanging from his wood and chain-link boson's chair, and he reminded himself to add Noxzema to his shopping list.

He pulled a worn canvas work glove from the back right pocket of his jeans, and slipped his fingers into the opening. When he gripped the ancient glove in his teeth to pull it onto his hand, Peter caught its scent: a blend of sawdust, earth, motor oil, and sweat—the smell of hard work.

He grabbed the thick, hemp pulley rope with his gloved hand and slowly, carefully lowered himself down the exterior lighthouse wall, thirty feet to the ground.

He stepped out of the harnessed boson's chair, grabbed the tip of the glove's middle finger with his teeth, removed it, and stuffed it back into his pocket.

He walked toward the light keeper's living quarters, and stretched his back and shoulders in an attempt to determine just how bad the sunburn was. He swept the lawn with his eyes and decided that the grass would need to be mowed soon, and that the forsythia should be trimmed.

Peter decided to wash off before heading inside. He turned the outside faucet on. Well water rushed from its underground prison like a captured animal whose cage door had sprung open. The rubber garden hose puffed out as water gushed through its coiled, fifty-foot length, and it coughed and sputtered as the last pockets of air were expelled from its mouth. Peter doused his neck and shoulders for a moment before taking several large, satisfying gulps of the cool liquid.

Two station wagons approaching the lighthouse caught his attention. Based on its color and markings, one of them belonged to the Coast Guard motor pool, the other was a light green 1969 Chevelle. The cars kicked up small dust clouds from the parched dirt of Rose Hip Point Lane.

Peter noticed that the Chief Warrant Officer who had conducted the inspection of the lighthouse the previous day drove the Coast Guard vehicle. He became nervous, and developed scenarios in his mind to explain why the CWO would be back so soon and why a civilian would be following him. Perhaps someone had lodged a complaint.

He knew he had been less than cordial with a few of the tourists who had peppered him with annoying questions while he tried to work. And he also knew that tradition dictated that a light keeper be courteous and accommodating to visitors. In fact, written instructions issued by the United States Light-House Board (USLHB) more than a century before hung on the wall of the tower watch room:

Keepers must be courteous and polite
to all visitors and show them everything
of interest about the station at
such times as will not interfere with

166

B. ROBERT SHARRY

Light-house duties…

Peter slowly turned the faucet off, grabbed his long-sleeve T-shirt and pulled it on over his head. He stared impassively at the two station wagons as they parked on the grass.

The crusty CWO, Kelly, was the first one out. Though he was middle-aged, he seemed to bounce from the car like a much younger man. Next, Kelly's passenger emerged—a commissioned officer, an Ensign who didn't look much older than a teenager. Both grinned at Peter, and then trained their gazes on the green Chevelle.

Peter's eye followed. A young couple that Peter did not recognize emerged from the front seat of the Chevelle and smiled and waved at him like he was an old friend. Peter shot CWO Kelly a puzzled look. Kelly just grinned enigmatically and held up an index finger in a *just-a-moment* gesture. Then he pointed that same finger at the Chevelle.

Peter watched as the rear car doors opened. An old man and young boy emerged. Peter immediately recognized them as the pair he had saved from certain death in the icy Atlantic.

The group approached. The young Ensign held what looked like a diploma in his left hand. He extended his right hand to shake Peter's.

"Keeper Ahearn, I'm Ensign LaChapelle. It's an honor to meet you, sir. I'm here on behalf of Admiral Bender to present you with this Letter of Commendation and the Silver Lifesaving Medal. The Admiral wishes to thank you and recognize

FOR RENATA

your diligence and courage in saving the lives of Mr. Fowler and his grandson, Billy."

"I just did my job," said Peter, still looking somewhat bewildered.

CWO Kelly stepped forward to shake Peter's hand.

"Well done, Pete. I'm proud of you." He leaned in and said in a chuckling whisper, "I came to inspect the place yesterday because I knew what was coming today. I wanted to make sure you weren't still living in a pigsty."

Next, Mr. Fowler stepped forward and shook Peter's hand. "Thank you, son, thanks for everything.

"Billy, can you say *thank you* to Mr. Ahearn?"

The reluctant boy took one tiny step forward. "Thank you, Mr. Ahearn."

Peter smiled and said, "Anytime, buddy."

The young woman whom Peter now understood to be Billy's mother rushed toward him in a flood of emotion. She stood on tiptoes and threw her arms around his neck. For a moment she examined his face through watery eyes, and then she kissed him on the lips and buried her face in his shoulder. She held him so tightly that he found it hard to breathe.

She wept as she whispered in his ear, "You saved my baby...and my daddy. I keep thinking about what would have happened if you hadn't been there. Thank you, thank you, thank you."

Peter felt her hot tears on his cheekbone, so close to his eye that they might have been his own. He felt the softness of her cheek against his, and smelled

B. ROBERT SHARRY

the sweetness of her breath and the citrusy fragrance of her hair. When her soft breasts compressed against his lower ribs, a sorrowful pang overtook him and caused a lump to form in his throat. He hadn't felt the warmth and touch of another human being for so, so long, and he was tired of being alone.

FOR RENATA

35

*N*ovember 3, 1973
 I helped Mrs. Gallagher gather rose hips today, and then we made jelly and jam. I eat so much of it, I figured it was the least I could do.

Christmas, 1973
 Ma, Dad, and Marybeth came to visit this morning. They're having Christmas dinner at Marybeth's today. She said it's time for her to start her own family traditions. She invited me, of course, but I begged off. Marybeth and I walked around outside for a long time and talked about Tommy. Seems like he's been gone forever.
 Mrs. Gallagher came by last night. She gave me a scrimshaw pipe that belonged to her father. It's carved in the shape of a schooner and the stem looks like ebony or mahogany. She said it's not for smoking — just looking.

B. ROBERT SHARRY

This morning I found myself wishing that she had brought some scones and rose hip jelly.
December 31, 1973

Guess who has a date for New Year's Eve? God, if anyone ever finds out. A few days ago I asked my old high school friend, Jimmy Vasconcelos, to put some fancy tea in with the regular grocery delivery. The other day I walked down to Mrs. Gallagher's to give her the tea as a thank you for the scrimshaw. She was so happy you'd think it was a pot of gold. She insisted on making some for us right then and served it with a gingerbread still warm from the oven. Then out of nowhere she said, "Do you have plans for New Year's Eve, dear?" I almost choked. What could I say? I said I would come if she'd have some scones and rose hip jelly for me to take home after. I will NOT stay until midnight – what if she tries to kiss me? Speaking of a pot of gold – I have to remember to have Jimmy bring me some more weed next week…

At 6:15 p.m. New Year's Eve, 1973, Peter Ahearn stepped from the warmth of the light keeper's quarters to the granite doorstep. It had been snowing steadily since midday. Absent even a trace of wind to make them change course, the flakes fell plumb from cloud to earth and formed a veil of insulation so dense that even breaking ocean waves were rendered mute.

Peter raised the collar of his navy blue, double-breasted pea coat. He wore no hat. His long hair and beard would keep his ears and face warm enough for the few minutes that he would be outside. He lit a joint, and began the quarter mile walk along Rose Hip Point Lane to Mrs. Gallagher's house. His own muffled footfalls were the only sound he could hear.

He remembered the last time he'd gone out on a New Year's Eve: He'd been a senior in high school, with two arms and two eyes. He'd spent the night with Cindy. That thought made him wonder what Cindy and Chip were doing this evening.

He pictured them fancily dressed, leaning toward each other from across a candlelit table, whispering and smiling their way through a romantic dinner at an elegant restaurant. Then he imagined them dressed casually, hosting a large house party attended by their once-mutual friends, and all of them eating, drinking, dancing, and laughing into the new year.

He became so lost in thought that he had overshot Mrs. Gallagher's by a hundred yards before he realized it. He dropped the roach into the snow and backtracked to the beige Victorian cottage with the gingerbread filigree and dark-green shutters. Soft yellow light spilled from the front windows and bathed the snow-capped shrubs below. Through the window, Peter could see Mrs. Gallagher scurrying about the outdated kitchen at the rear of the house.

He studied the Christmas wreath that hung on the oak front door for a moment, and then knocked. He brushed snow from his hair and stomped it from his chukka boots.

The heavy door swung open and Mrs. Gallagher greeted him. "Hello, Peter, and welcome," she said cheerily. "It's so nice of you to come and I'm so glad to see you, dear."

"Thanks for inviting me, Mrs. Gallagher," Peter said as he closed the door behind him.

"Now, Peter, it's past time for us to dispense with this 'Mrs. Gallagher' nonsense. Won't you please call me 'Bridey'? It's a nickname for my given name, Brigid. All my family and dear friends call me Bridey."

"All right," said Peter. "If that's what you'd like."

"Good. Now, let me take your coat, dear."

Bridey had worn a crisp, white linen apron when Peter spied her from outside. She must have removed it before she answered the door, and he could see her outfit now — a ¾ sleeve, high-necked, black velvet cocktail dress that was cinched at the waist with a wide black satin ribbon. The dress hung loosely on her, making her look as if she'd borrowed it from a heavier woman. Her grey hair was pulled back tightly into a bun, and she wore a single strand of slightly pinkish pearls around her neck.

The dining room table was set with Bridey's finest Limoges china, sterling silver, and crystal stemware. "It's been a while since I gave a dinner party, dear. I hope I haven't forgotten anything."

Peter was acutely aware of his own appearance: tan corduroy pants, an open-collared, denim work shirt, and a brown corduroy sport jacket. "I'm feeling a little underdressed, Bridey."

FOR RENATA

"Nonsense, Peter, you look very handsome. Now, I know there's one thing I haven't forgotten, and that's how to make a darn good Manhattan cocktail. You'll find some on the sideboard. There's a pitcher-full next to the ice bucket. Help yourself, dear, while I bring out some hors d'oeuvres, warm from the oven."

Peter and Bridey took their cocktails and hors d'oeuvres by the fire in the living room. Jazz music drifted from an aged stereo cabinet. Bridey pointed at the items on a silver serving tray. "These are shrimp puffs, dear. And those are chicken livers, wrapped in a blanket of bacon, and set on a toast point."

Peter felt the effects of the marijuana and rapidly popped the canapés into his mouth one after another. Bridey looked on in amazement. Then a big smile lit up her face. "I like a man with a healthy appetite."

"Mmm," was the only reply Peter could manage through his full mouth.

"The French have a phrase for these puffs, you know. *Vol-au-vent*, they say. I think it means *gone with the wind*, or something like that. Leave it to the French, eh, Peter?"

"Mmmhmmm."

"You just eat right up, dear."

"These are delicious," Peter meant to say, but with his mouth still half full, it came out as *ee ar dee ishush*.

"Do you have more?" he asked as he swallowed the last of the hors d'oeuvres.

"Well, I suppose I could make more, but I'd hate to see you spoil your dinner, dear."

"Okay."

They moved to the dining room, where Bridey served rack of lamb with mint jelly and roasted potatoes and carrots, followed by warm Indian pudding for dessert. The old woman managed to keep the rather one-sided dinner conversation going cheerfully.

She told Peter that she and her husband had bought the house as a vacation home. After Henry's death, some ten years ago, she had come to live full time at Cape Ann in order to be close to the sea.

After dinner, they settled once more by the living room fireplace. Bridey sipped port wine from a crystal aperitif glass while Peter ate more Indian pudding.

Bridey spoke fondly of her family and brought out an ancient photo album.

"This is my father, dear, the man who owned the scrimshaw pipe."

Peter sobered and sat up straight. "He's missing an arm."

"Yes, dear, he lost it in Cuba during the Spanish-American War. They sent his arm home with him and it was buried in the family plot in 1898. Father was reunited with it when he died in 1940.

"He wasn't one of Teddy Roosevelt's Rough Riders, but Father did meet the man himself while he was in the field hospital."

FOR RENATA

Peter was silent for a moment. Then he asked, "Did it change the way your mother...felt about him?"

Bridey looked up from the photo album, her brow furrowed. "Why, whatever do you mean, Peter?"

"I mean...I don't know what I mean. I just..."

The old woman was nodding. "Oh, I think I understand now.

"Well, I can tell you this: All of us children were born *after* he came home from Cuba. After all, he was the same man, and Mother loved him through and through. We all did. Is that what you were wondering about, Peter?"

After a long pause, Peter looked down and answered in almost a whisper. "Yes."

"Peter," Bridey said.

He raised his head and looked her in the eye.

Bridey rested her forearms on her lap and leaned in toward him. "People either love you...or they don't. It's just that simple."

36

January 1st, 1974
    Well, it could have been worse. Dinner was actually really good. Of course it could have been the doobie I did on the way over. She told me to call her by her nickname, Bridey. She's got one whole room just for books. Her house is like a Victorian museum with a library in it. She doesn't have any kids. I get the feeling she's kind of sad about that. I think she would have been a good mother. Walked home at about 10:30 last night and had scones and rose hip jelly this morning.

February 20, 1974
    This is the worst time of year. It's so dark all the time. You hardly ever see the sun and the sea looks so angry and unforgiving. And it's when I feel the loneliest.

April 14, 1974

FOR RENATA

I found an old Jon Gnagy "Learn to Draw" kit that Ed Boino left behind. I remember watching him on TV when I was a kid. So I'm learning to be an "artist" (ha ha).

I'm playing the piano a little – I rigged up a wooden extension that I duct-tape to my elbow. It has three tines on it and makes it so I can play a few simple bass chords. It looks really weird, but actually works pretty well.

I'm reading a lot too. In fact, I've read every book in the house and I'm borrowing books from Bridey now. My favorite so far is To Kill a Mockingbird.

June 20, 1974

Today there wasn't one cloud in the sky from dawn to dusk. I didn't bother whitewashing. I've already painted the shaded side. On a day like today, the white of the tower on the sunny side is so bright it would blind my good eye. Besides, I'd burn to a crisp if I was out there in full sun.

So, I goofed off for most of the day. I set up the easel where there's a little shade near the edge of the cliff and took a stab at painting the harbor.

There's a girl, a teenager who's been walking here almost every day for a couple of weeks now. She must have just finished high school for the year. She never comes closer to me than fifty yards or so. I know she watches me, but when I look over and wave she pretends not to see me and looks out to sea. Maybe she's afraid of me.

July 15, 1974

Starting to enjoy the fruits of the garden – mostly tomatoes and cukes right now. My new favorite

B. ROBERT SHARRY

sandwich: Take one ripe tomato still warm from the sun, slice it thick, a little salt & pepper, mayonnaise, and squishy Wonder bread. I think I could live on it.

The corn is looking good, it'll be ready in a month or so, and then Bridey and I are going to have a clambake.

July 21, 1974

The girl speaks. It's Sunday, and she looked like she was dressed for church – probably Our Lady of Good Voyage in Gloucester. I was picking up flotsam off the beach and I knew she saw me. I just waved and yelled "Hi" as loud as I could. It was kind of funny because she couldn't really ignore me. She gave a pouty look, a little wave, and a greeting that I could barely hear. I yelled "Beautiful day" but she just waved again and then headed in the other direction.

Oh, well, it's a start.

FOR RENATA

37

August 15, 1974
    I think I just had the best meal of my life. I'm so full I can barely move enough to write this. Bridey and I had our long-awaited clambake today...

At daybreak, Bridey pulled up in her station wagon. Peter, a mug of coffee in hand, stood at the cliff's edge, mesmerized by a rosy sunrise on the horizon. Bridey's perky voice shook Peter from his stupor.

"Ooo-hoo," she called. "Come on, dear, the clams won't dig themselves out."

Peter turned to see Bridey clad in her garden attire: a red and white short-sleeve gingham shirt tucked into high-waisted blue denim slacks. Her head was covered by a khaki fishing cap, and her feet by green, calf-high rubber boots.

"Wait till you see, Bridey: I used those old lobster traps I found in the garage. I baited all ten of them and caught six good-sized ones. They're in the water down by the dock."

Together they retrieved two large metal buckets, a shovel, and a pitchfork from the back of the station wagon. Equipped for their adventure, they descended the steep cliff path on the south side of the point to the beach below and scanned the soggy sand for clam holes and telltale squirting.

When both buckets brimmed with shellfish and saltwater, Peter said, "These are too heavy for you, Bridey. I'll carry one up and come back down for the other."

"All right, dear. Oh, Peter, there's a potato sack in the back of the station wagon. When you come back, can you please bring it down with you? We can use it to collect the seaweed."

"Seaweed? What for? Aren't we just gonna throw everything in a big pot?"

"Heavens, no. This is called a clam*bake*, not a clam*boil*. We have a good piece of work ahead of us if we're to earn our dinner."

It was after 10 a.m. by the time Peter had made the last of several trips from the beach to the lighthouse. Bridey put him to work digging a fire pit. "While you do that," she said, "I'll make a chowder. The bake will take some time and we'll need something to hold us over."

As she chopped potatoes, celery, and onions for the chowder, Bridey watched Peter from the kitchen window of the light keeper's quarters. The young man dug with his remaining arm. Several times he lost his balance. He fell once and the left side of his face struck the ground. She was about to run outside to see if he was all right when he jumped up, grabbed the shovel, and started again.

"That's just what Father would have done," she murmured. "You have stick-to-itiveness, Peter, and a good man can't be kept down."

Under Bridey's supervision, Peter made a fire in the pit. When it was good and hot, Peter and Bridey carried a dozen large round stones from the station wagon and placed them on the fire. After a time, Bridey abandoned her habitual dignified way, spat on one of the stones, and watched as her saliva sizzled.

"Good," she said, "Now we need more fire on top of the stones, Peter."

When Peter had done as instructed, Bridey said, "It will take a while for the fire to get just so. We can have some of that chowder while we wait."

They sat at the picnic table. They ate clam chowder from sturdy earthenware bowls and sipped Narragansett beer from pop-top cans.

"Bridey, this is the best chowder I've ever tasted."

"Thank you, Peter. I have a secret ingredient, you know," Bridey gave a mock-conspiratorial wink. "After I sauté the onions, garlic and bacon in butter, I like to deglaze the fry-pan with a little French brandywine."

When the flames from the fire had gone out Bridey spread the coals around the red-hot stones with an iron rake. She blanketed the hot coals with seaweed, followed by a layer of clams, another layer of seaweed, the potatoes, onions, and carrots, more seaweed, and the lobsters from Peter's traps. Then the whole mountainous pile was crowned with Bridey's seawater-soaked potato sack and a final layer of seaweed.

"There," said Bridey, "We'll give it about an hour and a half."

While they waited for the food to bake, Bridey and Peter made the final preparations for their feast. They set the picnic table, and then Bridey clarified butter and sliced lemons while Peter hosed down a bucket and filled it with ice and cans of beer.

When all there was left to do was wait, they sat at the picnic table sipping beer. Bridey kept the conversation going in her cheery way. She was on the subject of Longfellow's "Evangeline," explaining the story behind the epic poem, when Peter interrupted.

"Bridey, there's a girl…a teenager who comes around here. Long black hair…"

"Ah," said Bridey, "That sounds like the Raposo girl. They're in the next house down the point from mine, about another quarter mile."

Peter nodded in recognition. "I know Inacio. He comes here sometimes, mostly to borrow tools. She's his daughter?"

"Mm hmm, what about her?"

"Nothing, it's just that she seems kind of stand-offish and maybe a little sad. I just wondered…"

Bridey nodded her head. "I'm not surprised. I don't think she has a very pleasant home-life. The father is a fisherman. He's a hard enough worker, but he's partial to his drink. Most of the time he's at home, he's loud and drunk. And when he drinks, which is always, he gets awfully mean, and he takes it out on those poor girls. He's a bad apple, that one."

"Kids shouldn't have to deal with that. Life's hard enough," said Peter.

The two fell silent for a time until Bridey said, "I think our clambake is just about ready, Peter."

"Damn, Bridey, we forgot the corn."

"No, we didn't, dear. A lot of people put it in the bake, but I'm not one of them. You get some seawater boiling, but not too much—just enough to cover the corn. *Then* we'll pick it. Never pick the corn till the water's aboil. You may think you've had fresh corn before, Peter, but truly you haven't."

Bridey and Peter waited until the feast was unearthed and the seawater boiled before they headed to the garden. Bridey looked at the tall corn with admiration. "Now you'll have some *fresh* corn, kiddo."

"Maybe we should shuck it on the run," Peter joked.

Bridey got a mischievous glint in her eyes. "Good idea. Let's make a race of it. We'll each pick two ears. Last one to have them shucked and in the pot is a rotten egg."

"You're on," Peter laughed.

The old woman crouched in a wrestler's stance. "Ready...Set...GO," she cried.

Bridey pushed Peter back. She grabbed an ear of corn with each hand, yanked them from their stalks, and ran for the garden gate.

"Hey, no fair, Bridey."

"Whoever said life was fair, kiddo?" the old woman called over her shoulder.

Peter picked one ear of corn with his right hand, tucked it under his left arm, and then picked another. Bridey had already covered half the distance to the house, but Peter wasn't beat just yet. He began to shuck the corn with his teeth as he ran.

Peter burst into the kitchen. Bridey stood at the counter, next to the stove. She had shucked one ear already. She gave Peter a quick, furtive glance and went to work on her second ear of corn. But Peter had shucked one on the run and held it clamped in his left underarm. He held the remaining ear with his hand and shucked it frantically with his teeth. The race was a virtual dead heat.

But, in the end, Bridey dropped her second ear of corn into the pot a split second before Peter. She raised her hands in the air like a victorious boxer and danced around.

Peter feigned acrimony. "I'd have won if you hadn't cheated," he tried to say. But he had a mouthful of corn silk and his words were too garbled to be comprehensible. He clawed at the corn silk and spat it from his mouth.

FOR RENATA

Bridey stared at him in amazement, and then howled with laughter. "You look like you ate a bird's nest," she screamed.

The old woman's laughter was infectious and Peter couldn't help but join her.

"Maybe if I open my mouth wide enough, a chickadee will fly out."

Bridey laughed so hard that she bent over and pressed on her abdomen. "Stop it, Peter, you'll make me soil myself."

They let the corn boil for exactly one minute, and were still laughing as they carried it to the picnic table.

Then they sat and ate…and ate. Peter ate until he thought he might burst.

"Save room for strawberry shortcake, dear." said Bridey.

Peter loosened his belt.

Beer had them both acting giddy and silly for a time, but then the large amount of food and the heat of the afternoon turned them logy and somber.

After the silence between them had stretched on for a long moment, Peter said, "You know, Bridey, a while ago I was thinking about…"

Bridey showed no surprise. "I know, dear." After a pause, she looked out to sea. Sadness covered her face.

"I had a boy once," she said, her voice uncommonly quiet. "Jack was a beautiful child, an absolute joy. He was just about your age when the Second World War began. When he came home, I knew the war had changed him. I knew right away.

I could see the awful pain he was in. I tried to help him but I failed. And one night he just stepped off the Brooklyn Bridge and that was that.

"But it wasn't just *his* life, you know. After that I wasn't the same, and neither was my husband. *We* were never quite the same."

"I'm sorry, Bridey, I didn't know."

"It's all right, dear, not very many do."

Peter hesitated, and then said softly, "I came close last year...in February. But just when I was about to go through with it, you showed up with pie and tea, remember? You saved my life that night, Bridey."

Bridey expression became pensive. "I may have stopped you from taking your life, Peter, but only you can save it, only you can save it.

"But you don't think that way anymore, do you?"

"No, Bridey, don't you worry about me. Back then, I just didn't care. But I'm afraid of dying now."

"I'm glad to hear that. At my age, it's not so much dying that frightens me, but I do fear dying alone."

FOR RENATA

38

After hours of sitting quietly and watching as Renie read the Keeper's Log, Mark rose to stretch his legs and asked her if she'd mind if he made a fresh pot of coffee.

Renie closed her eyes and pinched the bridge of her nose with her thumb and forefinger. "No, let me," she said. "I could stand to rest my eyes for a bit, anyway."

She went through the mechanical motions of brewing a fresh pot and stared through the kitchen window at the sea. Peter's chronicle of his clambake with Mrs. Gallagher had triggered memories of her own from the summer of 1974. She remembered one day in particular, right at the end of the summer vacation, before her junior year of high school. She had gone to the lighthouse grounds to sketch...

The bright August sun had made her too warm, yet when she moved to the shade of a forsythia bush, it was too chilly. She tried to sketch the lighthouse, but her intermittent shivering made what should have been straight lines of charcoal become like tiny, crooked readouts from a lie-detector test.

She watched the thin, bearded light keeper from a distance as he weeded his vegetable garden. She was amazed by how quickly he worked with only one hand. He had slung a worn, canvas paperboy's bag over his shoulder, and he was yanking the weeds and tucking them into the bag with impressive speed.

He hadn't seen her yet, but he would. He always did. It was the reason she came here so often. Even though she'd never found the courage to talk to him, just seeing him smile and wave at her made her feel as though there was someone who was genuinely happy to see her.

A few months earlier she'd had such high hopes for her sophomore mock-prom. Somehow Mamãe had convinced her father to let her attend, the first time he'd ever allowed her to go to a dance. Her Auntie Branca had taken her shopping in Gloucester for something to wear, and afterwards they'd gone to a matinee of *The Great Gatsby*.

Though she would have liked to wear a mini-dress to the dance, Papai would never stand for it. So she settled for a burnt-orange, double-knit pantsuit of bellbottom hip-huggers and a modified bomber jacket. A wide-collared blouse of chocolate silk and beige platform shoes completed the look.

FOR RENATA

She was so excited she thought she might burst. For once she'd be dressed in style. She spent hours examining herself in the mirror, experimenting with hairstyles and makeup while listening to Barbra Streisand's "The Way We Were" over and over again, pretending that she was dancing to it with Robert Redford.

But on the morning of the dance a bright red pimple appeared on her chin, and her father attached a last-minute condition: Renie would be attending the mock-prom with a date of his choosing.

Ricky Alpande was a distant cousin. He was a senior at Gloucester High School, and in the fall he would attend UMass to study engineering. Ricky had short-cropped black hair in a cut that was long out of style. He was short, plump, and soft, with breasts that rivaled Renie's own. Scores of pimples and blackheads covered his bespectacled face and neck and, she felt certain, the rest of his body.

Ricky had come to collect her wearing a suit that was two sizes too small. A white carnation boutonniere graced his lapel, and he had brought a purple wrist-corsage for Renie.

At the dance, she felt the eyes of her peers, especially the other girls, on her and Ricky, and she knew that their titters and sniggers were directed at her.

"The Way We Were" began to play, and Ricky, with a confidence born of being the oldest student in the gymnasium, seized Renie and clumsily dragged her about the dance floor. He winked and gave her a self-assured grin, and Renie wished she were dead.

She looked up from her sketchbook in time to see the light keeper approaching. As usual, there was a broad smile on his face, and he waved his right hand and arm "hello" in a wide arc.

Renie smiled back, gave a small wave of her hand, and then stood up and headed home. Maybe someday she'd speak to him, maybe even tell him that it was she who had picked up two cans of food at the A&P parking lot long ago and placed them on his doorstep. Maybe someday, but not today. A few days ago, Papai had become enraged at the dinner table when he tasted Mamãe's fish stew. He had screamed that the meal wasn't fit for chum, and then flung his bowl at the wall. Mamãe had tried to flee, but Papai chased after her. When Renie tried to intervene, Papai had dealt her a back-handed blow, and her cheekbone was still bruised and swollen.

FOR RENATA

39

Renie carried two mugs of fresh coffee to the kitchen table. Mark noticed that her hands were trembling. But she made it without spilling a drop. She sat down and resumed reading the journal. Mark studied Renie's face as she read the words his uncle had written so many years ago. He watched her expression change as she read something trivial, funny, or poignant.

From time to time Renie would look up from the Keeper's Log, gaze at Mark, and comment on something she'd just read, or ask for help in deciphering Pete's scrawling cursive. He found himself wishing that Pete's handwriting had been even worse. When Renie asked him to interpret the particularly messy words, he had an excuse to lean in toward her and enjoy her fresh floral scent.

Having already read the journal, Mark knew exactly what Renie was reading, and he began to watch her reactions more closely as Peter's entries began to address a new subject: Renie herself.

August 28, 1974
The Portuguese fisherman's daughter still comes to the lighthouse grounds. Sometimes she sits and sketches, but she never gets too close to me. She's either afraid of me or painfully shy. I don't know why, but I have a feeling she'd like to talk, maybe even needs to talk. I think she actually smiled today, although it was one of those sad smiles. She reminds me of a wounded bird, so skittish and fragile.

A sad expression crossed Renie's face and her eyes welled up but no tears fell. Mark wondered what it must be like for her to read Pete's assessment of her emotional state from so long ago.

She looked up from the page and stared straight ahead for several moments. Mark could tell that her mind had taken her back to the 1970s.

After a silent moment, she continued to read. She hadn't progressed very much further when she sat up straighter and her eyes grew wide.

September 10, 1974
Her name is Renata and she is the most beautiful thing I've ever seen. Her hair is black as the night sky, and her eyes are the color of caramel. She was set up on the lawn, painting the lighthouse, and I marched right over and introduced myself. I didn't know what to expect,

but she just looked at me and smiled as though I had two arms and two eyes. She is so beautiful but there's a sadness about her, even when she smiles. I snuck a peek at the painting. I'm in it. Just a speck with an eye patch, but I'm in it. She's a really good artist and I told her so. She said that she'll come back tomorrow. I can't wait to see her again.

September 11, 1974
  Renata came back at about 9:00 this morning to paint. The day was warm and beautiful, not a cloud in the sky. I asked her if she'd mind if I set up my easel next to hers…

Peter had been watching for her all morning, hoping she would come back as promised. Finally he caught a glimpse of her walking up the lane from his kitchen window, and his heart leapt.

She was wearing the same thing she'd had on yesterday—a button-front, cap-sleeved dress with a round neckline. It was navy blue with a tiny white flower print. The full skirt was hemmed just above the knee. Her legs and feet were bare.

Renata's left arm was threaded through a small wooden stool, and she was carrying a large wooden paint box by its handle with her left hand. Under her right arm she carried a folded pine easel with the canvas secured to it with thick jute string.

Peter's first thought was to rush out the door and run to her. He could relieve her of the load she carried, like a lovesick schoolboy would carry a girl's books. The thought made him wonder if a boy had ever carried Renata's books for her.

But Peter Ahearn only had one hand. He worried that he'd look clumsy and awkward to her, and that his eagerness would frighten her away.

So he continued to watch her from the kitchen window as she moved gracefully closer. She carried her slim body with faultless posture. Her hips and breasts swayed with each step she took.

Renata stopped at the exact spot where she had been the day before and set up her equipment. Peter sensed something different in her face. Was it just his imagination, or did she look a bit less sad today?

When she finished setting up and finally sat down on the stool to paint, Peter's line of sight was blocked by the canvas. He was eager to go to her — more eager than he could remember feeling about anything — but he held himself back for as long as he could stand it. And while he waited, he went to bathroom and checked his hair, his beard, his teeth, his nose, his clothes, and then he checked them all again.

After what seemed like an eternity, Peter emerged from the light keeper's quarters and sauntered with forced casualness towards Renata. He deliberately altered his path so that she would see him coming from a hundred feet away and not be startled by the sudden appearance of a *one-eyed, one-armed, flying purple lighthouse keeper*. The thought made him cringe. He wondered if Renata had heard him called that, or worse, perhaps even recited it herself. What if the difference in her face wasn't an absence of sadness? What if it was amusement? Maybe she was laughing at him.

He stopped short. He held up the remnant of his left arm and stared at it for a moment. Then he brought his right hand up to touch the black patch that covered his left eye. *What a fool I am. Why would someone like her ever want anything to do with me?*

At least she hadn't seen him yet. He swallowed a lump in his throat, turned and walked back toward the lighthouse.

"Peter."

Peter turned back around when he heard her call his name. Renata was waving to him and smiling, her teeth gleaming.

"Good morning," she called, waving her right arm in a wide arc. "And isn't it just a glorious one?"

Peter felt such relief that it made his knees tremble a little. He quickly regained his composure and returned Renata's smile and wave as he walked toward her.

They stood a few feet apart, smiling at each other.

"Weren't you even going to say 'hello'?" Renata asked.

"Oh, I was coming to do just that when I realized that I shouldn't have come empty-handed. I was just going back to get you a cup of coffee."

"Oh? And how would you have made it?" she chuckled, "Would I take sugar or not? Do I like cream in my coffee? Do I even like coffee?"

"I hadn't thought that far ahead. Do you like coffee?"

"Is your coffee any good?"

"No," Peter said.

"Then, I would love some," she said, laughing.

"I'll be right back," said Peter. He had already taken a few steps toward the lighthouse when he stopped, turned back around and gave Renata a sheepish look.

"Cream and two sugars," was her answer to his unspoken question.

He returned a few minutes later, and carried a dinner plate with two mismatched ceramic mugs on it. Ordinarily he'd have placed the stump of his left arm beneath the plate for added stability. Hoping to draw less attention to the fact that he was missing half an arm, Peter carried the plate unsupported. He walked slowly, and watched anxiously as more and more coffee splashed over the rims and onto the plate with each halting, child-like step he took.

When he finally reached Renata, Peter could feel his face flush with embarrassment. The mugs had lost a third of their contents, and sat in a pool of coffee that had begun to drip over the plate's edge and onto his hand.

Renata put her hands on the edges of the plate. Peter stared at the ground. After a moment, Peter raised his eye to meet hers.

She smiled and spoke softly. "You should have used your other arm to help steady it."

She took the plate from Peter and placed it on the wooden stool, and then used a rag from her paint box to wipe his hand. She lifted the mugs from the plate and handed one to Peter. With her free hand she raised the plate and poured some of the spilled coffee into Peter's mug.

With a playful glint in her eyes, Renata put the plate's edge to her lips, tilted it, and slurped. She chortled with a full mouth and the coffee ran down the sides of her chin, her throat, and onto her dress. She laughed so heartily that she snorted.

Peter laughed as he hadn't in years. All of the tension in his body, all of the awkwardness he had felt, seemed to dissolve in that single moment.

When their laughter subsided, the two gazed into each other's eyes.

Peter broke the silence. "You know, I'm pretty well caught up on my chores. Would you mind if I set up my easel next to yours and painted a little?"

"I would be honored," Renata said.

Neither of them got much painting done, and Peter was certain that she'd seen through the ploy he'd used to be close to her.

They talked easily together throughout the cloudless morning, laughing often. At midday Peter said, "I could whip up some lunch, if you're hungry."

"Only if you'll let me help," Renata said, gently placing her hand on his arm.

In the light keeper's kitchen, Peter watched as Renata made sandwiches. He took a bag of potato chips from one of the scarred mint-green kitchen cabinets and a bottle of Blue Nun from the Frigidaire, and set them on the kitchen table. He sat down at the table, clamped the wine bottle between his thighs and twisted the corkscrew.

"Peter, it's such a lovely day. Why don't we take everything outside and make it a picnic?"

Peter picked up a large wooden cutting board from the countertop. He held one edge with his hand, rested the opposite edge on his half-arm, and grinned.

Renata smiled and nodded. "You learn quickly," she said, as she piled picnic items onto the makeshift tray.

They chose a lush, deep green patch of lawn near the cliff's edge, where the grass was warmed by the bright September sun. Renata lifted her skirt a bit as she knelt, and for an instant Peter glimpsed her smooth, pale thighs. Then she tucked her calves behind her so that the full skirt of her dress draped onto the grass and covered all but her bare feet and ankles.

Peter sat cross-legged as near to her as he dared, and then used the pretext of pouring wine to move even closer. He watched enthralled when Renata closed her eyes and lifted her face to a warm breeze. For the first time in a very long while Peter Ahearn felt happy and at peace.

At 3:00 p.m. Renata began to collect her painting equipment. Peter suggested she store the accoutrements in the light keeper's garage, where they would be safe and dry and she could access them at will.

They shook hands. Renata turned and walked toward home. She hadn't gone more than ten feet when Peter called her name.

"Renata."

FOR RENATA

She turned and blinked expectantly.

But Peter's head intervened and wouldn't allow his lips to utter the words his heart had fashioned: *Don't go. Don't ever go.*

Instead, trembling at the thought of what he had almost said, Peter paused and cleared his throat.

Renata smiled and asked, "See you tomorrow?"

"That's just what I was going to say."

He watched her as she walked down Rose Hip Point Lane, mesmerized by the way her flawless figure moved. Then, all too soon, she had passed Bridey's house, rounded the first bend in the lane, and was out of sight.

Peter turned on his heel and walked back to the lighthouse with a newfound spring in his step.

40

September 12, 1974

Despite having eaten sparingly, Peter had boundless energy. The awful heaviness that had plagued his chest for so long had vanished. He worked all evening and into the night so that he'd have as much free time as possible when she returned.

He slept little, but well that night, and woke long before dawn. He brewed coffee, took it outside, and sipped it by starlight. The dry air and cloudless sky prophesied that the coming day would be just as clement as the one before.

Peter didn't just hear birdsong that morning, he listened to it. And he didn't simply see the stars, he contemplated their beauty. The sun rose in all its magnificence at 6:18 a.m. Peter didn't just watch it: He experienced it and felt privileged to have done so. He felt strangely at peace and excited at the same time. Most of all, he couldn't wait to see her again.

Peter's stomach rumbled. He returned to the light keeper's quarters, soft-boiled an egg and buttered a piece of wheat toast. He took his breakfast to the picnic table at the cliff's edge and watched the sun climb into the sky.

By 7:00 a.m. Peter was getting ready for Renata, even though he didn't expect her to arrive until 9:00. He felt very self-conscious about his appearance and acutely aware of his limited apparel. He thought about calling Vasconcelos' Market to place an order for shaving gear and new clothes, but there just wasn't enough time. After rummaging through his meager wardrobe, he finally settled on tan corduroys, a white oxford shirt, and square-toed brown leather boots. He folded the left shirt sleeve and secured the cuff to the underarm seam with a safety pin.

He was showered and dressed before 8:00 a.m. He'd owned the pants and shirt since high school, and they hung loosely on his thinner frame.

Peter paced the lighthouse kitchen, and frequently peered through the window at the bend in Rose Hip Point Lane.

When he finally saw her, his heart leapt and a smile came to his face. Peter sprang from the light keeper's quarters and rushed out to meet her.

Renata wore a cream colored shirtdress with a tiny yellow and green flower print and a pale yellow cardigan with side pockets. She carried a large, woven cake basket.

"Here, let me carry that for you," Peter said, reaching for it. "Wow, this is pretty heavy. What's in it?"

"Food for us, for later, and something beautiful," Renata tucked her hair behind her ears. "Let's put the basket in the kitchen and then walk the beach for a while before we paint."

"Am I allowed to peek inside?"

"Not yet. It's a surprise that I hope you'll like."

Peter raised the basket over his head and made a pretense of looking for a gap in the weaving that he could peer through.

"Honestly," Renata frowned in mock reproach, "You're like a child who searches for his gift before Christmas."

Her captivating smile reappeared, and she clasped her hands behind her back as she walked. "You will just have to wait," she said in a sing-song voice.

The two of them walked across the lush green lawn to the south side of Rose Hip Point. They started down the steep, narrow, dirt path with Peter leading the way. About halfway down, there was a two-foot-deep drop in the path where it had eroded over the centuries. Peter stepped down first and turned to offer his hand to Renata. She hesitated.

"Don't be afraid, I've got you," he said.

"I'm not," she said, placing her hand in his.

Peter continued to hold her hand, gently but firmly, until they reached the base of the cliff. They turned right and walked westward to where the rocky shore ended and the long, narrow beach where Peter and Bridey had dug clams stretched on for almost a mile. Renata stopped, picked up a shard of glass from among a cluster of broken shells, and examined it.

"Give it to me. I'll throw it away," Peter said.

"You would throw treasure away?"

"Treasure?" Peter examined the smooth, brown shard. "I'm pretty sure that's a piece of a beer bottle."

Renata shook her head. "Where's your imagination? I think this glass is centuries old. It came from a bottle of madeira that a pirate captain shared with a young maiden he had kidnapped, and then fell hopelessly in love with."

Peter stroked his chin. "You obviously have a much better imagination than I do. You see, I imagined that it was from two teenagers who shared a beer about a year and a half ago."

"I like my story better," she smiled.

"I do too."

They meandered in silence for a while. Peter walked slightly behind, and he stole glances at Renata while she scanned the beach for more treasure. Renata examined each piece of sea glass they found, and then placed it in her sweater pocket for safekeeping.

Peter spotted it first: A thick, smooth piece of cobalt glass the size of a silver dollar. He picked it up and presented it to Renata.

"Oh, Peter, it's beautiful," she said with obvious pleasure, "and this color is quite rare."

Peter's eye grew wide. He looked around as if to see if anyone else was nearby.

"What is it?" she whispered.

Peter took the blue glass from her, held it high, and spoke in a low, conspiratorial voice. "A lowly cabin boy fell in love with a princess during an ocean voyage. The princess wore a tiara encrusted with an enormous sapphire…" Peter's inflection implied that the story was not complete.

Renata was delighted. "And… the princess was on her way to be married to an evil prince…"

"But," said Peter, "when the cabin boy delivered her supper one evening, he found her distraught and in tears…"

Renata took over. "What was she to do? Her marriage to the evil prince had been decreed by the King himself. To thwart it would mean certain death…"

Peter continued, "The cabin boy didn't care. He told the princess of his love for her and said *I'd rather die than see you unhappy…*"

"And so it came to pass," Renata giggled, "that they devised a plan of escape…"

"But their plan was discovered," Peter said, "and the cabin boy was tied to the mast and flogged to within an inch of his life. The captain forced the princess to watch, and said *Let this be a lesson: A princess may never love a commoner…*"

Renata took the sea glass from Peter's hand and became very animated. "*Then I will be a princess no more* she cried, and with that she removed her sapphire tiara and pitched it into the sea. She

FOR RENATA

grabbed the captain's sword and cut the rope that bound the cabin boy. She took the boy's hand and whispered, *now or never*. And hand-in-hand they leapt from the ship into the dark and stormy night."

Peter nodded his head in approval.

"See?" said Renata, holding up the blue glass, "Isn't that better than saying someone drank milk of magnesia?"

"Much better," Peter agreed.

"Here," she said, holding out the piece of cobalt sea glass, "You keep this one."

"Always," he said.

B y late morning they were back at the lighthouse. Renata had set up her easel and implored Peter to pose for her by the lighthouse door.

"But I'm hungry," the reluctant model said.

"You're just saying that because you want to know what's in the basket."

"Well, yes, that too. But I *am* hungry, aren't you?"

"Please, Peter, just for a little while? I want to paint over what I have and make it better. You have such a kind and handsome face. I want to capture it as best as I can."

"Well, how can I refuse when you put it that way?"

Peter posed by the lighthouse door, crossing his legs at the ankle and leaning against the building with his only hand. "How's this?"

"Perfect. Now, stay just like that, please."

Peter watched as Renata's caramel eyes alternated focus between him and the canvas as she painted. Her expression was pensive and she bit her lower lip.

When she finished, she called Peter over to her. "Well, what do you think?" She stood back to let him examine her work.

"Wow," Peter said.

"Yes?"

"I really am handsome, aren't I?"

"Oh, you…"

"No, seriously, I had no idea I was so good looking. But you have the patch on the wrong eye."

She looked at him, and then at the canvas. "I do not. You're impossible."

"And you," he smiled, "are very talented. It's beautiful. Thank you for making me look so good."

"Do you really like it?"

He looked into her eyes for a long moment. "I love…it."

Renata blushed and cast her eyes to the ground. Peter sensed that he had made her uncomfortable again and quickly tried to lighten his tone. "*Now* can we eat?"

"It's about time. I am *starving*," she said.

"Good, then I can have my surprise now too?"

"Yes, little boy, you may have your surprise."

Inside the light keeper's kitchen Renata opened the cake basket and took out a covered record album. "You told me yesterday that you love music. My mother gave this to me but I'd like you to have it now. I hope you'll accept it. That would make me very happy."

Peter studied the cover. "Amália Rodrigues? I've never heard of her."

"She's Portuguese. She's not so well known here, but in Portugal and the rest of Europe she's known as *Rainha do Fado*, Queen of Fado."

"Where is Fado? I've never heard of that either."

"Fado isn't a *place*," Renata laughed, "It's a state of mind, a genre of music that's kind of like the blues here. Fado means *destiny*. The songs are about love, loss, and desire. They're often sad, but not always."

"Can we listen to it now?"

"Of course. Put it on the stereo. Let me choose the first song for you to hear, though. You think you've never heard her, but there's one song I think you might recognize. The song is called "Coimbra" or, sometimes, "April in Portugal," and it's known throughout the world. Coimbra *is* a place, a place in Portugal."

Peter put the album under his left arm and walked the few steps to the living room. He turned the stereo on and raised its black, smoked plastic cover, and then carefully slid the album from its cardboard envelope and placed it on the turntable. Renata took over, raising the record player's arm and delicately lowering the needle into position. After a few seconds of scratchy noise, the dulcet guitar introduction began and Amália Rodrigues's voice filled the room.

Coimbra é uma lição

de sonho e tradição…

Peter's face lit up in recognition, and then something else…pleasure. "You're right. I have heard this song."

…I found my April dreams
in Portugal with you…

Peter closed his eye and leaned his right ear toward the speakers, as if to soak in the music. When the song ended Peter opened his eye to find Renata standing close to him. Her soulful eyes studied his face.

"I'm so happy that you like it," she said.

"I love it. It's a lovely gift. Thank you."

Renata raised the turntable arm and started the album from the beginning. "Now we'll have a Portuguese picnic here on the floor and you can listen to more of Amália."

Renata went to the kitchen and returned with the basket. She sat on the floor and emptied it one item at a time.

"Here we have *frango escabeche*. It's marinated chicken that's cooked one day and then served cold the next. These are *papo secos*, fresh rolls that I baked this morning—the kitchen smelled *so* good—a little salad, and a bottle of wine."

"Everything looks wonderful. I'll get some plates and glasses and things," said Peter.

"No, sit, sit," said Renata. "Listen to the music. I'm sure I can find everything. Later, you can make some of your terrible coffee to go with our dessert, a custard tart called *pastel de nata.*"

"You made that too?"

"I like to cook, but I *love* to bake. It's a passion for me."

The afternoon passed too quickly for both of them. At precisely 3:00 p.m., the same time that she'd left the day before, Renata said, "I must go now, but this has been a wonderful day, the best I can remember, Peter. Thank you."

"Will you come tomorrow?"

"I can't. I wish I could but there's someplace else I have to be."

Peter grimaced with disappointment.

"Maybe I could come in the evening," she said, adding quickly, "just for a short while, though."

Peter's eye lit up. "I'll make dinner for us."

"I really can't stay very long."

"Then I'll make a short dinner," he smiled.

"It will have to be an early one. Will 6:30 be all right?"

"I'll be waiting."

Once again Peter watched her walk down the lane and, once again, he had to stop himself from calling out to her.

Renata turned around at the bend in the lane. Smiling, she raised her right arm high in the air and waved enthusiastically. Peter did the same.

When Renata disappeared from view, Peter hurried to the light keeper's quarters. He telephoned Vasconcelos's Market and placed his order with Mr. Vasconcelos for delivery early the next morning.

41

September 13, 1974
Friday the 13th. It may be unlucky for some, but this has been the best week of my life. Every day I spend with her is heaven on Earth. I want to know everything about her, absolutely everything. Her favorite flowers are lilacs, her favorite color is yellow. "Not just any yellow, daffodil yellow," she told me. Her favorite meal is veal Marsala with little red potatoes and asparagus. Her favorite book is Gone with the Wind, *and her favorite movie is* Splendor in the Grass.

Renata means "born again." And that's how I feel every time I see her. But I die a little each time she leaves and I watch her walk down that lane. I think about her every waking moment and I dream about her every night. I want to hold her and take care of her and be with her always. Renata. RENATA.

Peter's disposition seemed to match the warm, picture-perfect weather. He ate and slept sparingly but still felt revitalized. He rose before dawn and attacked his chores with a vigor and purpose bordering on exhilaration.

He had once climbed the eighty-nine spiral steps of the tower as wearily as a doomed man ascending the gallows. Now he effortlessly bounded up the steps two at a time. As he cleaned and polished the Fresnel lens, Peter caught himself whistling. He smiled at the realization that the tune was "April in Portugal."

Just after 8:00 a.m., Peter heard the distinctive clattering approach of Vasconcelos's Market's delivery van. The driver, Jimmy Vasconcelos, had a stocky, muscular body forged by a decade of hard work at the family market. His olive complexion had been darkened by the summer sun, and his face and body seemed to be entirely covered with thick black hair.

Jimmy steered the van past the end of the lane and pulled up onto the lawn, next to the house's kitchen door.

Peter flew down the spiral steps at a breakneck speed, and exited the base of the tower just as Jimmy turned off the ignition. The engine seemed to ignore his command, and continued running for several more seconds, rattling and pinging as if suffering from automotive death throes.

Jimmy stepped from the van and immediately noticed the uncharacteristic broad smile on Peter's face, an expression he hadn't seen since the two of them were in high school.

"How's it goin', man?" Jimmy asked.

"Great, couldn't be better."

"Yeah, I can see that. You seem really stoked."

"Did you get everything?" Peter asked eagerly.

"I think so. This is the list my father gave me. I thought it was a mistake, though. I said to the old man, *You sure this is for Pete? 'Cuz it sure don't look like his usual order.*

"You really gonna shave your beard, man?"

"Thinking about it."

"'Stache too?"

"Maybe. Why, you don't think I should?"

"No, man, it's *your* face. I'm just so used to seeing you with the beard and mustache, that's all. I haven't seen you without it since…"

Peter interrupted, "So, let's see what you've got for me, Jimmy."

Jimmy pulled a list out of his pocket. "Okay, besides the shaving stuff, I got olive oil, a pound of veal medallions, a pound of mushrooms, a pound of butter, all-purpose flour, fresh garlic, beef broth, red skin potatoes, asparagus, a bottle of Marsala wine, two bottles of Chianti. That's it for food and wine. Then I picked up the other stuff over at Kresge's: underwear, socks, and aftershave—Old Spice okay?"

"Anything but Bay Rum. I love my grandpa, but I don't want to smell like him," Peter laughed.

Peter laughing was something else Jimmy hadn't seen in years. He regarded Peter for a long moment. "You look good, Pete. Life out here must agree with you."

Peter just smiled in response.

Jimmy snapped his fingers. "Hey, I know this ain't on the list but I brought a couple of bottles of Seagram's and a nickel bag..."

"Thanks, Jimmy, but not this time."

"No problem, man. Here's the receipt from Kresge's, I'll just add it to our monthly bill."

Jimmy Vasconcelos loaded up as many of the bags as he could and Peter grabbed the rest. They entered the light keeper's quarters and set everything down on the kitchen table.

"Anything else you need, man?"

"You don't carry arms and eyes at the market, do you, Jimmy?" Peter asked.

Jimmy was thrown until he saw the broad grin that was spreading over Peter's face. He shook his head slowly and chuckled. "Sorry, man, we're fresh out of arms, and we only got brown eyes."

Peter's playful grin became a sincere, close-mouthed smile. "Hey, thanks for everything, Jimmy. You've been really good to me over these past couple of years. Don't know what I would have done without you."

Jimmy turned the delivery van turned around and it rattled across the lawn to the road. "Catch you on the flip-side, man. Don't let your meat loaf," he called out.

Peter waved and went back to work. He hurriedly completed his essential lighthouse duties, skipping the tasks that could be left for another day.

By 11:00 a.m. he had finished his labor. He stood in the light keeper's bedroom and tried to decide what to wear for dinner with Renata. His choices were sparse, ill-fitting, and worn. It was early yet. He could still call Jimmy and ask him to pick up some new clothing. He went downstairs to the living room, picked up the heavy, black handset and began to dial the number for Vasconcelos's Market. He stopped mid-dial and hung up the phone.

Peter walked outside and swung open the garage door, revealing the 1966 red Dodge Dart. He had started it and let it run weekly but hadn't driven it since the day of his last foray to the A & P, almost two years ago. Since then, this tiny piece of Rose Hip Point, less than two acres in total, and just beyond to Bridey Gallagher's house had comprised Peter Ahearn's entire physical world.

He felt strange sitting behind the steering wheel — unsettled. He had felt the same way when he drove for the first time after he returned from the war. At the time, he hadn't driven since leaving for basic training – almost a year.

He started the car to let the engine run for a while. The car radio came to life, blaring a song he didn't recognize, "*I shot the sheriff…*". He turned the radio off and slowly backed out of the garage. He stopped abruptly when he caught sight of the two easels in the corner. His and Renata's paintings sat side by side, patiently awaiting the return of their artists.

Looking at Renata's painting, Peter could see himself through her eyes — a thin, long-limbed young man dressed in worn, ill-fitting clothes, and

FOR RENATA

an eye patch, leaned against the lighthouse door with his only hand. His bearded, boyish face smiled as if he had everything any man could want.

The Dodge Dart crawled down the lane, past Bridey Gallagher's house and the house he now knew to be Renata's. He'd been by the little cottage in the past and had never paid much attention to it, but now he saw it differently. It wasn't just a house anymore, it was where *she* lived. At the end of the lane he turned right onto Route 127 toward Gloucester. Twenty minutes later he stood in Foster's Men's Shop where they had been "*Offering the Finest in Men's Clothing since 1947.*"

Dean Foster stood behind the counter, and eyed Peter with suspicion. It wasn't often that a hippie entered Foster's Men's Shop. They all seemed to favor the Gloucester Army/Navy Surplus Store.

"Hi, Mr. Foster," said Peter.

"Who's that?"

"It's Peter Ahearn, Mr. Foster."

"Oh, for heaven's sake, Peter Ahearn." Foster scurried out from behind the counter, and extended his hand as he approached.

"Peter, I didn't recognize you with the, um, beard. Why, I haven't seen you since…gosh, it must have been Memorial Day a few years back. I heard you were out at Rose Hip Point now. Keeping the light burning, are you, son?"

"Doing my best, Mr. Foster."

"Gosh, you don't have to wear some type of uniform or…"

"No, it's a civilian job."

B. ROBERT SHARRY

"Well, good for you, Peter. Good for you. I see your dad from time to time over at the VFW. You should come down sometime, we'd be glad to have you."

"Thanks, I might do that. But right now, Mr. Foster, I need some clothes."

"Well, judging by the sign on the window, I'd say you've come to the right place. Looking for anything in particular?"

"Nothing special, really, just a few shirts and a couple of pairs of pants—casual stuff."

"Let me show you what we've got."

On the drive back to Rose Hip Point, Peter stopped at Margaret's Flowers. The last time he had been to the flower shop was more than four years ago. He'd come before his senior prom to pick up a boutonniere for himself and a corsage for Cindy. Margaret Anderson had told him to behave himself and not embarrass his parents.

Now Margaret greeted him with the same distrustful glare he'd received from Dean Foster, her shaky, deeply-wrinkled hand perched on the telephone, as though she might call for help at the slightest encouragement.

"It's me, Mrs. Anderson, Peter Ahearn from Hollistown Harbor—John and Katherine's son?"

The woman's expression changed from fearful to something less distinct. Perhaps it was pity. "Oh, my soul, Peter, I didn't recognize you."

"Yeah, I guess it's the beard."

FOR RENATA

"That's not a beard. A real beard is kept trimmed and neat. You look like a scraggly mountain man. Don't be one of those hippies, Peter, you'll embarrass your parents and break their hearts."

Peter felt his face flush. "Do you have any lilacs?"

"Lilacs? No, not at this time of year."

He pointed to a bouquet of white flowers that sat in a refrigerated display case.

"I'll take those," he said.

"Don't be in such a hurry. Are they a gift?"

"Sort of."

"Now then, what's the occasion?"

Peter bit his lower lip. "No occasion, I'd just like to buy the flowers."

"Peter, I can't help you if you don't let me. Getting the wrong flowers can send the wrong message. Those are white dahlias. They symbolize a lifelong commitment of love..."

"Mrs. Anderson, are those flowers for sale or not?"

Mrs. Anderson let out a sigh of exasperation. "It's $3 for the flowers, $4.50 if you want them in a vase."

"Thank you, I'll take the vase too."

Peter drove home carefully with the dahlias stowed in a cardboard box on the passenger-side floor of the car.

At 2:00 p.m. he stood shirtless before the bathroom mirror, scissors in hand. He blew out a great sigh and began to cut away more than three years of cinnamon growth from his face. After trimming as closely as he could with the scissors, he wet a facecloth with water as hot as he could stand and held it to what remained of his beard and mustache to soften them. Peter placed the red and white striped Barbasol can on the edge of the bathroom sink, then pressed down on the nozzle with his thumb and released far too much lather into his palm. He worked the foam into his beard and mustache and then rinsed the excess from his hand. Though he tried to be careful with the double-edged safety razor, he still nicked himself multiple times.

After he showered and toweled off, Peter examined his face in the steamy bathroom mirror. The cuts were still bleeding. He splashed Old Spice onto his face and almost cried out from the sting. The cologne did nothing to stanch the bleeding. He dressed the tiny wounds with little wads of toilet paper.

Later, he stood before the full-length mirror that hung on the back of his bedroom door, pulled his eye patch on to cover his lifeless eye, and assessed his reflection. His right eye was clear and deep blue. Long, wavy, blond hair, parted haphazardly in the middle, fell almost to his shoulders. His sideburns were auburn and flared slightly where they ended parallel to his earlobes.

Except for his square-toed brown boots, everything he wore was new: the socks, the underwear, the long-sleeved, brown and white patterned, wide-collared, polyester shirt, and the tan, double-knit polyester bellbottom pants that were held up by a wide, white patent leather belt with a shiny faux-brass buckle.

He stood erect and felt another of emotions that had been buried beneath his heavy heart: confidence.

He glanced at the alarm clock on his nightstand. It was 4:00 p.m. Renata was to arrive at 6:30, and he had much to prepare.

42

Peter was bent over, holding the oven door open, when he heard a soft knock at the door. He glanced at the kitchen wall clock. *6:30 already?*

"Come on in," he called over his shoulder.

Renata entered the kitchen and immediately caught sight of Peter bent over the oven. Her eyes were drawn to his narrow hips and tight buttocks. She stared for a moment and imagined… She blushed at thoughts she shouldn't be having, and quickly diverted her gaze, as if she had walked in and found him standing naked before her. Renata cleared her throat. "Good evening, Peter."

Peter straightened and turned around. He broke into a broad smile. He was surprised to see that Renata's cheeks were red, and there was a stunned expression on her face. "What's wrong?"

FOR RENATA

He watched her blush dissipate as she brought her hand up to her mouth and giggled.

"Oh, yeah," he said, "I forgot. I shaved. Is it that much of a shock?"

"No. Well, yes, but it's not just that," she shook her head and laughed harder.

"What, then?"

Renata took his hand. "Come, look in the mirror."

She led him to the mirror in the living room. His face was covered in all-purpose flour and speckled with a dozen tiny toilet paper bandages stained with dried blood. And his brand new shirt and pants were covered with flour images of his own handprint.

"God, I look like *The Mummy*. I'm surprised you didn't run from the house, screaming."

"It's not that bad," she chuckled.

"It's not?"

"Yes, it is." she laughed and snorted. "Come."

Back in the kitchen, Renata wet a dishcloth with cold water. She faced Peter and rose up onto her tiptoes. She placed her left hand on his shoulder to steady herself.

Peter was captivated by the way she tilted her head, her lovely smile, and her spellbinding eyes, caramel with microscopic flecks of green. She brought the cool, wet cloth to his face and slowly washed him with gentle dabs and strokes.

"There," she half-whispered when she had finished. They stood face to face, their lips just inches from becoming a kiss.

Peter slid his arm around her slender waist, and gently pulled her close to him. Just then, the kitchen timer buzzed and broke them out of their trance.

Renata felt disoriented, as though she had been sleepwalking and had come awake in Peter's embrace. Her face reddened, her eyes sought the floor, and she pushed herself away from him.

It took Peter a moment to collect his thoughts. "The...the potatoes are done," he said in a quavering voice.

Renata raised her focus from the floor and saw his hardness straining against a white flour handprint on his trousers. She diverted her gaze once more.

"You...you have flour on your...pants," she said. She handed him the dishcloth and took a good look around the kitchen for the first time since her arrival. Two bottles of red wine sat on the kitchen counter next to an ancient cookbook titled *The Butterick Book of Recipes and Household Help*.

"Oh, good, you have wine. May I have some? Please?"

"Renata, I..."

But she cut him off. "Don't." she said. She walked toward the stove. "Can I do anything to help with dinner?"

"No, I can do it. I want to surprise you."

"You already *did*."

Peter smiled sheepishly. "I meant with dinner."

"I know," she smiled.

"Why don't you have that glass of wine and just relax?"

FOR RENATA

"Maybe I'll take the wine outside. When I arrived, the sun was very low in the sky. I'd like to watch it set."

"Good idea. I'll have dinner ready before you know it."

Renata stood near the edge of the cliff on the south side of Rose Hip Point and looked to the west. The gold September sun inched its way into hiding behind the tiny village of Hollistown Harbor, taking the warmth of day with it. She sipped from her wineglass, wrapped her arms around herself, and shivered.

How close they had come. She could almost still feel Peter's powerful arm grasping her, pulling her so close to him that her whole body was enveloped in his. In that moment, in the warmth of his embrace, she had felt sanctuary and belonging.

She imagined how his lips might feel against hers, and how the sensation of drawing her fingertips over his lean body would make her tingle.

Twice she started for the light keeper's quarters, and twice she stopped. She was frightened by the strength of her own desire.

She had all but decided to bolt, to run home and avoid temptation altogether. But as she stole through the dusk, past the kitchen window, she caught sight of Peter. He stood over the stove, looking happier than she had ever seen him. She imagined how that look on his face would change if he discovered that she wasn't coming back. Renata steeled herself and went inside instead.

Peter heard her and turned around, beaming. "Two more minutes, I promise," he said, waving a spatula. "I set the table in the living room, have a seat, and I'll be right there."

The table stood by the old stone fireplace, illuminated by the flickering, buttery glow of a diminutive fire. A folded white bed sheet served as tablecloth. A basketed Chianti bottle cum candlestick sat at the center of the table and threw soft light on an open bottle of wine and a bouquet of white dahlias. A pair of scuffed wooden chairs had been commandeered from the kitchen.

Renata noticed that the forks and knives were placed on the wrong sides of the plates, only the spoons were where they should be. She smiled and thought, *He's twenty-three years old, and I think this is the first time he's set a table.*

The Queen of Fado sang softly in the background. The record's jacket was propped on top of the stereo. Its cover image — a youthful, pretty Amália Rodrigues clad in a green sundress, wore her dark, wavy hair short, with sideburns so long and wide they looked boyish.

Renata refilled her wineglass and stared transfixed at the short, hopping flames of the fire. Presently, she heard a clatter from the kitchen followed by a muffled curse from Peter. She listened for a moment, and then called, "Are you all right?"

"Just hunky dory," Peter said as he entered the living room carrying a dinner plate. He stopped beside Renata, set the plate in front of her, and said,

FOR RENATA

"I give you: Veal Marsala with little red potatoes and asparagus."

"Oh, Peter, it looks wonderful."

"Be right back," he said, and in a moment he returned with his own plate of food and sat down across from her.

"Surprised?" he asked.

"You remembered my favorite."

"Well, you did tell me just yesterday."

"I know, but it's so...so..." Her caramel eyes welled up.

"Renata, what's wrong?"

"Nothing."

"Did I do something?"

"No. Yes, you did something beautiful. Everything is just...beautiful."

"Then why are you crying?"

"Because I'm happy."

Peter was dumbfounded.

"Peter, no one has ever done anything like this for me—*just* for me."

"So, you're happy."

"Yes, very."

"But you're crying."

"Yes."

"I don't understand."

"I know," she said, laughing through her tears. "I'm sorry. Let's eat."

The veal was burned and tough, the potatoes undercooked and hard, and the asparagus a soupy mush. But Renata was done crying, and the rest of the meal was seasoned with laughter.

After they finished eating, Renata stood, stepped away from the table, and beckoned to him with her arms. "I want to dance to Amália."

Peter stood and walked toward her.

Renata realized that, from habit, she had raised her right hand. She lowered it and raised her left.

Peter clasped her left hand with his right and only hand. He kept the remaining half of his left arm at his side.

She questioned him with her eyes.

"I don't want to make you feel uncomfortable," he offered.

"Quite the opposite," she said with a sly grin. "It's very comforting to know that your *other hand* can't stray and grab something it shouldn't."

And they both began to laugh. Renata laughed so hard that she snorted.

"You snorted."

"Yes, I did," she said, laughing even harder and snorting again.

When their laughter subsided, Peter took her left hand in his right and placed the stump of his left arm against her ribs. Renata put her right hand on his shoulder. She turned her head and laid it on his chest. They moved slowly in each other's arms to the rhythm of Fado.

Peter had no way of knowing that Amália Rodrigues sang of doomed love.

FOR RENATA

43

September 20, 1974
 This has been the longest week of my life. She won't let me call her, so I just have to wait. Every day I look down the lane hoping to see some sign of her. Nothing. Last night I walked down to her house and stood outside. It sounded like the whole family was arguing and yelling at once. The fisherman must have been drunk. I wanted to rush in there, take her by the hand, and rescue her from it all. No one should have to live like that, especially not her.

September 22, 1974
 I saw her coming up the lane today and ran out to meet her. She looked so pretty all dressed up for church...

But as Peter drew closer, his smile evaporated. Renata's face was swollen. As he got closer, he could see the bruises that her heavily applied makeup was meant to disguise. Her stunning eyes were puffy and the lively glint he'd seen in them the previous week had vanished.

"*He* did this to you?" Peter said through clenched teeth.

Renata's eyes sought the ground. Peter put his hand on her left arm. "Renata, there's no reason for you to be embarrassed." He looked beyond her, down the lane, and said "Stay here."

Renata grabbed his arm with both hands and stopped him.

"No." she cried.

"Don't worry. Just wait here."

"Please, Peter, you don't understand...you'll only make things worse. He gets this way when he drinks. You're a good man, but if you intervene it'll only bring more suffering.

"I only came to tell you that I can't visit you anymore."

"But..."

"Please, Peter, you have to trust me, trust that I know what's best."

She lifted her fingers to Peter's cheek. "You've been very kind to me. Thank you."

She turned and walked away.

"But I love you." he called.

She turned back to face him, her eyes studying him as though she wanted to lock every detail of him in her memory. "Don't...don't love me," she said. She brought her hand to her mouth, turned, and ran.

FOR RENATA

44

Tears slid down Renie's cheeks. She closed the Keeper's Log as though the act itself might put her memories to rest. She stared blankly at nothing, and Mark second-guessed his decision to ask her to read it. Maybe he should have just told her the truth upfront. Or maybe he shouldn't have said anything to anybody, ever.

"Do you want me to go?" he asked.

Renie blushed as if she'd just remembered Mark's presence and was embarrassed by the realization that he'd read every word in the journal too. "No, I just need a moment."

Mark rose from the table, crossed over to the kitchen counter and grabbed the carafe. "Do you mind?" he asked, breaking her trance.

"Help yourself."

"You want more coffee?"

"No," she said, "but I'm going to excuse myself for a moment." She rose from the kitchen table and hurried from the room, down the short hallway to her childhood bedroom. She closed the door behind her, leaned her back against it, and began to hyperventilate. The memories reared in her mind like monsters from under a child's bed.

After a time, Renie did her best to compose herself. She wiped her tears away and made a hasty repair to her mascara before opening the bedroom door.

The longer he waited for Renie's return, the deeper Mark's discomfort grew. He had just upset a total stranger and was now sitting in an unfamiliar house that was so quiet he could hear the ticking of the mantel clock in the living room. He had learned that while fifteen minutes can fly by, they could also be nine hundred ticks of a clock.

When the Portuguese fisherman's daughter returned, she avoided eye contact. She glanced at the clock on the kitchen wall, sat down, and said, "Perhaps it *would* be better if you left now, Mark."

Mark felt himself blush for the second time in as many hours. Somehow, the idea that she hadn't read far enough into the Keeper's Log to learn Peter's terrible secret did not bother him nearly as much as the thought that he might never see her again. He frantically searched his mind for a graceful argument that would buy him some time, but couldn't come up with anything remotely plausible.

FOR RENATA

"Of course," he finally said. "I understand."

He rose and scooped up the Keeper's Log. Knowing how it ended, he couldn't just leave it with her. He had planned to interrupt her at just the right moment, hoping that he could somehow prepare her for the final entry, and cushion the shock that she would unavoidably feel.

"I'm really sorry," he said, "You've been so kind, and the thought that I've upset you is just…"

Renie's face softened. "I'll be all right." She glanced again at the kitchen clock. "But please, please, just go now."

Mark nodded. If he couldn't stay, at least he could make sure that she had the ability to contact him. He placed his business card on the kitchen table. "In case you change your mind."

Renie looked at the card but not at Mark, who turned and left the room. Mark closed the front door of the Raposo home as softly as he could, and walked down the flagstone path to his pick-up. He stood at the driver's door and looked back at the picturesque cottage. When he was satisfied that Renie was not watching him from any of the windows, he kicked his front tire and muttered, "Smooth move, Mark. You just managed to alienate the most enchanting woman you've ever laid eyes on."

45

Mark went to bed each night thinking about Renie. He considered calling her to apologize, just so he could hear her voice. And he felt guilty that he'd been more concerned with her perception of him — and the thought that he might never see her again — than the fact that there remained a terrible secret she deserved to know.

With so much on his mind, he found it impossible to concentrate on work, which wasn't at all like him. Mark loved his work. He had a satisfying career as a marine mammal biologist and was recognized as one of the world's leading experts on the behavior of humpback whales.

He was eight years old when he had his first sighting of a humpback breaching, sailing into the air, and then falling back into the sea with a mighty crash. He had become determined then and there to learn all there was to know about the imposing behemoths. There had been many a long, lazy summer day when he had peered at the ocean from the shore in the hope that he might glimpse a humpback as it breached, pec slapped, or lobtailed. He could even identify individual whales by their flukes — the undersides of their tails — long before he knew the term itself. As a teenager he had worked summers on charter fishing boats and whale watch excursions — anything to be on the water.

Mark's professional existence was not without its perks. He was an expert diver and worked each winter in the Caribbean, where humpbacks gathered by the thousands to mate or give birth to the next generation. But as exciting and satisfying as his career was, there were holes in his life, an emptiness that work could not altogether fill. He had no siblings, and he'd lost his mother to cancer a few years earlier.

And there was no woman in his life. There hadn't been anyone special since Jill.

They had been very happy at the beginning. But as Mark's career progressed, his work kept him away from home for longer periods of time, sometimes weeks or even months. Jill became unhappier with each goodbye. Mark could sense it, and the guilt stung him. He was torn between the passion that had driven him since he was a child and his longing to be with Jill.

One day Mark returned home early from a work trip. He had bought flowers and two plane tickets to Paris, determined to surprise his wife. Instead, she surprised him — he found her in bed with her boss.

Mark had dated other women since their breakup, but Jill's betrayal had stayed with him, and those who came after her had met the impenetrability of a hardened heart.

He had opted to avoid the Memorial Day onslaught of tourists by staying at home in Annisquam instead of driving through holiday traffic to the Institute. Ostensibly he was doing "field work," but in truth, he had spent most of the day pacing the back portion of the wide, covered porch that wrapped around his house. There was a splendid view of Ipswich Bay, but he was so distracted that he didn't even look at it.

This is insane. How could he be pining like an adolescent over some middle-aged woman he'd spent all of a few hours with and knew nothing about?

But that wasn't true. He'd learned a lot about her from the Keeper's Log. His feelings for Renie had begun while reading about her. Seeing her in the flesh had only solidified an already burgeoning infatuation.

And he realized something else: He hadn't thought about Jill in weeks. Though he had thought of her less with each passing year, it was rare for more than a few days to go by without him wondering where she was and what she was doing. But the last time he could remember thinking about her was during his first trip to the Soldiers' Home, almost two months ago.

FOR RENATA

Mark leaned his elbows against the porch railing and cradled a ceramic coffee mug imprinted with the slogan *Massachusetts' Other Cape*. His eyes followed a small sailboat as it tacked lazily over the calm waters of Plum Cove. But his mind kept returning to memories of Renie — the enticing smile she had given him when she first opened the door of her mother's home, then the sadness that had come over her while she read the Keeper's Log. He had caused that sadness. Did she hate him now? Did she think of him at all?

The soft, doorbell chime of his iPhone brought him back to the present. He pulled the phone from the front pocket of his tan cargo pants and held it far enough in front of him that he could see the number on the screen. He didn't recognize it, but he knew the area code, 413, was Western Massachusetts. He returned the phone to his pocket when he remembered something: Renie had said she used to live in the Berkshires. That was in western Massachusetts. He pulled the phone back out and almost fumbled it over the porch railing.

"Hello?" he said with more excitement in his voice than he would have liked.

"Mark?"

"Yes?"

"Mark, this is Renie Bennett. Am I calling at a bad time?"

"Not at all. I was just having my coffee."

"Good. First of all, I'd like to apologize for the way I treated you. I was not a very good hostess…"

"No, I'm the one who needs to apologize. I just showed up out of the blue, and hit you with this thing. I should have handled it differently. I'm so sorry to have upset you."

"Thank you. Anyway, I *would* like to finish reading Pete's journal, if that's all right."

"Of course, I can be there in an hour, if you'd like."

"No," she said, "not here. Would it be all right if I came to you?"

"Of course, I'll make a fresh pot of coffee."

"Actually, later in the day would be better. I'm looking at studio spaces today. I teach dance and, well, I've had to close my studio in the Berkshires…"

"There's no need to explain."

"I could come around five, if that works for you."

"Five will be perfect."

"All right, five it is. I'll just need your address for my gps."

Mark gave her his address, and ended the call with, "See you at five."

The closer it came to 5:00 p.m., the more nervous Mark felt. Renie arrived shortly after five, and Mark watched her from the bay window of his living room as she parked her SUV and got out. Her hair was pulled back tightly into a long ponytail, and she wore black capris with a tan T-shirt and black flip-flops.

FOR RENATA

Mark's iPhone chimed. He looked at the screen. It was Jake Carvalho, a Gloucester fisherman and friend. Jake never called without a good reason.

"Hello?" Mark answered.

"Marko, it's Jake. I'm about a mile out and I've got a baby humpback caught in fishing net. It hasn't come up for a while, so chances are it's done for, but I thought you should know."

Mark's brow furrowed. "They can hold out for quite a while when they need to, Jake. Give me your coordinates, and I'll be there as soon as I can."

Renie had barely raised her fist to knock when Mark pulled open the front door.

"I'm sorry," he said, "But I have to leave for a work-related emergency. I'm a marine biologist with the Oceanographic Institute. A baby whale is caught up in fishing net. It probably won't survive, but I have to at least try."

"Of course," said Renie. "Good luck, and call me when it's convenient to reschedule."

"Listen, Renie, I can't say exactly how long I'll be gone, but you're welcome to wait here for me. Better yet, would you care to come along? You won't be in any danger."

"I'm sure I'd just be in the way."

"No, I'd like for you to come — really. But we have to hurry."

"All right," she said. Her eyes were wide, and she looked startled.

Mark led Renie down the narrow path that led from his backyard to his boat dock. He calculated that it would take twenty minutes to reach the coordinates that Jake had given him. They had to hurry if they were to make it in time to make a difference.

Mark pulled up to the port side of the fishing boat and cut the engine. His Bayliner bobbed gently against the larger trawler like a puppy nuzzling its mother.

Jake Carvalho was the personification of a harbor seal. His head and face were almost totally covered with dark, short-cropped hair. On the bridge of his short nose sat round glasses that magnified large, brown eyes bordered by long eyelashes.

Jake helped Mark aboard first, and then each of them took hold of one of Renie's arms, helping her onto the trawler's deck.

"Thank God you're here, Marko. I spoke too soon. It's not dead. It surfaces every few minutes to breathe."

"But I thought it was too caught up in the net for that," Mark said.

"It has help," Jake replied.

"You mean...the mother?"

"Uh-huh. As soon as I hung up the phone with you, I saw it surface. The calf was up for just long enough to take a breath, and a minute later Mama surfaced along the starboard side. She dives every few minutes, and then she helps junior surface for long enough to get some air. They've been doing that for a while now."

"Well, that's how a mother helps her newborn take its first breath. Okay, I'll change into my wetsuit."

"Mark, you're not going to…"

"I don't have much choice. They can't keep this up forever. If the calf's not freed, it'll die."

"Yeah, what about *you*?"

"I'll be fine."

Jake shook his head slowly and stroked a hand over his beard, but Mark's tone implied that he wasn't asking for anyone's feedback.

Mark crossed back over to his own boat to change.

Renie turned to Jake, eyeing him curiously. "What's going on?"

"Look, the mother must weigh in at about eighty thousand pounds. If she makes a wrong move around Mark, even accidently, he could be crushed. When I called him I didn't know the mother was around."

"Couldn't you have just called the Coast Guard?"

Jake laughed.

"Why is that funny?"

"It's just that…I guess you haven't known Mark for very long, have you?"

"No, not very."

"You see, if I had called the Coast Guard, they'd have called Mark and asked him what they should do. He's like the world's leading expert."

B. ROBERT SHARRY

A few minutes later Mark emerged from the Bayliner dressed in a wetsuit, snorkel, and facemask. After giving a wave to Jake and Renie, he slipped into the sea. Through his wetsuit he could feel the seawater cool his body and he shivered for a moment before he swam around the larger boat's bow, toward the young whale.

When Mark went underwater, he could see where the fishing net was tangled around the whale's fins and tail. He drew his knife from its sheath and was about to make his first cut in the net when something dark and enormous approached in his peripheral vision. He turned his head to the left and was startled to see a black eye the size of a grapefruit just a few feet away from him—the mother.

He struggled to keep his composure and stay still. He stared directly into the giant eye for a few seconds and thought, *God, I hope you know that I'm the best friend you've got right now*. Then, turning back ever-so-slowly, he began to saw through the net, pulling it away from the young whale's body as he went.

But he was one man with one knife and his progress was slow. After several minutes of cutting, surfacing for air, and re-submerging to continue, he heard the young one cry out.

The enormous silhouette of the adult whale appeared beneath her offspring and the calf began to rise to the surface with Mark on top of it. Holding fast to the net, he surfaced along with the whale. It took all the strength he could muster just to hold on.

FOR RENATA

Renie and Jake gasped simultaneously when they saw Mark rise up with the baby whale. Mark clung to the net like a rodeo rider would hold onto a bronco. An enormous, violent gush of water and air spewed from the animal's blowhole and was followed by a huge, desperate-sounding inhalation of air. Then the calf fell back below the surface, and took Mark with it.

Mark sawed furiously at the net. His strength was being sapped and he feared he wouldn't be able to last much longer. Finally, lungs bursting, he cut through the last strands that were tangled around the whale. It bolted quickly, its mother by its side.

After a few tense moments Mark surfaced and Renie and Jake sighed with relief. Jake hauled his exhausted and weakened friend over the side. Mark collapsed onto the deck.

"Are you all right?" Renie rushed to his side.

"I'll be fine." Mark said. "I just need to rest for a little while."

Renie knelt beside him and watched with concern while he lie on his back, gasping.

A few minutes later, Jake murmured, "I'll be damned. I think you have a fan club, Marko." He pointed out to sea, and his hairy face spread into a smile.

Renie helped Mark to his feet, and they both turned to look. The cow and calf were engaged in a display of lobtailing and fin slapping. The whales' breathtaking dance lasted for several minutes. At the end of the performance, in the backdrop, the sun melted into the sea like a dollop of butter on a griddle.

Mark steered the Bayliner back toward shore. He felt Renie's eyes on him, and turned from the helm of the boat to meet her stare.

"What?" he asked.

"That was the most incredible thing I've ever seen."

Mark nodded. "I know. They put on quite a show, didn't they?"

Renie leaned in to him, and placed her hand on his forearm. "Not them. I mean you. What you did was the bravest, most selfless act I've ever witnessed."

Mark felt himself blush and tried to conceal his embarrassment with nervous chatter about whales—how they had been hunted almost to extinction, and why it was essential to save them.

With twilight came a rapid drop in air temperature, and the breeze created by the boat's speed made Renie shiver. Steering with his left hand, Mark used his right to lift up a seat bench and pull out a blanket for her. He draped it over her shoulders, and pulled her in close.

"Better now?" he asked.

She looked up at him, smiled, and nodded her head.

When they got to Mark's house, Renie offered to brew some tea.

FOR RENATA

"If it's all the same to you, I think something a wee bit stronger is in order," Mark said.

Renie laughed when Mark grabbed a bottle of Jack Daniels from a kitchen cupboard.

"I guess you've earned it," she said.

"Join me?" Mark asked as he poured a good measure into an ice-laden tumbler. The warm, honey-colored liquor caused an ice cube to split with a loud *crack*.

"I'll stick with tea, thanks."

"Here's to swimmin' with bowlegged women," he said with a devilish grin.

While Mark showered, Renie meandered around the living room. The decor was both attractive and inviting—a mix of newer upholstered sofas and chairs and older tables, lamps, and artwork, which Renie imagined Mark had grown up with.

Two large, overstuffed sofas in dark green brocade sat opposite each other in the center of the room, perpendicular to the fireplace. Between them, an antique, stenciled mahogany hope chest acted as a coffee table.

Renie moved about the room until she arrived at the fireplace. Several family photos were displayed in stylish frames on the mantelpiece. One was of a five-year-old Mark and his parents. Mark's hair was in a long, Dutch-boy cut and he sported the same devilish grin she'd seen just moments before. It made her smile.

Then another photo leapt out at her and her smile faded. An older teenage girl was flanked by two younger boys, one of whom Renie recognized instantly, even though it was the first time she'd ever seen him with two eyes and two arms.

The long-haired children stood with their arms strung over each other's shoulders, smiling broadly. Their happiness showed in their clear, young eyes — not a care or a doubt in the world. Renie surmised that Peter posed with his older brother, Tommy, who would soon die in Vietnam, and his sister, Marybeth, who would become Mark's mother.

In her mind's eye she remembered what Peter had looked and sounded like when she knew him in the early '70s. For a few precious moments it was as if she was sixteen again. The memory brought a bittersweet smile to her lips.

Renie heard the shower abruptly stop, and was jostled back to the present. Young Peter was once again exiled to the back of her mind. She was here with Mark now. But as much as she had come to like and admire Mark in their brief time together, and as much as she wanted — *needed* — to know what Peter had written in the rest of his Keeper's Log, she was determined that no one, not even Mark, would ever learn the truth of what had happened at Rose Hip Point.

46

Mark emerged from his bedroom. He was barefoot, and wore jeans and a black, long-sleeve T-shirt. His dark, wavy hair, still wet from the shower, was combed back.

He scanned the living room and said, "Now, where did I leave my old friend, Jack?" Eyeing the tumbler of bourbon on the coffee table, he added, "There you are. Come to Papa."

On his way to retrieve the drink, Mark passed close by Renie and she took in his clean scent and the aroma of his lightly spicy cologne.

"Feel better?" she asked.

Mark was still so pumped with adrenaline that he was almost hyper. He looked directly into her eyes, smiled, and said, "I feel positively human. Then he added, "Hey, I've been so wrapped up in myself I almost forgot to ask. How'd the studio search go?"

"Actually, quite well, there's a nice, big space available off of Main Street in Gloucester. It's just a little way up the hill on Elm Street. It has a beautiful hardwood floor. All I need to do is add mirrors and a ballet bar. I think it will be perfect."

"That's great, I'm glad things are falling into place for you."

Their eyes locked for a long moment before Renie nervously broke the spell. "I think you have some reading material for me?" she said, and looked away.

The Keeper's Log, the damned Keeper's Log. At that moment Mark just wanted it to go away. He wanted to say, *Oh, that. It's not important. Listen, saving that whale made me hungry. I have a couple of steaks in the fridge and a bottle of Côtes du Rhône. Let's just forget all about the Keeper's Log. We can light a few candles, and have dinner on the porch overlooking the bay.*

But he didn't. Of course, he didn't. Instead he said, "Right, one Keeper's Log coming up."

He disappeared into his home office, and returned a few moments later with the journal in hand.

They sat together on the sofa. Renie slowly, reverently turned the pages until she found the place where she had left off.

*N*ovember 27, 1974
  Marybeth and Bridey both invited me to Thanksgiving dinner, but I begged off. I just don't feel like being around people right now…

FOR RENATA

Peter heard a soft knock on his kitchen door and peered through the window. A frail-looking Bridey Gallagher stood on the granite stoop. The old woman held a large willow laundry basket whose contents were concealed by a gleaming white bath towel. He pursed his lips and shook his head.

When he opened the door a swirling gust brought the damp, gray cold and scent of November into the light keeper's house.

"Bridey," he said.

But the old woman pushed by him as brusquely as the autumn wind. "Peter, be a dear and set the oven to 325 while I lay the table? Everything's cooked. I just need to warm a few things."

"But, Bridey, Thanksgiving's not until tomorrow. Besides, I *told* you…"

"Oh, too bad aboutcha. Since you wouldn't come to the mountain, dear, I decided to bring the mountain to you."

"You're just…just…"

"I think *exasperating* is the word you're searching for. Now stop your noise and start the oven. Oh, and build a fire too, won't you, Peter? It's awfully chilly in here."

Peter threw up his hand in acquiescence. He turned the oven on, and then headed for the living room fireplace. When he had a good blaze going, he returned to the kitchen.

"Anything *else*?" he asked.

Bridey gave him an appraising look.

"Yes, you might want to have a shave, because I invited Renata."

"Oh, my God, she's coming *here*?"

"Well, what choice did I have? I invited both of you to my house, but you couldn't be bothered…"

Peter flew up the narrow staircase. A few moments later Bridey heard the bathroom shower start. She smiled to herself and continued to set the table for three. Then the old woman leaned on the kitchen counter and watched for Renata through the window above the sink. Renata arrived ten minutes later. She carried a brown-glazed earthenware bowl covered with aluminum foil. Bridey opened the door wide as she approached.

"Hello, dear," Bridey said, "I'm so glad you could make it. You look lovely, as usual."

"Hello, Bridey, and Happy Thanksgiving to you in advance."

They kissed cheeks, first the right, then the left. The bowl Renata was holding poked lightly into Bridey's stomach and the older woman winced.

"I'm sorry, Bridey. Are you all right?"

"Of course, dear, I'm fine."

"You're looking very svelte these days, what's your secret?" Renata asked.

"Oh, no secret. At some point we old ladies just begin to eat like a bird, that's all."

Renata set the bowl down on the kitchen counter. She removed her coat and looked around the light keeper's quarters. Her eyes fell upon the spot in front of the fireplace where Peter had served up her favorite meal, and a sad smile came to her lips. She turned back to face Bridey.

"How is he?" she asked.

"Oh, he's sad and miserable and broken-hearted and brooding. He misses you so."

Renata gave a heavy sigh. "I feel the same way, but I have to do what I think is best."

"I understand, dear."

"Where is he?" Renata asked.

Bridey smiled. "When he learned you were coming, he ran upstairs to shower and shave. I expect he's preening his feathers right now, and that our little peacock will come bounding down the stairs at any moment."

Bridey gave Renata a once-over. "If I didn't know better, I might think you did a little extra preening yourself."

Renata smiled and blushed.

"Sorry, dear," Bridey continued. "That wasn't at all fair of me."

Bridey walked over to the bowl Renata had brought and took an edge of the aluminum foil in her hand. "May I?"

"Of course," Renata answered.

Bridey removed the foil and bent over the bowl.

"Some type of pudding, dear? It looks yummy."

"Well, I hope it tastes better than its name. In Portuguese it's called *baba de camelo.* But I'm afraid to tell you what that means because you might find it offensive."

"Ooo, is it naughty, dear? Because I might be old, but I'm no prude, you know. Once, when I was a girl, my best friend, Sally, and I made our own variation on a cream Swiss roll. We shaped it just so," Bridey gestured with her hands, "and we called it…" She leaned in toward Renata and lowered her voice to a whisper, "Adonis's Dick."

Bridey howled with laughter and then covered her mouth with her hands. Renata began to giggle.

"And then…" Bridey said, still laughing. "And then…when we heard Sally's mother come home, we dove in and gobbled the whole thing up as fast as we could so that she wouldn't see what we had done."

Both women were so convulsed with laughter that they had to dab tears from their eyes. Renata snorted. Finally, Bridey ended her laughter with a long, drawn-out sigh.

"Ahhhhhh," she said, "Now what does *baba de camelo* mean?"

Renata closed her mouth and held her breath, trying to stave off more laughter. "Camel's drool," she finally managed to blurt out.

Bridey was silent for a moment, and looked befuddled. "Drool? But that's not naughty, that's just…disgusting."

Both women began to howl again. Through her laughter Bridey was barely able to say, "You simply *must* give me the recipe."

"I'll trade you for Adonis's Dick." Renata screamed.

When their hysterics had died down again, Bridey said, "Seriously, dear, tell me how you make it."

"It's so simple," said Renata, "I cook a can of condensed milk for about an hour. Then I beat half a dozen egg yolks into the milk. I whip the egg whites and mix them in. I put it in the fridge for a few hours, and then sprinkle the top with almond slices just before I serve it."

"Sounds lovely. I can't wait to try it. And I'll bet you're anxious to try Adonis's…"

Peter bounded down the stairs. "Hey, what's all the commotion down here? I can't leave you girls alone for five minutes…"

Peter got to the bottom of the stairs, and his gaze locked with Renata's. Bridey looked on, shifting her attention back and forth between the two.

Peter and Renata were wearing the same outfits they'd had on the night Peter had made her dinner, their best outfits.

"Hello," Peter said.

"Hello" was Renata's only reply.

"It certainly sounded like you girls were having a lot of fun down here, what'd I miss?"

Renata and Bridey looked at each other and smiled.

"Oh," said Bridey, "just girl talk, swapping recipes…"

"I should put the dessert in the fridge, if there's room," Renata said.

"Oh, there's plenty of room," said Bridey, "All I saw in there was some beer, eggs, butter, and sour milk. Oh, and something growing, which I assume is a science experiment you're doing, Peter?"

Peter hurried over to the fridge and grabbed the moldy leftover, and then dropped it, plate and all, into the trash. He held the refrigerator door open for Renata as she placed the *baba de camelo* inside.

"Heavens," Bridey said, "I'm developing the forgetful mind of an old woman. I just realized I left the gravy on the countertop. I'll just run over and get it."

"I can go for you," Renata said.

"Thank you, dear, but no. You keep an eye on the turkey for me. I'll be back in a jiffy," she said, putting her coat on and heading out the door.

Renata walked over to the kitchen window and watched Bridey as she made her way down the lane.

"I was surprised when Bridey told me you were coming," Peter said. "Pleasantly surprised, I mean."

"Well, I didn't think I should, but I find it impossible to refuse Bridey."

"I know what you mean," Peter agreed. "She's like an irresistible force. Trouble is, she's so cheerful and well-meaning that it's hard to be cross with her for long, even when she meddles."

"I'm worried about her," Renata said. "She's lost a great deal of weight."

"I noticed that too," said Peter. "But she's still the same old Bridey. She enters a room like a little tornado. She causes a commotion, and before long everything and everybody is disrupted, but somehow it's in a good way."

Renata smiled and nodded her head in agreement. She turned around to face Peter. "So, how is your painting coming along, and your music?"

"I haven't done either since I lost my muse."

Renata blushed. "Peter, I…"

FOR RENATA

"I'm sorry, that was unfair. I just…miss you so much," the young man groped for the right words. "My life started to make some sense again after you came into it, and now…now, nothing feels right. It's selfish, I know, but it made me happy to have you here. And I hadn't been happy for a long, long time."

The kitchen door opened and Bridey burst through it carrying a Limoges gravy boat. "It's a bit lumpy, but it'll just have to do," she said, placing it on the table. Hearing no response, she looked up at Peter and Renata, who were searching the floor with their eyes.

"Well, I don't know about you two, but I'm famished. Renata, be a dear and take the turkey from the oven before it dries out completely, and scoop the stuffing into a bowl. Peter, you're in charge of opening the wine. I'll pop the rolls into the oven and give the potatoes and butternut squash a final stir."

When they sat down to eat Bridey said how thankful she was to have two young friends who were willing to share their time with an old woman. Renata said, "No, Bridey, we're the lucky ones, you're a joy to be with."

"She's right, Bridey, we're the lucky ones," Peter agreed.

Before long laughter reentered the room as Bridey regaled her audience with reminiscences of growing up in a small town in upstate New York. When something struck her funny, Bridey would stamp her feet as she laughed, giving Peter a glimpse of the young girl she had been. He also noticed that Bridey's once-double chin had shrunk to a thin, wrinkly wattle that shook when she laughed.

"...And we really did roast chestnuts over the fire too. Father had fashioned a long-handled roasting basket. We'd wash the chestnuts and then cut a little "x" in the shell with a sharp knife. Then we'd hold the basket over the flames and shake them from time to time, like popcorn. We took turns because that basket would begin to feel like it was made of lead. After half an hour or so, the shells would pop open where we'd cut the "x," and we'd know they were done. Then we'd peel them and dip them in melted butter, and dust them with cinnamon. Mmm, I can almost taste them now.

"But then the blight came and all the chestnut trees were wiped out."

Bridey let out a wistful sigh. "You don't know what you're missing, dears, you don't know what you're missing."

Later that day, Renata carried the laundry basket, and she and Bridey walked arm-in-arm down Rose Hip Point Lane. Peter stood in his doorway and watched them until they rounded the bend near Bridey's house and disappeared from sight. He closed the door, walked to the living room, and felt a pang of emptiness.

Renata followed Bridey onto her porch. Now the basket only held Bridey's clean Limoges gravy boat and the white towel. The rest of the food and dishes had been left behind for Peter's use.

"Come in for some tea, dear," Bridey said.

While Bridey put the kettle on to boil, Renata set the willow basket on the kitchen table and stared out the window to the backyard and the sea beyond it.

"I'm remembering those lovely summer days when we sat in your backyard and you read that tragic poem to me," Renata said. "Do you remember?"

"Of course, dear, it was Longfellow's "Evangeline," my favorite. "This is the forest primeval. The murmuring pines and the hemlocks, / Bearded with moss, and in garments green, indistinct in the twilight,/Stand like Druids of eld."

"Yes, that was it," Renata spoke as if entranced. "I remember one perfect summer day in particular, the sun was so warm, the cicadas were singing loudly, and butterflies were everywhere. I remember the smell of your crisp, clean bed sheets hanging on the line. You made iced tea with fresh mint from your garden, and you served that delicious, cool lemon dessert. And I remember thinking, *Life can be beautiful*."

Bridey walked over to the window and put her hand on Renata's shoulder.

"I remember, dear. I sat in the wicker chair under the arbor and you rested at my feet with your head on my lap while I read to you."

B. ROBERT SHARRY

"I thank you for that day, Bridey, and so many others like it over the years. I thank you for opening your home and your heart to me."

The women embraced, and Renata began to weep.

"What's all this?" Bridey asked tenderly.

"I'm afraid, Bridey."

"Why are you afraid, dear?"

"I'm afraid because I think you're not well."

Bridey paused. "Oh, I see," she said.

"Are you *very* sick?"

"Yes, dear, I am," Bridey was serene. "I have a cancer in my bowel, and the doctor tells me it's too far gone for a surgery."

Renata's whole body shrank. "What can I do?" she pleaded.

"Just what you've always done, come and see me often and bring your beautiful spirit."

The weeping women embraced again, and the kettle screamed.

FOR RENATA

47

December 25, 1974
    Bridey called last night…

Peter hung up the phone and ran to Bridey Gallagher's house. The beige Victorian cottage sat in darkness. No electric candles shone through the windowpanes. No evergreen garland threaded the front porch railing. No ribboned wreath hung on the front door. Peter bounded into the house.

He flew about the rooms, calling her name and switching on lights as he went. He reached through the doorway of the first-floor bedroom, brushing the wall with his hand until he found the light switch. He pushed the button in, lighting a scene that shocked him.

Bridey lie motionless, her wan complexion, hollow cheeks, and vein-riddled translucent skin rendering her almost unrecognizable. Her sunken eyes were closed, and Peter feared the worst.

"Bridey," he said softly. He repeated her name, a little louder.

Frantically, he cried, "Bridey!"

Bridey's eyes fluttered open. "Peter, is that you?"

"I'm here, Bridey, I'm here. What is it? What's wrong?"

The old woman took several breaths, as though she were about to go under water. "It's just my time, dear."

Peter reached for the pale-blue princess phone at the bedside. "I'll call for an ambulance."

"No, Peter, please, no."

"But…"

"Peter," Bridey said calmly, "Please, no ambulance, no hospital. It's just my time, that's all."

"But I have to do *something*, Bridey."

"Just stay with me," the old woman said. "I don't want to linger in some hospital surrounded by strangers. That's what happened to my Henry. I don't want it to be that way for me.

"I told you once that death doesn't frighten me. I just don't want to be alone, that's all," Bridey smiled, holding out her hand.

Peter fought back the lump in his throat, and returned the phone to its cradle. He grabbed a cushioned stool from Bridey's vanity, and dragged it to her bedside. He sat down, took her hand in his, and smiled with welling eye. Bridey closed her eyes, and whispered, "Thank you, Peter."

FOR RENATA

A grandmother clock in the front hall chimed six times.

Peter held Bridey's brittle hand while she slept. He looked about the room, which reflected so much about its owner. Bridey's spindle maple bed was covered with a lightweight crazy quilt, and it sat upon a wool Victorian carpet with a willow and tulip design. A maple dresser was flanked by two windows hung with white lace curtains. Several framed black and white photos sat atop the dresser included a wedding portrait of Bridey and Henry and a snapshot of the young couple with their beaming toddler, Jack. From an ornate silver frame, a young army officer smiled confidently, his dress visor cap angled rakishly above clear, youthful eyes.

Throughout the evening Bridey drifted in and out of consciousness. She told Peter that she'd willingly stopped eating after Thanksgiving because she'd wanted to control her death rather than allow it to control her. For the past month she'd only taken tea. If her pain had become unbearable, she would have brewed a final cup from belladonna she'd grown in her own herb garden.

Peter could tell that consciousness brought agony to his elderly friend. Mostly she trembled and moaned softly when awake. But one time tears streamed from those pale blue eyes, and she cried out, "The burning! Oh, the burning!"

Peter had never felt so helpless in his life. He leaned in, his voice choked with emotion. "I wish I could take the pain for you, Bridey. I would if I could."

Bridey squeezed his hand. "I know you would, dear," she said, and then mercifully drifted into oblivion.

Later that evening, Bridey's eyes opened and she turned her head to look at Peter. "I have something to say to you." Her voice was weak. Peter leaned in closer.

"Life has been unkind to you and Renata, just as it was to me when I lost my Jack. For the longest time I withdrew from everyone, even my husband. I wallowed in self-pity, thinking I had every right to. For months I was sullen and inconsolable. And I was absolutely horrid to Henry.

"One day I snapped at him for the umpteenth time. And over what? He had forgotten to put out the trash can. He left the room without a word. Soon I heard the sound of the trash can being plunked onto the sidewalk. A few minutes later, I heard him drive off.

"An hour later he came back, and I was ready. I would let him know how inconsiderate he was to just drive off without even so much as a goodbye. I stood by the kitchen door, ready to let him have it.

"He came carrying a bouquet of daisies, my favorite. *Hoped these might cheer you up*, he said.

"I screamed at him, *Cheer me up? I've lost a* child, *not a pair of earrings*.

"He said, *I know, I know. I lost him too, Bridey. And now I'm losing you. I need you. I need you to come back to me. Without you, I don't think I can bear it.* And he began to weep."

FOR RENATA

Bridey blinked tears away and swallowed hard. "That's when it dawned on me how selfish I'd been. I wasn't the only one who had lost a child. He'd been like a rock the entire time, but his heart was just as broken as mine. And he *needed* me. To be loved and needed is a marvelous thing, Peter."

The old woman let out a heavy sigh. "From then on we helped each other. We still felt the pain, but we shared it, and made a good life for ourselves.

"This life, this...gift can't be wasted, even if it's sometimes heartbreaking and unkind. You and Renata can help each other heal. You both have such beautiful spirits under all of that pain. You're young, and there's so much time left for you."

Peter shook his head. "She won't let me see her, Bridey."

"She will, dear. She will when she's ready, because she needs you."

Bridey squeezed his hand and drifted back to sleep.

Midnight arrived and the old clock struck, stirring Peter from half-sleep.

Eyes closed, Bridey asked, "Is it Christmas now?"

"Yes."

"Merry Christmas, dear."

The old woman's grip tightened on the young light keeper's hand, and Bridey Gallagher spent her final breath.

B. ROBERT SHARRY

48

April 25, 1975
    Last night there was a terrible storm, wind and rain like I've never seen this early in the season. I was sitting on the couch, reading...

A loud clatter came from outside. Peter grabbed the fireplace poker, tucked it under his left armpit and opened the kitchen door. He stood, listening intently while his eye adjusted to the darkness. But he saw nothing out of the ordinary. He turned around and was poised to close the door when he heard another sound—an unnerving moan.

He stepped into the driving rain and followed the sound to a hedgerow of forsythia. But the noise stopped as he approached. He stuck the poker into the bushes several times and hit nothing but branches. Then he made contact with something that wasn't a branch, and it moved.

"Ahhhhh, please, no more."

Peter shoved the greenery aside. Renata Raposo cowered in the bushes, drenched by the rain. Peter reached for her.

"No, God, please, no more." she cried.

"Renata, it's me—Peter. You're safe now. Nobody's going to hurt you."

Placing his right arm beneath her knees and the remnant of his left arm at her back, Peter lifted her. He carried her into the house and climbed the narrow wooden staircase to his bedroom.

Renata shook with cold and fear. She clung tightly to Peter's neck and became hysterical when he tried to loosen her grip. He sat on the edge of the mattress and held her in his lap while waves of convulsive sobs wracked her body. After a long time, Renata quieted but still trembled. Her head was buried in Peter's shoulder. He whispered into her ear. "Renata, you have to trust me. You can't stay like this. We need to get you warm." Peter reached up, grasped her wrist, and gently tugged her hand away from his neck.

"No," she said.

"Just for a few minutes. I'm going to make you some hot tea while you get out of these clothes. We need to get you warm and dry. I'll be just downstairs, and I won't let anything happen to you, okay?"

Renata nodded and raised her head from Peter's shoulder. For the first time he could see how battered her face was and how it had begun to swell. Patches of crimson and purple puffed up around her eyes, and a path of dried blood stretched from her lower lip to the base of her chin. Peter seethed with shock and anger, but he was determined to act calm for her sake. He smiled reassuringly and gestured toward the adjacent bathroom.

"I'll start a hot bath for you. There's a clean towel on the rack, and my bathrobe's hanging on the door."

Peter plugged the claw foot tub's drain hole with its rubber stopper and adjusted the hot and cold spigots until the water temperature was just right. "I'm afraid I don't have anything in your size, but there are T-shirts and pajamas in the middle drawer of my dresser."

He left the bedroom and descended the stairs to the kitchen. When he returned half an hour later, he carried a tray that held a cup of hot tea and a bowl of ice cubes. Renata lie on the bed with her back propped against the heavy brass headboard. She wore a tie-dyed T-shirt beneath Peter's plaid, flannel bathrobe.

Peter placed the tray on top of the dresser, and then brought the tea to her. He placed some ice cubes on a dry washcloth and gathered the ends into a compress. "You should hold this against the bruising. It'll help keep the swelling down."

"Peter, I don't know how to thank you."

"No thanks are necessary. I'm just glad you're all right. You need rest more than anything.

"I have to go out for a while. Will you be all right?"

FOR RENATA

A look of panic crossed Renata's face. "No, Peter, no. Please don't do anything." She cast her eyes on her teacup. Then she raised her head, looked directly into his eye, and her words began to flow with her tears.

Peter sat down on the bed and listened to her. When she was finished, he took her in his arms and held her. She buried her face in his chest and sobbed.

They sat in silence for a long time. Finally, Peter said, "Rest, now. I'll be right downstairs if you need me."

"Stay with me a little longer, Peter. Just until I fall asleep?"

"Of course."

Renata put her tea aside, got beneath the bedcovers and closed her eyes. Peter sat beside her and stroked her forehead and hair until her breathing turned slow and steady. When he was sure she was sleeping, he turned off the lamp and quietly walked downstairs.

Peter slipped outside and retrieved the poker. Holding it, he paced the first floor of the house like a sentry, constantly peering through windows for any sign of trouble.

He kept this vigil until the small hours of the morning, until he felt confident that the Portuguese fisherman would not come. At 3:00 a.m. he went back upstairs and lie on the bedcovers, next to Renata. He slid the poker under the bed. Out of habit, he started to remove his eye patch, but kept it on instead. He watched her sleep until he himself was overcome with fatigue.

Peter began to stir just before dawn. The window beside his bed was open just a little. Cool salt air flowed through the crack, carrying the familiar, faint sounds of waves breaking against the cliff and seagulls cawing.

He felt her lips on his. Startled, he twitched slightly. He opened his eye and saw that hers were closed. Her left cheek was swollen and bruised. He raised his hand and gently touched her face. She opened her eyes and gazed at him. Peter took a breath to speak, but Renata brought her hand to his lips.

"Shh, don't speak. And don't see me like this. We'll both keep our eyes closed."

They kissed tenderly for a long time, and she whispered things to him that he did not understand. When she explained, he asked her to repeat them over and over again so that he would never forget.

She undressed him, and then herself. She took his hand in hers, kissed it, and pressed it against her cheek. Peter traced her shape with the soft press of his fingertips, from the nape of her neck to her straight shoulders, down her side to the flair of her hip, then on to her thigh, calf, and foot.

"You are the most beautiful woman in the world."

She leaned in to kiss him. Her nipples brushed his chest, and he wondered if they were pink or dark. She sat astride him and took him inside her, moving on him slowly, almost imperceptibly. Peter placed his hand on the small of her back.

She stopped moving, leaned in and whispered into his ear. They held each other like that for a long time—not moving, just kissing and whispering with eyes closed.

Afterwards, they lie facing each other, kissing. In time they fell back to sleep, mid-kiss, in each other's arms.

When Peter awoke again, she was gone.

It was midnight when Renata Raposo Bennett closed the Keeper's Log once more. "Well, your uncle has a vivid imagination, I'll give him that."

"What do you mean?" Mark asked.

"Don't get me wrong, Peter was very good-looking: Even that eye patch looked good on him. But it just wasn't that way between us. I'm sorry, but this never happened."

Mark felt stunned. Was everything a lie? But then why had Renie gotten so upset before, when Mark had first approached her at her house?

"Look," Renie said. "He had one *arm*, remember? Do you really think he could carry me upstairs to his bedroom? He probably saw this on an episode of *Dark Shadows* or something."

"You're saying that he...he just..."

"Look, I'm sorry. Your uncle is a nice man, but he was lonely. I think he was just fantasizing when he wrote this."

Mark shook his head. "No, I'm the one who's sorry. I never should have bothered you with any of this."

"How could you have known?" she said, handing the Keeper's Log back to him. She rose from the sofa, and Mark felt the same wrench of panic he'd experienced after their first meeting. He feared that he would never see her again.

"But you haven't finished it," he said desperately.

Renie had started for the door. She turned back to face Mark and said, "Thank you, Mark. I know you meant well."

And a moment later she was gone.

49

Mark was irritated when he pulled into the parking lot of the Soldiers' Home. He had been upset since the previous night, when Renie had walked out of his life while he sat on the couch feeling like a fool. Over the course of a long, sleepless night on the sofa, his thoughts had naturally turned to the person who was responsible for making him look foolish to the only woman who had captured his interest in more than a decade. Tired and wrung out, he had loaded himself into his truck. He wore the same jeans and black, long-sleeve T-shirt he had put on after his shower the previous evening.

He grabbed the Keeper's Log from the passenger's seat, hurried up the building's marble steps, and made his way to his uncle's room.

Uncle Pete sat in his chair, looking like he hadn't moved since Mark's last visit. His roommate Horace lie propped up in bed, and shakily dabbed at his chin with a paper napkin. He must have just finished his breakfast.

Mark circled around to face Peter only to realize that his eye was closed. He was asleep.

"Uncle Pete," Mark said. There was no response. "Uncle Pete," he repeated, this time giving Pete's good arm a gentle shake.

Peter's eye fluttered open and Mark wasted no time in explaining why he was there. "Pete, I know you're not well—not yourself—but there are some things I need to know the truth about." Mark's tone was a mixture of compassion and frustration. He placed the Keeper's Log on Peter's lap.

Peter stared at Mark, then down at the Keeper's Log, and then back at his nephew. He looked confused, and Mark felt sorry for the old man.

"Renata?"

"Yeah, Pete, I found her, and you know what? She told me you made all of this stuff up. She said you were lonely, and it was all a fantasy.

"How do you think she felt, reading what you wrote about her? She was hurt and embarrassed."

"Renata," said Peter.

"Yeah, and she's a really nice woman, Pete. Thank God she didn't finish reading it. Or have you forgotten the little bombshell you saved for the end of your story?"

FOR RENATA

When Peter opened the Keeper's Log, his eye latched onto the yellowed envelope that was still there, still sealed. "Renata, no."

"Renata, yes, Renata. And if you really knew her, you'd know enough to call her Renie.

"Pete, what were you thinking? You can't just…"

"Mee nall may soo ah."

"Oh, God, that's enough, Pete. I can't do this anymore." Mark shook his head and started for the door. He wasn't sure how he'd expected Peter to react—whether he had wanted to hear a denial or perhaps even a confession—but his inability to communicate with the older man was driving him around the bend.

To Mark's surprise, Peter sprang from his chair with unexpected agility. He stood eye to eye with Mark, and slapped the Keeper's Log into his nephew's abdomen.

"Renata," he repeated forcefully.

Mark was so startled that he was almost frightened for a moment. The look of determination in his uncle's eye made the man look like a stranger. Left with little choice, Mark took the book and stormed out of the room.

When he got home, Mark tossed the Keeper's Log into the trash bin, which he wheeled to the end of the driveway. He was done with this dance with the past. Done.

It was early the next morning, and a raw, grey fog sat atop Ipswich Bay. Sipping his coffee, Mark found himself pacing and pining once more, pacing the length of his back porch like a caged wildcat, and pining for a woman with whom he had spent a grand total of eleven hours.

How is this possible? He asked himself. *I'm forty-seven years old, not a schoolboy. Why am I thinking about her this much when we hardly know each other? She obviously doesn't feel the same way about me – not after so little time. And yet, the whole time I was with her my heart just soared. So, if that's possible…*

His thoughts were racing. Something started to nag at him. He couldn't quite figure out what it was, he felt as though he had walked into a room to get something, and, once there, had forgotten what it was he had come for.

He shrugged, and his thoughts turned to Uncle Pete. He felt guilty for the way he had treated the older man. Sure, he was infuriating, and his stories had caused Mark a world of embarrassment. But if not for Peter and his Keeper's Log, Mark would never have met Renie at all. He shouldn't have tossed the Keeper's Log away, it obviously meant a great deal to the old man and…

The Keeper's Log. Mark heard the rumbling of the trash truck and realized what had been niggling at the back of his mind.

He plunked his coffee mug down on the porch railing, bolted down the stairs, and ran to the front of the house. The truck had already left his house and was now a quarter mile away and rounding the bend. Mark yelled and flailed his arms, but in seconds the truck was out of sight. The Keeper's Log was gone forever.

Mark sighed. His shoulders slumped as he shuffled to the empty tote, and then rolled it back to the garage.

He told himself: *Well, I tried*. But then he corrected himself: *No, I didn't – not really. If I can save a baby whale, I can damn well get my own trash back.*

Mark raced into the house and grabbed his car keys. Seconds later, he was speeding to catch up with the garbage truck. Within a few minutes he spotted the truck, and beeped his horn.

The huge truck, which was a familiar sight to everyone in the small town, came to an abrupt stop. The driver's door, with the words *Another Man's Treasure* hand-painted on it, opened. Dave Nelson climbed down onto the gravel road. He smiled as Mark jumped from his vehicle.

"Hey, Mark, did you decide that your cottage cheese didn't expire after all?"

"Very funny, Dave," he said, panting a little. "No, but I did throw something away I shouldn't have."

"Don't tell me: *Your* trash is the one in the dark green plastic bag, right?"

"Jeez, Dave, I don't know what you're doing driving this truck when there are so many comedy clubs around."

"Naw, this is my calling, Mark," Dave said as he pulled a lever to hydraulically open the back of the truck.

A few minutes later, Mark had found what he was looking for and jumped down to the ground. "By the way, your truck smells lovely."

"It's called a *garbage* truck, Mark. And, hey, it could have been worse. You might have *flushed* by mistake. There's always a silver lining."

Mark shook his head as he walked to his vehicle and tossed a wave back at Dave.

While driving back to the house Mark realized that he hadn't just reclaimed the book for Peter. There were some things in the Keeper's Log—and something he had seen—that just didn't make sense when taken together with Renie's claims.

50

Mark sat at the bar at Nellie's restaurant and moved food around on his dinner plate with a fork. Frosted glass light fixtures dangled from the ceiling, their dim bulbs reflecting blurrily on the rich dark mahogany paneling of the walls. Flickering tea lights, spaced at regular intervals along the bar, and a live pianist's soft renditions of Andrew Lloyd Webber love songs added to the warm ambiance.

Bob Hascom, Mark's closest friend since grammar school, took the last bite of his New York strip steak, pushed his plate away, and wiped his face with a linen napkin. "How's your uncle doing?" he asked.

"Well, he's there, he's just not *all* there," Mark said.

"Do you have any idea where he's been all this time?"

"Not a clue. One day some mysterious stranger just dropped him off at the Soldiers' Home. Their social services department tracked me down as his closest living relative. And, suddenly, he's my problem."

"Is that why you're being such a dick?"

Mark dropped his fork, and turned to look at his friend. "What, I'm a dick now?"

"Yeah, is it because of this stuff with your uncle?"

"No. What do you mean I'm being a dick?"

"Okay, then who is she?"

"Who's *who*?"

"Don't give me that. Who is *she*?"

"What are you talking about?"

"The last time I saw you like this—I mean a mess—was after you and Jill broke up. That was over ten years ago, and I had to hold your hand for the next three years until you started to act normal again. I mean normal for you…"

"Why? What am I doing differently?"

"Well, first of all, although you've never exactly been Chatty Cathy, you haven't said two words all night. Second, you're not eating your scallops — which just so happens to be your favorite meal in the entire world — and third, and most importantly? There's a hot woman on the other side of the bar who's been sizing you up all throughout dinner, and you haven't even noticed her."

Mark looked over at the woman. "Wow, she *is* hot."

"I rest my case. So, are you gonna tell me who she is?"

"It's no one you know, and besides, it's not going anywhere. I promise I won't take three years to get over it this time." Mark smiled. "Buy you an after-dinner drink?"

"No, thanks," Bob reached over and speared a scallop from Mark's plate. With a full mouth, he said, "I gotta go. I'm a married man. My real life is over, remember? All I have left is a vicarious existence, and you better not let me down. Promise me you'll follow up with that woman at the other end of the bar so that we'll have something to talk about next week?"

"We'll see."

"God, you're pathetic. Okay, buddy, catch you later," Bob said, slapping some bills down on the bar.

"'Night, Bob, and say hi to Michelle for me."

Mark asked the bartender for a Jack Daniels on the rocks and sipped it while he indulged himself with thoughts of Renie. It had been more than three weeks since she'd denied having an affair with Uncle Pete.

He had seen her earlier tonight. She hadn't seen him, but he'd seen her. On his way to Nellie's he had parked his car on Elm Street. He'd forgotten that Renie had talked about finding the perfect space for her studio there—that is, until he saw her.

As he walked down Elm toward the restaurant, he'd happened to glance across the street. There she was, visible through the window of her new dance studio. Dressed in a leotard, she was holding onto the ballet bar and demonstrating demi-pliés in first position to three young girls who sat cross-legged on the floor.

Mark took a final swig of whisky, paid his bill, and walked from the air-conditioned restaurant into the humid night air. He walked along Main Street and stopped for a moment at the intersection of Main and Elm. He took a deep breath before he turned onto Elm Street's sidewalk.

She won't still be there at this time of night, he thought. But as he walked up the slight incline toward his truck, he noticed that the light was still on in the studio.

From the angle of his approach, he only saw the left profile of the back of her head and shoulders. His heart raced as he made his way along the sidewalk and more of her came into view.

But then he saw that she wasn't alone. A man wearing a well-tailored business suit stood facing her. Mark's heart sank and his head bowed as he continued on up the sidewalk. He turned back for one final glance, did a double-take, and stopped short in his tracks. Renie was grimacing and the man in the well-tailored suit was clutching her wrists tightly in his hands.

Mark bounded across the street and flew through the building's doorway. He found himself in a short hallway that served as a windbreak to the main studio space.

"Stop it, Gerry, you're hurting me." Mark heard Renie say.

"Did you really think I'd let you just walk out on me?" the man said.

Overhearing this short exchange told Mark all he needed to know. He raced around the corner, and into the studio. "I think the lady asked you to leave her alone," Mark said.

Both Renie and Gerry turned to look at Mark.

"And who the fuck are you?" Gerry spat at Mark. Then, turning back to face Renie, "Who is he? Is this your new boyfriend? You didn't waste any time, did you?"

"He's not my boyfriend."

"I'm just a friend," said Mark.

"Well, then get lost, *friend*. This is my wife, and this is private property, and a private conversation. I'm a lawyer, and you're trespassing. So, you better leave right now, before I call the cops and have your bumpkin ass thrown in jail."

"Let me save you the trouble," Mark said, pulling his iPhone from his pocket. "I just had dinner with the chief of police, Bob Hascom. We've been friends since we were kids. He's a bumpkin too, and he might misinterpret what I've witnessed here as an assault. And, being a bumpkin, he might decide to play it safe and arrest you. Then there might be an assault charge, a restraining order, and who knows what else? Maybe even the Bar Association would hear about it, and your license to practice would be in jeopardy. Of course, I'm not a lawyer…"

Gerry shot a venomous look at Renie as he released his grip on her wrists. He straightened his tie and walked toward the door, sneering at Mark as he passed. Over his shoulder, he called out, "You're really robbing the cradle, Renie. It's pathetic for a woman your age. You shouldn't be traipsing around in a leotard either, considering the way you've let yourself go."

On his way out, Gerry slammed the door so hard it made Renie jump and the front window of the studio shudder.

After a moment, Renie let out a long sigh, as though she'd forgotten to breathe for a while. Her eyes held Mark's for a moment. Then she blushed and averted her gaze.

"I was just passing by, and I happened to see what was going on through the window," Mark said. He took a closer look at her. "Are you okay?"

"I'll be fine."

Mark eyed her wrists. "Did he hurt you?" he asked.

"What, this?" Renie held up her wrists. "This is nothing," she said with a chuckle that Mark found perplexing.

"Do you want me to call the police?"

"No, I just want him gone. Please don't call your friend and have him arrested."

Mark grinned. "That's not likely to happen. Bob Hascom's an insurance salesman."

Renie looked surprised but then a smile spread across her face. "You lied."

"I lied," Mark admitted, "but it was for the greater good."

"Well, I'm glad you did. That was quick thinking. You managed to defuse the situation rather easily.

"God, you save whales and ladies in distress too? Are you Superman?"

"Well, if I am, then my Kryptonite is a Death-by-Chocolate dessert they serve at Le Pegase. Can I interest you?"

Renie hesitated. "No. Thank you, but no. It's past time for all cradle robbers to be in bed."

"Don't listen to him. He was just trying to manipulate you into feeling bad about yourself.

"Please?" he added with a warm smile, "I'd really love for you to join me."

"All right, just give me a few minutes to change."

At Le Pegase, Mark chose a table for two at the front of the restaurant. "Let's sit by the window and watch the world go by."

A slim waiter, dressed all in black, appeared to take their order.

"Two Death by Chocolates…"

"One," Renie said. "I'll just have a taste of yours, if that's okay."

"Are you sure?" Mark asked. "It's called *Death* by Chocolate, so if you just have a taste, you might only go into a coma."

Renie laughed and said, "I'll take my chances."

"Okay, one Death by Chocolate, two spoons," Mark said to the waiter. "And two espressos with lemon zest?" he added, turning to Renie for confirmation.

Renie nodded her approval.

The waiter returned a few minutes later with their order. He'd forgotten dessert spoons, so Mark and Renie used the demitasse spoons that had come with their espressos.

"Ladies first," said Mark.

He watched as Renie took the spoonful of chocolate into her mouth and withdrew the empty spoon through pursed, red-coated lips.

"Well?"

Renie closed her eyes. "Mmm, this is really, really good."

"I told you."

When they'd finished coffee and dessert, Mark ordered pastis on the rocks with water on the side.

"I want to apologize, again, for my uncle's fantastic delusions. I tried to set him straight, but I don't think, given his current condition, that he understands he did anything wrong. It's just baffling to me as to why he would do that, especially when so many things in the journal don't seem to be made up. Do you have any ideas?"

Renie's eyes were downcast. "Don't be too hard on him. He was very kind to me, and he never did anything that was remotely untoward or inappropriate."

She quickly changed the subject, asking Mark questions about his work and telling him about her younger sister, who was a second violinist with the Boston Symphony.

FOR RENATA

"Tanglewood is the Symphony's summer home. I was visiting my sister one summer, and met Gerry. That's how I came to live in the Berkshires."

Mark and Renie spent over an hour in pleasant conversation, smiling constantly and laughing often. At midnight, they slowly ambled up Elm Street and discovered that their vehicles were parked just a few spaces apart.

"Thank you, Mark...for everything."

"There's one thing I'd like to thank *you* for."

"What's that?"

Mark broke into his devilish grin. "You look absolutely fantastic in a leotard."

51

Mark waited several days before trying to contact Renie again. There were questions about the Keeper's Log that gnawed at him, but it hadn't felt right to say anything specific about that at Le Pegase.

He wanted answers, but more than that, he wanted to see her — he wanted to have her in his life. He tried her phone a few times over a period of several days, sent texts, and left voice messages twice. Soon it became obvious to him that she didn't want to have contact.

Mark reluctantly accepted that, aside from the possibility of a chance encounter in the small community of Cape Ann, he would never see her again. He sat on his sofa holding the Keeper's Log and the yellowed envelope marked *For Renata* just as he had that first night after Peter had thrust it into his hands.

How readily he had believed what Peter had written in the Keeper's Log. Why wouldn't he?

What would compel Peter to have invented such an astonishing story and confession?

And he had just as readily accepted Renie's repudiation of the journal's contents. She had told him that Peter had fantasized the whole thing, and he'd believed her. Just like that.

But she hadn't said the whole thing was made up, had she? In fact, she hadn't refuted anything until she read Peter's description of their lovemaking. Mark had watched Renie closely as she read each and every word of the Keeper's Log, and never once before had she challenged its veracity. Perhaps she was just too embarrassed, or perhaps she was telling the truth and that part was a fantasy. But that didn't mean *everything* in the Keeper's Log was a lie.

But with Bridey Gallagher long dead and Peter Ahearn incoherent and oblivious, Renata Raposo was the only viable, living witness to what had really happened at Rose Hip Point.

Or was she?

Mark sat upright when the realization hit him like a thunderbolt. There was one other person who was very much alive and very much coherent who might be able to shed some light on the truth.

Mark parked his truck on Washington Street in Gloucester and walked across the road to Vasconcelos's Portuguese Market.

Jaime "Jimmy" Vasconcelos stood behind the meat counter. His hair was thinning but still very dark. A pencil was tucked behind his ear, and bifocals perched on the end of his nose. He smiled broadly when he recognized Mark.

"Mark Valente, it's been a while since you've been in here."

"I know, Jimmy — it's been too long."

"That's because you don't eat right. All you bachelors eat that processed pre-packaged crap. You gotta shop here. You get fresh food here, you'll live longer."

"Okay, Jimmy, you win. I've been sufficiently rebuked."

"Good. Now is it true what I hear about Pete?"

"I don't know what you've heard, but it's true that he's alive. He's not well, though. He has some kind of Alzheimer's, and he's being cared for at the Soldiers' Home near Boston."

"I'm sorry to hear that, Mark. Pete was good people. I liked him a lot."

"That's actually what I wanted to talk to you about, Jimmy. Didn't you used to deliver groceries to him at the lighthouse?"

"Among other things," Jimmy punctuated this statement with a sly grin. "You remember that?"

"Well, no, I was pretty young back then, but Pete remembered it."

"Pete's got the Alzheimer's but he still remembers me?"

"Well, not exactly. He wrote about it a long time ago."

Jimmy looked around the store, and then leaned toward Mark and half-whispered. "Did he write about the weed?"

"Yeah, he did, Jimmy, but that's not why I came to see you."

"What do you need?"

"This is going to sound kind of weird, but did Pete have a woman in his life then?"

"Oh, yeah, definitely."

"Really? Who?"

"I have no idea."

"You didn't recognize her?"

"Recognize her? I never even saw her."

"I don't understand, Jimmy. If you never saw him with anyone, how do you know there *was* anyone?"

"New underwear."

"Excuse me?"

"New underwear…and other stuff, of course."

"Of course. Could you maybe elaborate a little?"

"Look, I really liked Pete. He's a couple of years older than me, but he was always real nice to me when we were kids—he was always nice to *everybody*. I looked up to him.

"You don't remember, because you're too young, but Pete was a mess when he came home from the war and that girl threw him over. Kids used to taunt him. I mean, just think about it: He loses his brother, he gets maimed so bad he can't play his music no more, and his fiancée dumps him. And it all happens almost at once. It was like he got hit by the perfect emotional storm. He didn't even wanna go out no more. So he asked me to deliver everything out to the lighthouse so he wouldn't have to go nowhere.

"He didn't even shave after he got home—not for like three years. I don't mind tellin' you he didn't smell too good some of the time either. He just didn't care. He didn't see nobody and nobody saw him, so what the hell?

"Anyway, I used to bring him everything—groceries, beer, booze, a little weed...

"Then, all of a sudden, there was a change in him. He tells me to bring him shaving stuff, cologne, new underwear...and he doesn't want any more hard liquor or weed. Oh, and instead of macaroni and cheese and canned stuff, all of a sudden he wants fresh veal.

"But, the biggest change of all? Pete. was. *happy*. He was like his old self again. He had that gleam in his eye, and he was smiling, joking, even. Now, let's review: What makes all of that happen in a guy?"

"Hmm," Mark said.

"Precisely, hmm." Jimmy agreed.

"When did this happen, Jimmy?"

"I don't know exactly, but it was several months before he disappeared."

"And you have no idea who this person might have been?"

"No, but come to think of it, I know somebody who might."

Jimmy told him about a conversation he'd overheard one night long ago, and it reminded Mark about another Keeper's Log entry that deserved a second look.

FOR RENATA

52

April 27, 1975
File this one under bad timing: I was waiting for Renata when I saw somebody coming up the lane pushing a baby carriage…

An April shower had passed and now the noontime sun shone, and made mirrors of the water-filled ruts that dotted the lane on Rose Hip Point. A young woman maneuvered a baby carriage around the potholes as she approached the lighthouse grounds.

Tourists usually arrived in automobiles, but it wasn't unheard of for locals to walk the picturesque, mile-long lane to reach the tip of the point and admire the stunning views for a time before trekking back.

Whenever Peter saw strangers approach, whether by car or by foot, he'd disappear into the house until they had left the property. He had turned his back to the stranger in the distance and walked toward the light keeper's quarters when a flash of recognition made him spin back around.

The last time Peter had seen Cindy Everhart was the night she had broken their engagement, and his heart.

Then, her blond hair had been straight and long enough to touch the small of her back. Now it was darker and cut into a wavy, gypsy cut that barely reached her shoulders. The top half of a red and white flip-top box of Marlboros protruded from the front pocket of her cutoff denim shorts. She wore a white peasant blouse, and brown leather sandals. When they were fifty feet apart, Cindy gave Peter an exaggerated wave, a broad smile, and yelled, "Hi."

Peter remained motionless and expressionless, but Cindy's smile didn't lose any of its luster. When all that separated them was the length of the carriage, she said, "How are you, Pete?"

"How *am* I? Cindy, what are you doing here?"

"I think about you a lot, Pete, and I just wanted to say *Hi* and see how you were. So, how are you?"

"I don't get it, Cindy. I haven't seen you for how long? Not since you…"

Cindy tilted her head and batted her eyes. "Don't be like that, Pete. I know I hurt you, but I was young and immature back then. I'm sorry. You didn't deserve that. We were really close once, and I was hoping that we could at least still be friends.

"And look, I'm a mommy. This is Parker, isn't he cute? Thank God he's sleeping right now. He'll be six months old next Tuesday."

"How's Chip?" Peter's tone oozed sarcasm.

"How should I know? He split like three months before Parker was even born. Get this: He's never even seen his own kid. He's shacking up with some chick over in Rockport. He was boffin' her the whole time. Good riddance. But I don't even get a dime because he works under the table.

"I was so far behind on the rent that I got evicted from my apartment. What was I gonna do, not buy formula?

"So, I'm back at my mother's for now, and I work part time as a chambermaid over at Rocky Neck."

"Sorry, Cindy, that's really tough."

"Tell me about it. The whole thing is so bogus. He always wanted to party, but I could never count on him for anything in real life, you know? He's just an immature asshole."

Cindy began to tear up. "You were never like that, Pete. You never treated me like shit. That's why I've been thinking about you so much. I know I was awful to you, and I was hoping you could forgive me, and maybe we could try again."

"What? What are you talking about?"

"I miss *us*, you know? And I thought maybe we could give *us* another chance, find the love again."

There was a time when Peter had been fixated on all the things he wanted to say to Cindy, all the names he wanted to call her. But now he just said, "Cindy, you don't know what love is, and I doubt that you ever will. But one thing I do know…" He was about to say *I'm too good for you*, but he wondered what Renata would think if she heard him say something so spiteful. Instead he said, "Never mind. Good luck, Cindy. I'm sure you'll find somebody."

At that moment little Parker started to cry. Cindy's eyes were baggy and red from exhaustion. "Yeah, right, who's gonna want me now, Pete?" She turned the carriage around and went back the way she had come.

Peter watched as Cindy made her way down the lane. He felt sorry for her, but his feelings for her had been childish, and they were firmly in the past. Then he saw Renata walking toward the lighthouse and his heart soared.

When the two women met on the lane, they stopped and chatted for a moment. Peter saw Renata point in the direction of her house, and then bend over to coo at little Parker.

Minutes later, Peter was drawing Renata into a welcoming embrace and kissing her passionately. When their kiss ended, Renata looked back at the lane. Cindy had reached the bend in the road near Bridey Gallagher's house.

"Do you know that woman, Peter?" she asked.

"Just someone I used to know in high school."

FOR RENATA

They made love all afternoon and saw each other's bodies for the first time.

"You're still the most beautiful woman in the world."

"That's how you make me feel. And that's why you're the most beautiful man."

At sunset he watched with a sinking heart as she walked down the lane.

But she returned every day that week. Each morning he waited for her to appear at the bend in the lane near Bridey's house. He would come down to meet her and together they would walk hand-in-hand to the lighthouse.

When Renata spoke, Peter studied the movement of her lips as she formed each syllable, took each breath.

They smiled constantly. In fact, it was rare when they didn't. Only the passion of their lovemaking could erase their smiles.

B. ROBERT SHARRY

53

Mark Valente and Linda Gonsalves sat on two of the four grey plastic patio chairs on the backyard deck of Linda's tiny rented house in East Gloucester. The chairs were grouped around a round table that was covered with a blue-and-white-checkered tablecloth. On it, Linda had placed an acrylic pitcher of iced tea and two matching cups.

Linda had the leathery skin of one who has worshiped the sun too fervently. She wore ill-fitting dentures and her mouth looked sunken.

"I knew your mother," Linda said in a husky voice. "She was a real lady."

"Thanks. I kind of liked her," Mark smiled.

"We were friends once—not close friends—but you couldn't be friends with Marybeth Valente *and* Cindy. Your mom never forgave Cindy for the way she treated Pete. I can't say I blame her. But I was Cindy's best friend, so I guess I was guilty by association.

"Is it true what I hear around town about Pete?"

Mark repeated the same few paragraphs he'd become accustomed to delivering whenever anyone in the small community of Cape Ann asked about Peter. Then he turned the conversation back to Cindy.

"When did Cindy pass away?" Mark asked.

"It'll be a year ago on September 27th. It was breast cancer."

"I'm sorry."

"Somehow I doubt that. But what else can you say? You want something, or else this is the last place on Earth you'd be."

"Please, Linda, I didn't even know her."

"Well, let me tell you a few things about Cindy: She was my best friend since kindergarten, and she was always there for me. We were always there for each other. We helped raised each other's kids, and took them camping together and to baseball and soccer practice.

"We worked together at the processing plant— we made the fish sticks—not very glamorous, but we liked to think of ourselves as the Laverne and Shirley of the North Shore. We partied together too. Man, did we ever party."

"That sounds nice."

"Cindy was really generous with me. We'd swap clothes, lend each other money, and tell lies to cover for each other, especially where men were involved.

But I was the only person that Cindy would ever do that for. When it came to the rest of the world, she didn't give a shit about anybody. She would use people for whatever she could get. And if something was the least bit inconvenient for her? Forget it. If you were on fire, and Cindy happened to be standing right next to you, *and* she had to pee anyway? You might stand a chance. Otherwise, you'd be toast."

Mark grimaced at the image.

"She was so pretty, though. I always felt like a frump sitting next to her. We'd go to a bar and guys would, like, flock to her. In thirty years, I don't think we ever bought a drink for ourselves.

"But that was her downfall. She never had trouble *getting* a guy, but she didn't keep 'em. It was like that was where she got her self-esteem. She always had to feel like another guy wanted her. Dr. Phil would say it's where she got her validation.

"I'd always be telling her, *This is a great guy, why do you want to screw it up by going out partying?* And she'd be, like, *I'm bored.*

"But she wasn't bored. She just had to have that next guy flirting with her to make her feel…I don't know…worth anything, you know?"

Linda must have seen something in Mark's expression that didn't sit well with her. "Hey, Mr. Fancypants, before you go judging, consider this: Not every girl gets to go to college and be a teacher like Marybeth Ahearn, you know. All some of us got is our looks, for however long and far that will take us."

FOR RENATA

"I didn't mean to offend, I just came here hoping to find some answers," Mark said meekly.

Linda paused and took a gulp of her iced tea, and then examined her airbrushed fingernails. Somewhere in the small yard, two squirrels chattered loudly to each other.

"Anyway, what do you want?" she asked.

Mark wanted to both give her a plausible reason for his questions and make them seem as inconsequential as possible. "Well, like I said earlier, Pete has these memory problems, and the court has appointed me his guardian because I'm his closest living relative. I have to take care of all his affairs, but I was so young when he disappeared that I don't really know much about him. So I've been talking to a bunch of people who knew him back in the day, and one thing leads to another, you know?

"I was chatting with Jimmy Vasconcelos down at the market because he used to deliver groceries to the lighthouse. Out of curiosity, I asked him if Uncle Pete ever had a girlfriend after Cindy. Jimmy said he didn't know, but he remembered being down at The Wharfside Bar one night when you and Cindy were talking about her and Pete. She had gone to see him at the lighthouse. Do you remember that?"

Linda thought for a moment. "Oh, yeah, Cindy was really pissed off that night."

"Pissed off? Why?"

"Well, her husband, Chip, had bolted. People who didn't know any better thought that I'd be pissed at Cindy when she and Chip hooked up, but he was never anything to me. We just played a little kissy-face when we were younger, that's all."

You protest too much, Mark thought.

"Anyway, Cindy was left flat broke with a new baby. And she was living back at home with her mother, which she hated. So, knowing Cindy and how her mind worked, she probably figured she could move into the lighthouse, have Pete be her built-in babysitter, and go out and party whenever she wanted."

Linda lit a long, thin menthol cigarette and took a deep drag. "But when she got up there, Pete wasn't putty in her hands like she thought he'd be. In fact, he kind of blew her off.

"Cindy used to brag about how she had never been dumped by a guy. She was always the one who did the dumping, that was a big thing with her. Now that I look back on it, I wonder if she didn't dump all those guys just so they couldn't dump her first. I don't want to get all Freudian, but Cindy was devastated when her father left. I don't think she ever really got over it.

"Anyway, when she was leaving the lighthouse, another girl with black hair down to her ass shows up and this girl and Pete are, like, all over each other."

"Did Cindy say who it was?"

"No, she didn't know. But she said she knew where the girl lived and was going to find out who she was. I got the feeling that what pissed her off the most was that this other girl was drop-dead gorgeous.

FOR RENATA

"But that was it. I could tell she was done talking about it."

Linda sipped ice tea, and then dragged on her cigarette. "Within a few days Cindy had roped in another guy, a mechanic. She moved in with him, like a week later."

"Can you think of anything else, Linda? Anything Cindy might have said?"

"Not then. But not long after, I was helping Cindy move into this new guy's apartment, and we were sitting at the kitchen table having coffee and reading the newspaper. All of a sudden, she says, *He did it.*"

"Who did what?" asked Mark.

"That's exactly what I said, *Who did what?* And Cindy gets this faraway look in her eyes and says, *Pete, and it's all my fault.*

"So I said, *What?* And then she came out of her trance and said, *Nothing.* But I knew Pete must have done *something.*"

54

Mark eased his truck to a stop in front of the cottage on Rose Hip Point Lane and parked it behind Renie's SUV. Renie hadn't answered any of his messages, including his latest plea that he urgently needed to speak with her. Now he felt like he had no choice but to come to her and tell her the rest of the story.

He was tired, tired of being lied to, tired of carrying around secrets, and tired of feeling guilty for not believing Uncle Pete, and even guiltier for falling so hopelessly for the woman his uncle loved.

He dug his iPhone out of his trousers and hit redial one more time. The call went straight to her voicemail. He took a deep breath and hopped out of the truck. He strode up the flagstone path, and knocked on the red door.

Renie opened the door just a crack. She looked exhausted and embarrassed.

"You shouldn't be here," she said.

"I'm sorry to just show up like this, but you haven't given me many options. You don't answer my calls or return my messages. There are important things I need to tell you about the Keeper's Log. Believe me, I wish I'd never even seen this damn thing," he said, holding the book up.

"But I did. And I know what's in it, and — believe me — it's something you need to know too."

Renie let out a sigh of resignation and opened the door wider. "Come in, but you'll have to make it fast, my mother and aunt will be home soon."

Renie led Mark through the living room. The oil painting of Uncle Pete leaning against the lighthouse door hung above the mantel. Mark followed her into the kitchen. She glanced at the clock, and then folded her arms across her chest and turned to face him.

"When did your father die?" he blurted out.

"My father passed away a *long* time ago."

"When did he die?"

"I don't see what…"

"Please."

Renie sighed again. "May, 1975, all right? Are we done now, Mark?"

"No, you have to finish the Keeper's Log."

"*Excuse* me? I don't *have* to do anything."

"No, of course, you're right. What I mean is you really *should* finish it."

She appraised him for a few moments, and then stared at the Keeper's Log in his outstretched hand before fully extending her hand, palm up.

*M*ay 2, 1975
        That bastard fisherman is back. We had such a beautiful week: talking, painting, making love. Renata knows all about plants, and it's a good thing, because I've already forgotten a lot of what Bridey taught me. She helped me get a lot of veggies into the ground and told me what kind of annuals to get. She doesn't know it yet, but the three lilac bushes I ordered through a catalogue arrived today: one purple, one pink, and one white. She's gonna be surprised.

Mark knew that Renie was about to turn the page to the final entry, dated May 4, 1975. This was the moment he had been dreading. He needed to somehow prepare her for what was to come.

"Renie, wait."

Startled, she looked to Mark for an explanation.

"Before you read any more," he said, "there's something I have to tell you…"

The kitchen door opened. Mamãe and Branca walked in carrying brown paper bags full of groceries. Branca looked at Mark. With a deep Portuguese accent, she said "Ooo, who have we here?"

Renie said, "It's not what you think, Auntie Branca." Renie turned to her mother. "Mamãe, this is Mark Valente…"

Auntie Branca cut Renie off. "Nice to meet you, Mark Valente." She stuck out her hand to shakes Mark's. "You be good to my little niece, she is a keeper. Are you Portuguese, by any chance?"

FOR RENATA

"Half," Mark said, flustered. "From my father's side of the family."

"Auntie Branca, please," Renie said. "Mamãe, Peter Ahearn, the light keeper, is Mark's *uncle*."

Mark noticed that Renie had put a strange emphasis on the word *uncle*.

Mamãe turned to Branca. In an identical accent she said, "Thank you, Branca, I will call you later."

"Let me at least help you put the groceries away," said Branca.

"Branca, I love you like a sister, but go now."

"That is because I *am* your sister, and, as your sister, I forgive you. But you better tell me everything later," Auntie Branca cooed as she left, closing the door behind her.

Mamãe turned back to Renie. "What's wrong, meu coração?"

"Oh, Mamãe," Renie cried as she fell into her mother's arms. Mamãe glared at Mark as she comforted her daughter.

"Mrs. Raposo, my Uncle Pete is at the Soldiers' Home near Boston…"

Mamãe gasped.

"…Pete suffers from dementia and can't live on his own anymore. This is a journal he kept when he was the light keeper here, and in it he…well, he confesses to something that impacts you and your daughter."

Still holding on to Mamãe, Renie looked up at her and then at Mark. "I was just about to read the final entry. It's dated May 4th, 1975."

Mamãe spoke after a long silence. "Thank you for coming, Mr. Valente. I am certain that this was a very difficult thing for you to do. I hope you'll understand, but my daughter and I would like to be alone now."

Mark's every instinct told him to stay. He wanted to be there for Renie. But Mrs. Raposo's tone was adamant, and he had absolutely no justification to stay after being ordered to leave.

"Of course," Mark said. "There's just one more thing, and then I'll leave you alone." He reached to the inside breast pocket of his sport coat. "My uncle has written a letter to you, Renie. It's sealed, and I want you to know I didn't open it." He held out the yellowing envelope marked *For Renata*.

The kitchen door cracked open. Auntie Branca's head popped through it. "Renata, just one quick question: Are we still meeting for lunch tomorrow?"

Renie hesitated before she answered. "Sure, I'll call you later."

"Not *you*, Renie, I'm talking to your mamãe. Of course you are welcome to come with us. Renata?"

Mark looked alternately from Branca to Renie to Mamãe. There was a long pause, and Auntie Branca looked increasingly perplexed.

Finally, Mamãe answered her, but kept her eyes focused on Mark. "Yes, lunch tomorrow, Branca."

Branca was bewildered. After a moment she shrugged. "Was that such a difficult question?" she asked. She pulled her head outside and shut the door.

FOR RENATA

Two Renatas! Mother and daughter share the same name, and one gets a nickname to avoid confusion: Renie.

Mamãe and Renie studied Mark as his eyes darted here and there, and he tried to fit this new puzzle piece together with the old ones. He thought back to the Keeper's Log and rearranged the characters in his mind, substituting mother for daughter. Not everything fit yet, but he was certain of one thing. He held the envelope out to Mamãe. "Mrs. Raposo, I think my uncle meant for *you* to have this."

Renata Raposo took the envelope from Mark slowly, turned it toward her, and read Peter Ahearn's cursive *For Renata* through misty caramel eyes. At last, she spoke. "I will go to my bedroom for some privacy, but please, both of you, wait here."

She gathered up the Keeper's Log and left Mark and her daughter standing in the kitchen.

After a while, Renie led Mark out into the backyard. Hydrangea and wild rose bushes shared a view of the sea. Speaking little, they wandered around the yard for a long time. Eventually, they found themselves on Rose Hip Point Lane, and strolled the half mile to the lighthouse.

The Atlantic Ocean pounded the cliff as it had for millennia. The two milled around the grounds in silence. Mark realized that he'd never actually been to the lighthouse, except in his imagination. He'd only seen it from ships and boats from the sea below. When a gentle mist began to fall, Mark and Renie returned to the cottage. Renie asked if he wanted coffee.

"No thanks," he said.

Renie nodded absently and turned to look at the ocean through the window above the kitchen sink. Mark moved close enough to her that he could smell the tropical scent her shampoo had left on her thick black hair.

"You knew the truth right away, didn't you?" he asked quietly.

"Not right away, but I'm sorry."

"No, that's not how I meant it. It's not an accusation. I know that you were only trying to protect your mother. But I'm still a little confused. Earlier in his journal my uncle clearly talks about a teenager."

Renie hesitated for a moment, and then turned to face him.

"That was me. I was very timid and Pete tried to draw me out. It worked. Eventually we had some lovely conversations.

"I didn't realize the truth until I read, *Her name is Renata and she's the most beautiful thing I've ever seen.* I knew then because that entry was in September, and I was back in school. And I had never painted the lighthouse, only sketched it. The painting he wrote about—the one with him in it—was done by my mother, and it's hanging in the living room. And Pete, like everyone else, called me Renie."

Renie shook her head and spoke softly, as if to herself. "After my father died, my mother never showed interest in another man. But, believe me, many men showed an interest in her. I think I understand now. I think she had found her true love in Pete. All this time…just…wasted."

"I'm sorry," Mark said. "I should never have come here."

"No, Mr. Valente," came a voice from behind him.

Mark turned around to face Renata Raposo. Her eyes were puffy and red, and she clutched the Keeper's Log and the opened letter to her breast. "You have done us a great service."

Mark gave her an embarrassed half-smile.

Renata held out the letter. "I want both of you to read this."

"That's not necessary, Mrs. Raposo."

"Please, I insist. I see from Peter's journal that you know some very intimate things already, as does my daughter." The three seemed to blush in chorus.

"But before you read the final entry, meu coração, and this letter, you deserve to know the whole story, including some things that even Peter did not know."

Renata Raposo slowly paced the kitchen floor. Mark studied her closely and realized what a handsome woman she must have been, and indeed, still was. Her hair was streaked with grey now and piled atop her head, but her skin was smooth and her body, erect and slim, like that of a dancer's — like her daughter's. Her face assumed a faraway expression and she began to speak.

55

Renata Raposo stared through the kitchen window at the sea. "I have held too many secrets for too long a time. They scratch at my heart and disturb my sleep. It is time for confessions.

"I was born in a village called Horta, on the island of Faial. The Azores were not yet the stylish tourist destination they are today. When I was young, Horta was like so many other simple fishing villages of the islands. My father was a fisherman, as was his father, and his father's father, just as my mother, and all of the women in my family were the wives and mothers of fishermen for as far back as any of us could remember. It was August 7, 1956, the evening of my fifteenth birthday. I remember feeling so happy.

"I had been running on the beach, running like the wind with my friend, Mateus. My mamãe called me to supper and told me, with great excitement, that I had been promised to a fisherman in America.

"It was quite a coup for her to have arranged my marriage to an American. It guaranteed that I would enjoy a life of comparative luxury, complete with modern appliances and even a family automobile.

"Inacio's family had emigrated some twenty years before, when he was six years old. Many people on the islands had relatives in the United States back then, but I would be the first from my family to move here. Once settled, it would be my responsibility to find a suitable husband for Branca, when she came of age.

Now the hint of a smile came to Renata's lips. "But I loved Mateus. We had been inseparable from the time we were little ones. We went to school together, and we loved to spend time together — swimming, walking for miles and hours. Sometime, at night, we snuck out to go to our Secret Place. We would lie on our backs, look at the night sky, and talk about our hopes and dreams.

"For the next year I sulked. I wrote terrible, sad poetry. I listened to mournful Fado songs of despair. And I entertained the many romantic ways in which I would end my life in the name of love."

She saw the shock that registered on Mark's face, and chuckled as she explained, "Girls of that age are often melodramático."

After a short pause, her face turned serious again.

"In a final act of defiance, I gave myself to Mateus one week before I was to leave for America.

"I saw him only once more after that. I taught myself to hate him then. But now I know it wasn't meant to be."

The old woman paused and bowed her head. Renie and Mark looked at each other and then returned their focus to Renata, who had started to speak again. "My marriage had been planned for the Saturday following my arrival in Gloucester. During the trip I had resigned myself to the arranged marriage and was determined to make a good wife and a good home for Inacio. But when I arrived, I learned that Inacio was ill with the rheumatic fever. The wedding was postponed until his recovery. At first, I was relieved."

Renata looked directly into her daughter's eyes.

"But my relief soon turned to panic as the weeks went by, and my "monthly visit" did not come. I had been too clever for my own good. Of course, it had occurred to me that I could be made pregnant, but I had assumed that I would be a married woman two weeks later. I had sinned and God was punishing me."

The realization made Mark look for Renie's reaction. Her brow furrowed a bit but Mark couldn't tell if she fully understood what her mother was telling her.

Renata took Renie's hands in hers.

"What could I do? I begged Inacio's mother to let me help care for him. I did everything I could to speed his recovery. And I prayed that my sin would never be revealed.

FOR RENATA

"As I nursed him, I flirted and stoked his desire for me. Fortunately, Inacio was young and strong and was eager to have me.

"We married five weeks after my arrival. When my time came, I tried not to let my guilt show. Inacio accepted that Renie was born prematurely."

Renie's mouth was agape and her eyes were fixed on her mother.

"My mother-in-law looked at me with suspicion, but said nothing. My deception had worked. I was spared the humiliation of being labeled a whore and shipped back to Horta.

"I was so thankful to God for a second chance that I vowed to be a virtuous and hardworking wife for Inacio. For a time we were a very happy family and, perhaps because I felt remorse for having betrayed him, I made myself love my husband. I know he loved me once."

Renata looked at Renie. "And he loved you once too, meu coração, very much."

Renata gave a heavy sigh. "But in time the truth was revealed."

56

Renata sat at the kitchen table and examined her wrinkled hands as she told Renie and Mark about the day Inacio had learned that he was sterile. "The beating began on the drive home, and then continued in the kitchen. After a while he dragged me to the bedroom, stripped me of my clothes, and whipped me like a dog. He left me there while he drank whiskey in the kitchen, then he returned to beat me more. This he repeated throughout the day and into the night.

"I remember thinking that I must accept my penance and give thanks that Renie was not there to learn the truth about me or the shame that I had brought to her. I wanted to die."

Renata rose from the table and looked at the sea through the kitchen window. "I wanted to die, and Inacio wanted to kill me.

"He came back for what I thought was another beating. But he held a knife this time instead of his belt. I thought, *I'm only twenty-one years old, but now I will die and never see my Renie again. God, I know I cannot enter Heaven, but please don't send me to Hell. Please let it be Purgatory so that I may someday be with my daughter again.*

"I cowered naked in the corner of the room, closed my eyes, and waited for death. He grabbed my hair and set the knife against my throat. He put his mouth close to my ear and I smelled whiskey. He whispered, *You deserve to die, whore. But you won't die this day. You will be the one who is barren. If you ever tell anyone otherwise, I will kill you. If you ever again become pregnant, I will slit your throats and drop you and your bastard bitch into the sea. Do you understand?*

"Yes, yes, I understand.

"He wanted to kill me. I knew he did. It was his pride that saved me. He would rather let me live than have it be known that he was not man enough to father a child and that his wife had been with another.

"Our bargain was struck. To the world, I would be the one who could no longer conceive. His reputation as a man would remain intact.

"He said, *Once a whore, always a whore.* And then, for the first of countless times to come, he used my body in shameful, unspeakable ways."

Renata paused, took in a deep breath, and turned to face Renie and Mark again.

"Around the time my sin was discovered my sister, Branca, was ready for a husband. At first Inacio forbade me to find a husband for her, but I convinced him that it would appear odd if I did not arrange for a suitable match. Eventually, he allowed it but insisted that prospective husbands not include his family or friends.

"The sister of a whore is likely a whore, he said.

"At Our Lady of Good Voyage I was able to find Fabio, a kind man. Branca and Fabio made each other very happy until the sea took him some twenty years ago.

"I often wished that the sea would take Inacio. I did not pray for it, though. God would not approve of that kind of prayer, and I hoped that He did not know of my secret wish. But God knows all.

"As the years passed I kept our bargain. I accepted my torture as God's punishment. Perhaps, I thought, I may endure purgatory here on Earth. Perhaps God will see it that way too, and take me directly into Heaven when it is time."

Renata's eyes became even sadder as she turned to look at Renie and addressed her alone. "But also, as time passed, Inacio's hatred of you grew. At first he shunned you but did not harm you physically. I could see the disgust in his face whenever he looked at you. I suppose you were, like me, a constant reminder of my treachery and of what he regarded as the challenge to his *masculinidade*.

"As you matured, you grew to look more and more like the young girl I had been: The sixteen-year-old who had betrayed Inacio—even before we met—and had tricked him into falling in love."

Renata turned to Mark. "Now his drinking was worse and the beatings more frequent. And they

included poor Renie. I did the best I could to draw
Inacio's wrath away from my daughter."

Her voice choked with emotion. "It made me
sick in my heart to know that she suffered for my
sin.

"When she was small—before my sin was
known to my husband—she was light itself, happy
and smiling from dawn to dusk. Then, in the blink
of an eye, the man she thought was her papai
spurned her. What is a little girl to think of that?
How could she understand that the fault was not
hers? There was no escape for this beautiful,
innocent lamb."

Both women had given in to tears. Renata
opened her arms wide and Renie rushed into her
embrace.

"God forgive me, meu coração, I am truly sorry
for how you suffered because of me."

They held each other tightly for a long time.
Renata broke away and cupped Renie's face in her
hands for a moment before resuming her tale.

"Because my husband was a fisherman,
moments of relief were brief but frequent,
particularly during trips to the Georges Bank, which
would take him away for several days.

"Still, we were prisoners of a sort. Although we
had an automobile, Inacio forbade me from getting
a driver's license. He or his uncle, Pio, would take
me to church, to the market, and to family
gatherings. When I was not here at Rose Hip Point, I
was under constant surveillance.

"The grounds of the lighthouse became my sanctuary. They were secluded and within walking distance. I could go there, lie down, look at the sky and pretend that Mateus was lying next to me. And I could write poetry.

"Mr. Boino, the keeper before Peter, was a very kind old gentleman. I always enjoyed drawing pictures, and when Inacio was away and Renie was at school, Mr. Boino would teach me what he knew of painting. And he gave me the supplies I needed.

"Mrs. Gallagher was also very kind to me. When Mr. Gallagher was alive, Bridey would come to Cape Ann for the summer and her husband would join her on weekends. But I did not come to know her well until her husband passed away and she came to Rose Hip Point to live the year round. I think she made an effort to befriend me because she sensed that my home life was not easy. I would go to her house and we would bake together. And as we worked, we talked of music, poetry, flowers, and other beautiful things. And we laughed. God, she could always make me laugh.

"After Mr. Boino retired and Peter became the light keeper, I stopped going to the lighthouse grounds during the daylight, but would often walk there at night.

"In Peter's journal he writes of the night he almost took his own life. I was there, outside in the cold. I saw him drape a rope across a ceiling beam — a rope with a *noose* on it. I did not know what to do. I ran down the lane to Bridey's and told her what was happening.

"She acted strangely. She cried out something I didn't understand at the time: *Oh God, Jack.*

"Then, even more strangely, she ran to the kitchen and came back with a pie and a box of tea. It was winter and very cold. She had stopped for pie and tea but no coat. She ran to the lighthouse so quickly that I had trouble keeping up with her. When we got to the lighthouse we could see Peter through the window. He was standing on a chair, the noose around his neck. Bridey pounded frantically on the door. Thank God Peter answered.

"I waited outside in the cold for almost three hours for Bridey. I draped my coat over her shoulders as we walked home. She said, *I think the danger has passed for now, but that poor boy needs help. Self-preservation is the first law of nature. If he wants to die, then his mind is not right, he's not thinking clearly. He needs a friend.* And then she told me of the tragic death of her own son, Jack. I do not think Peter ever really knew what an *anjo da guarda* he had in Bridey, what a guardian angel we both had.

"I had seen on his face the awful pain that Peter was going through. I did not know him, but everyone knew of him and what had happened during the war. I wondered if that was why he was so tired of life.

"While Inacio was away or in a drunken slumber, I went to the lighthouse to spy on Peter night after night for weeks that winter. He seemed to improve after he saved two people from drowning. His face was not pinched in torment as it had been. I think he had found purpose. This I understood, for my purpose was my daughter. If not for her, I would certainly have fashioned my own noose long before then."

Renie's head tilted and her lips quivered.

"It would be another year and a half before Peter and I would meet. In the summer of 1974, Renie had begun to spend a lot of time sketching on the lighthouse grounds. She would come home in the late afternoon and tell me of the young man who was keeper and how nice he seemed.

"You know from his journal that Peter and I met for the first time that September. Inacio was at the Georges Bank and Renie was back at school."

Renata looked to her daughter with pleading eyes. "You must believe me when I say that I never intended or imagined anything more than friendship at that time. The memory of my first sin was always with me and I had no desire to bring more shame to my family.

"But as Peter and I spent time together I began to rediscover feelings that were long lost to me, the way I had felt as a carefree girl with Mateus. My heart became lighter and raced with anticipation instead of fear. And I blushed with affection instead of shame. For the first time in a dozen years I heard words of kindness and encouragement instead of insult and blame.

"God forgive me, I was so hungry for compassion and affection that I could not stop myself from loving this man. And what a man! Without an arm and an eye, still more of a man than any ten together I have ever known. You will never grasp the depth of his kindness and understanding from this journal. He was far too modest for that. Nor could you ever sense the depth of our feelings for each other.

"It was the end of April, 1975. We were at the lighthouse and I told Peter of my sin because I did not want to keep secrets from him or to allow a lie to pass from my lips to his ears. Do you know what he said to me? *You were guilty only of being a young girl in love. The God that I know would never punish a girl the way you have punished yourself. And He would never want you to be tortured by a sadistic husband. Go home, look at your daughter, and ask yourself: If Renie did the same thing would I want the rest of her life to be spent in a living hell? Does God not forgive, especially the young?*

"*Go home, look at your daughter, and then forgive yourself.*

"I did. I went home and embraced my Renie and forgave myself. Forgiveness from within.

"I gained new strength after that. Peter had implored me to take Renie and come to stay at the lighthouse under his protection until he could make arrangements for the three of us to move elsewhere and begin anew. But I did not have the courage. I was certain that Inacio would come to the lighthouse and kill us all.

"We would have just ten more blissful days after that. On the evening of May third, Inacio was already drunk and in a foul mood when he came home. I knew what our fate would be for that night. When the violence started, I drew his attention to

320

me and away from Renie. This I had accomplished before by baiting him with insults to his manhood. It would increase his fury, I knew, but aim his blows at me."

The tears had stopped and Renata's voice was stronger.

"Now you must read Peter's final entry in the Keeper's Log, and then the letter he wrote to me so long ago."

FOR RENATA

57

May 4, 1975
Last night I walked down to Renata's house and stood in the lane, watching. It was deathly quiet for a long time before the yelling started. I heard the bastard's voice first, slurring his filthy words, and then I heard the smacks followed by screams. I wanted to break the door down and beat the shit out of him. But I didn't. She had begged me not to do anything. It would only make things worse, she'd said. The house went quiet again, so I had started up the lane for home when I heard the bastard yell, "Don't worry, I'll come back." as the front door creaked open...

Inacio Raposo slammed the front door as hard as he could and almost broke the whiskey bottle he carried. He staggered down the steps and out to the lane, then turned in the direction of the lighthouse. Peter stepped back into the bushes and watched Inacio zigzag up the lane, stopping every once in a while for a chug.

Then he started singing. "He's a one-eyed, one-armed, flying purple lighthouse keeper."

When Inacio got to the lighthouse, he quieted. He tiptoed up to the living room window and peeked inside. After a few moments, he shrugged and then staggered to the cliff's edge. He chuckled, tossed the empty whiskey bottle into the dark abyss, and unzipped his fly.

Peter stepped quietly from the shadows. He looked at Inacio's back. How easy it would be—a little shove, and Renata's suffering would be over. He extended his right arm, locked it like a football player who is straight-arming, and started forward. But then he stopped. *This would be murder. What would I say to Renata? Say to her! There would be nothing to say, I'd lose her forever.*

Just then, Inacio finished and pulled up his zipper. He turned around, and was startled to find Peter staring at him from a few feet away. The fisherman recovered his composure and sobriety quickly. He tossed his head back. "Hey, *Branquelo*, I've been looking for you."

Peter neither moved nor spoke.

"I met an old friend of yours," Inacio grinned. "You remember Cindy. She told me she dumped you because you were not enough of a man for her. She said she needs a whole man.

"She told me how you like my wife. I was laughing so hard I almost pissed my pants. I told Renata and she couldn't stop laughing either. She said *What would I do with half a man?*

"Don't you know what a joke you are, *Branquelo*? No woman wants half a man.

"I feel sorry for you but, still, this is a matter of honor. I can't let this go unpunished, even if you are a gimp."

Inacio pulled a large switchblade from the back pocket of his blue jeans. He flicked the knife open and flashed a greasy smile as he tossed it from hand to hand and shifted his weight from foot to foot in a show of dexterity and balance. Peter's eye widened and he stepped back.

"Don't look so scared, *Branquelo*," Inacio said. "I won't kill you this night. I'll just leave you with a few mementos, scars that will remind you not to fuck with a *whole* man.

Then he shrugged, adding, "Or maybe I'll take your other arm. I don't know, I'll see how I feel."

Keeping his eye on the knife, Peter took another step back. Inacio moved to his left, and Peter did the same. The fisherman grinned as he made feint lunges at Peter. He pretended to stumble, and followed with a lightning-speed backhanded slash that left a deep slice in Peter's right cheek.

Peter tasted his own blood. Inacio continued to move left. The two men matched each other move for move in a circular dance. Peter's whole body stiffened when he realized that his heels were touching the edge of the cliff. For a split second he looked to his right and saw only darkness below.

Inacio chuckled. He wagged his knife at Peter, and sneered, "This is your lucky day, *Branquelo*. All this excitement has my blood racing. I think I need to go home and fuck my wife's ass."

Peter became incensed and charged the fisherman.

But Inacio brought the knife to Peter's throat and stopped him in his tracks. "You should have listened to me when I tried to help you: There are skanks down by the waterfront that will fuck even a pathetic freak like you. That's the only kind of woman you'll ever have."

Inacio took a step back, and turned. Then he stopped, swiveled his head back, and shook the knife at Peter one more time. "Remember, *Branquelo*, stay away from her."

Adrenaline coursed through Peter. "NO!" he cried, "*You* stay away from her."

Peter lunged forward and grabbed hold of Inacio's collar, and the two men locked eyes.

Rage showed in Peter's deep blue eye. His breaths were short and rapid.

Inacio inhaled deeply and swallowed hard.

After a long moment, the madness in Peter's eye drained away and was replaced by sadness.

The fisherman breathed a sigh of relief, and then smirked.

But in a heartbeat the look in Peter's eye changed again. The sadness became a steely coldness.

With his right hand and arm, over the years grown half again as strong the average man's, Peter Ahearn gave a mighty pull and launched Inacio Raposo over the cliff's edge, and into the blackness.

FOR RENATA

58

It was late at night when Peter returned to the lighthouse. Far out at sea faint bolts of lightning, veiled by dark clouds, flashed randomly in the night sky. He stood on the wide granite doorstep, worn smooth over time by the elements and the boots of light keepers. He looked around, and pondered the place that had been his home since he was barely twenty.

It was too dark to make out the detail of the lighthouse grounds, but Peter could picture every square inch of its two acres in his mind. An expanse of rolling lawn scarred here and there by jutting limestone covered most of the land. He had fertilized the lawn, and tender green shoots of grass had begun to overtake the brown scrub left by winter.

Peter knew that a low hedge of forsythia near the shed was in bloom now. He had seen its bright yellow flowers earlier that day. But he could also picture the same bushes in late summer, blossomless and lush with green leaves, or winter-bare, with thin branches coated with ice or sprinkled with snow. He kept the hedge trimmed low. Nothing was allowed to grow high enough to obscure the tower light.

A few days ago, three mail-ordered lilac bushes had arrived, a surprise for Renata. He planted them near the picket fence that enclosed the vegetable garden. It occurred to him now that, as they grew, the lilacs would rob the garden of sunlight. There would be no time to move them.

He had lived with the Atlantic through all of her moods. He'd seen her docile, so calm and smooth she might be sleeping. At times she was playful, rippling and rolling, and changing her color because some cottony clouds had floated across the blue sky and eclipsed the sun. But she angered easily, especially in autumn, and could turn choppy and aloof without warning. And on occasion she became crazed, conspiring with wind and rain to raise a fury such that women scorned and all of hell should sit quietly and take notes.

The narrow point had been home to Peter for only three years of his young life, but it was the place where he had known his greatest elation, and his deepest despair. And now he would pack up the few things that were his and leave it forever.

He wiped his boots on the doorstep. Despite a cool east wind that gusted from the sea and made his khaki pants and denim shirt billow, he streamed sweat that stung his eye and plastered his long hair to the back of his neck. The storm would be fast-moving, he knew, with winds quite possibly reaching gale-force. He had checked the back-up generators. The beacon had to shine even if electric power was cut by the storm. People counted on it.

Peter stepped into the light keeper's quarters and slowly surveyed the place. His gaze settled on the one thing he had put on the wall since becoming light keeper. His Silver Lifesaving Medal hung crooked. Bridey Gallagher had framed it for him, and together they'd chosen the spot to hang it, between the two front living room windows. Peter had held the nail while Bridey held a hammer in her wrinkled hand, and gingerly tapped until the picture hook became anchored in the brittle horsehair plaster.

Peter trudged across the room and reached out to straighten his award. When he pulled his hand back he saw that the picture frame now had a small dark-red smear on it. He examined his bloody fingers, brought them to his cheek, and felt the slice that stretched from his right earlobe to almost the corner of his mouth. The wound was fresh and sore. There was Mercurochrome in the medicine cabinet, he was sure of it.

Thunder rumbled. He looked down at his shirt to where the pocket should be. The flap was there but the pocket itself was missing. Tiny pieces of white thread showed around the seam where it had been sewn to the shirt. He wondered if the dead fisherman still clutched the cloth in his hand.

He thought about the Mercurochrome again for a moment but decided he should call the Coast Guard first. The light couldn't go unattended, even for a day.

The lightning grew brighter and the thunder louder. The wind whistled and groaned as it struck the house, and then caromed off. Peter reached for the phone. A blinding flash of light was followed shortly by a loud *CRACK*, and all of Rose Hip Point, and the village of Hollistown Harbor at its base, were plunged into darkness so complete that he could see nothing between flashes of lightning. A moment later he heard the main generator kick in. The light would continue its signal.

Peter felt his way along to a kitchen drawer that held a flashlight. A bright lightning strike revealed an obscure form outside as it floated past the window, toward the front door. Several eerie seconds of silence passed before a deafening thunderclap grabbed the tiny house and shook it.

More silence.

A soft rap on the door.

After a moment, the raps became thumps and his name was called.

"Peter."

Renata. Why is she here?

"Peter, please." There were tears in her plea.

He moved to one side of the window, peeled the curtain edge an inch from the window frame, and peeked into blackness.

Another flash and he saw her for an instant. She stood on the granite doorstep. Her long black hair, hair he had coiled playfully around his fingers, was so saturated with the driving rain that rivulets of storm water trickled from the ends. Her eyes, entrancing caramel eyes in which he had so happily become lost, were swollen and streamed mascara to the corners of her coral lips. Her dress was soaked and clung to her body—the body that had fit his as if it had been fashioned for that purpose alone.

My soul is yours, and my body too, she had whispered to him. And he had discovered the depths of each. He had looked into her soul and felt it within his own. He had explored every region of her body, joined and moved with her until they were spent, and then rested his head upon her warm breast and listened to the beating of her heart.

Renata pounded on the door. Peter moved away from the window, toward the door, and the pounding stopped. Perhaps she sensed him there, sensed that only two inches of ancient wood stood between them.

He imagined the door opening and the two of them rushing into each other's arms, never to let go. Their pain would be over, their hearts weightless again.

He reached out for the heavy bolt with a trembling hand-and then stopped. He brought his hand to his forehead and backed away from the door. He drew his fingers through his long, blond hair, made a fist, and pulled it tight. His face reddened and twisted.

Renata called out to him, "Eu te amo," *I love you*, and it was more than he could bear. He turned and fled along wide, glowing pine floorboards. He crossed the kitchen, and followed the short passageway that led to the tower. He raced up eighty-nine spiral steps to the lantern room and began to pace. He walked the catwalk encircling the enormous glass lens, and pumped his fist in angst. He cried out, "NO!" He punched the thick, rippled glass with all his might, and then disregarded the pain that shot through his fist and traveled up his arm to his shoulder.

The giant lens was unscathed and continued to flash its intermittent beam through the maelstrom and across the roiling sea for miles upon miles.

The lightning was closer and had grown to the power of a thousand lighthouses. It seemed to mock with each violent blaze and following roar. A lengthy flash turned night into day, and Peter saw her again.

Renata stood in the center of the lighthouse grounds and looked up at him with pleading eyes. She screamed to him but her words were swallowed by the howling tempest and didn't reach him.

He felt an aching in his chest. Never had he felt so helpless, or so hopeless.

Pitch-black returned. At once, Peter felt relieved that he could not see her agony, and yet squinted to find her again. Another flash...Renata stood with arms outstretched, and screamed up to him again, her beautiful face twisted in anguish.

"I can't," he whispered.

Again she was lost to him in the darkness. His heart was breaking, he could feel it.

FOR RENATA

When, at last, the lightning flashed again, Renata fell to her knees. She tilted her head back. Merciless, slanting rain pelted her face and throat. She clutched her breast and cried out to the heavens. Peter knew she was beseeching God.

He whispered, "Forgive me, Renata. Amo-te com todo meu curacao." *I love you with all my heart.*

59

Renie finished reading. She closed the Keeper's Log slowly and then looked at her mother through teary eyes.

Renata Raposo stood ramrod straight, and with a resolute expression, unfolded the yellowed letter, placed it on the kitchen table. "Now the letter. Both of you."

My One True Love,

I know how much I hurt you. I stood in the lighthouse and listened to you pound on my door and cry out through the rain. It tore me apart to hear you in such pain. I wanted to run to you and hold you and never let you go. But I couldn't come to you, not after what I've done. Your husband's death was no accident. I killed him.

I just couldn't stand the idea of him or anybody else hurting you. And now I have to live with what I've done. But how can I face you? If I tell you what I've done, you will never look at me the same way again. If I don't tell you, how can I ever look into your eyes again? I knew at the moment I made my decision that I would lose you forever.

I never told you this, but you healed me. You brought the pieces of my broken heart together and made it feel light again. But now there is a hole in my heart, in the shape of you, which no one else can ever fill.

I wish for two things with all my soul: that you and Renie live happily and without fear, and that you will find it in your heart to forgive me.

I love you with all my heart.

Renie and Mark finished reading within moments of each other. Renie broke the silence.

"Oh, Mamãe," she cried as she rushed to her mother's embrace.

"It's all right, meu coração, it's all right." Renata looked at her daughter, gently brushed a few strands of tear-stained hair away from Renie's eyes, and then kissed her forehead.

After a moment, a far-away look crossed Renata's face. Her story was not over.

"My attempts to draw Inacio's attention away from you did not work for long that night. He had hurt you worse than ever before. Inacio slapped you so hard you were knocked to the floor.

Renie remembered: "Papai, please," she had begged. He had stood over her, kicked her, and screamed hateful things that made no sense to her until now. *Don't call me that anymore. You're nothing to me— just the filthy spawn of a filthy whore.*

B. ROBERT SHARRY

Renata continued, "You were in shock, I think, and almost unconscious. I helped you to your bed and told you to stay there.

"Something else was different that night—the way he looked at you. It was not the way a man looks at a daughter.

"*Do not even think it, pig*, I said to him.

"He beat me to the floor, kicked the breath out of me, and stood over me. *Before you dare tell me what to think, whore, let me tell you what I know. I know about you and your gimp. I know what you do when I am gone. Is half a man the best you could do? Did you think I wouldn't find out? Whores are always found out for what they are. So, don't tell me what to think, puta. I think the little bitch is no relation to me — just the bastard daughter of a whore who will be a whore herself, if she isn't already. That little cona has to be broken in sometime. It would be nice to have some that's not so old and stretched out.*

"Then he laughed and said *Now, if you will excuse me, puta, I have a matter of honor to attend to. Don't worry, though, I'll come back.*

"I knew he was going for Peter. And then I heard him singing that awful song the children used to chant about Peter. And I wasn't afraid any more. I stopped crying and I stopped shaking and I went to the kitchen and grabbed the biggest knife. I went out the back door and moved as quickly and as quietly as I could. I remember thinking *One of us will not survive this night.* I was going to kill him, and then I was going to come home and get you, and run away. I could not think beyond that.

FOR RENATA

"When I got to the lighthouse, I hid behind a forsythia bush. I saw him standing on the edge of the cliff with his back turned and thought, *This is my chance.* Just as I started toward him, Peter came from the shadows.

"There was a brief scuffle, but Inacio had begun to walk away. Then, all of a sudden, Peter grabbed Inacio and threw him from the cliff. It all happened so fast. I stood there, stunned. Now I was staring at Peter's back where just a moment before I had been staring at my husband's.

"I started to go to Peter, but I stopped when I saw the way his shoulders were slumped and his head was bowed. I knew he felt ashamed.

"After a long time he turned away, and I ducked back behind the bush and watched him walk into the lighthouse.

"I started for home but stopped short when I had an awful thought: *What if he's not dead?*

"I crept down the cliff path and looked for him. But before I saw him, I heard him. He was not moving, but he was moaning, and that meant he was still alive. And if he was still alive, he could still hurt us."

Anticipating what her mother was about to say, Renie shook her head slowly from side to side.

"Inacio lay on his back in water up to his chin. I knelt beside him, turned his face sideways and held it there. And when I was sure he could not hurt us anymore, I said, *See how they like your singing in Hell.*"

Stunned, Mark and Renie exchanged glances.

What Renata *hadn't* told them, had never told anyone—even Padre Abade when she later confessed to him what she had done—what she *would* never tell anyone, were Inacio's final words.

As she knelt beside him, Inacio stopped moaning and opened his eyes. His face was serene. He gazed into her eyes and she had the feeling that he knew what she was planning, what blackness and rage was in her mind and heart. Then he shocked her.

"I loved you so much," Inacio said softly.

Renata was already weeping but Inacio's surprising declaration made her hesitate and choke with emotion. Scenes from their happy years together played through her mind. She mourned those years, and regarded her husband with eyes full of sorrow and remorse.

Then, in an instant, the serenity left Inacio's face. He sneered and added a final word. "Whore."

Renata's head was bowed. She looked up to find Mark and Renie staring at her, expectantly. She cleared her throat. "The wind had picked up and it had begun to rain. I returned to the lighthouse. As you read in Peter's letter to me, I pounded on the door. I had to tell him what I had done.

"But he would not come to me. I ran out to the middle of the yard and, for just an instant, I saw his silhouette high up in the lantern room. I screamed until I became hoarse—telling Peter how much I loved and needed him, and the truth about Inacio. But the storm was louder than I and drowned out my words. Finally, when no more sound could come from my throat, I fell to the ground trembling, pleading with God to reach down and wrench the aching heart from my breast.

"I was hysterical. I screamed and wept, wept and screamed until I fell unconscious. I remember opening my eyes and seeing Peter's face above me for a moment. I thought I was dreaming. But when I awoke again, I was at home, in my own bed, and knew that he had carried me there.

"I went into my daughter's bedroom. I lay down beside her, held her, and slept too well for what I had done.

"The next morning the police arrived. They said they had found Inacio's body. But the place where he was discovered was far from the lighthouse. It occurred to me that I had left Inacio at low tide. During the night, the tide had risen some ten feet and carried him away.

"I told part of the truth to the police, that Inacio had been drunk, had beaten us, and that I had heard him singing as he went for a walk. But I told them that I was certain he had walked in the opposite direction, toward town. I told them all of this as evenly as if I was saying nothing more significant than *have a nice day*.

"One of the officers was Portuguese. I knew him from church and knew that he was the son of a fisherman. He looked at our battered faces and bruised arms and hung his head as if in shame.

"That day Peter was gone, and two coastguardsmen had taken his place. As far as I know the police never looked for Peter. They must have accepted my story. Inacio's death was ruled *accidental*.

"One month later Father Abade from Our Lady of Good Voyage took me to the rectory after mass. He gave me a thick envelope that contained an enormous amount of cash, twenty-four thousand and three hundred dollars. I begged him to tell me where Peter was, but he swore he did not know.

"I was able to pay off the debt on the house, and with the remainder, open my little bakery.

"Over the years, there were more envelopes of cash — usually a few hundred dollars at a time. They were always delivered by the same priest."

Renata stared into the middle distance. "We were ten years apart in age, but there was no distance between our hearts. We were two broken souls who, for a brief, beautiful time, became one whole."

A long silence followed, after which Mark stood from the kitchen table, and addressed the two Renatas. "I don't know if I've done the right thing or not, but I can promise you both that I will never repeat what I've heard here today, and that I won't ever bother you again."

Renata Raposo smiled kindly. "But you must come back, Mark, you are family. You see, I have *two* daughters: My youngest was born after Inacio's death. People assumed that God had blessed me with a miracle baby to honor Inacio. She has luxuriant, black hair like Renie's...and like mine when I was young. But her eyes are not like ours, they are the deep blue of the sea—the eyes of her father. She is called Pedra. In Portuguese this is the feminine form of Peter."

Renata's smile slowly evaporated. She stood very erect and locked hers eyes with Mark's.

"Take me to him."

B. ROBERT SHARRY

60

Renata, Renie, and Mark walked the hallway of the Soldiers' Home toward Peter's room. Renata stopped short when a familiar figure approached from the opposite direction.

"Padre Abade?" Renata said.

The priest stopped and answered sheepishly. "Hello, Renata."

"Why are you here, Padre?" she asked in a tone that said *I already know you're your answer but I want to hear you say it.*

"I came to visit an old friend," the priest said.

"Is this friend known to me, Padre?"

The priest's eyes sought the floor.

"You said you didn't know where he was, Padre. It was you who brought him here."

"No, Renata, I've never lied to you."

"Then how…" she regarded the priest, and then darted her eyes around as she thought. Her expression changed when the truth came to her. "You can't say. You're bound by the seal. He confessed to you—long ago, he confessed to you when he gave you the money for me."

She turned her eyes back to the priest. "But you heard my confession too, Padre, and you never told Peter? I would have released you from the seal of the confessional."

The priest looked into her eyes. "Sometimes, one's sacred vow and one's heart can be at odds with each other.

"Go to him, Renata. He needs you." With that, the priest went on his way.

The three continued down the long hallway until they reached Peter's room and stood just inside the doorway. The image of Warren Beatty and Natalie Wood filled the muted television screen. Peter sat in the same chair beside his bed that he had been in every time Mark visited. An orderly was changing the bed linen.

Renie addressed the orderly while staring at Peter's profile. "I understand Mr. Ahearn speaks sometimes."

"Yeah, if you can call it that. Doc says it might be Vietnamese, or it might be just plain nonsense."

Renata moved in front of Peter and slowly knelt down before him. Around Peter's neck hung a piece of cobalt glass, held in place by a rawhide shoelace. Peter turned his gaze from the television to the caramel eyes before him.

"*Mee nall may soo ah*," Peter said softly, a smile lit his face.

B. ROBERT SHARRY

"See? I told you," said the orderly.

But to everyone's astonishment, Renata answered him, tears streaming from her eyes.

Renie gasped and raised her hand to her mouth. "My God," she breathed.

"What?" Mark said. "What is it?"

Renie shook her head slowly from side to side. "It's not Vietnamese and it's not nonsense. It's Portuguese."

Without moving her eyes from Peter's, Renata repeated the words softly. Minha alma é sua...e meu corpo também. Amo-te com todo meu coração. These are the words of love I spoke to him the first time...and every time."

Renata's voice choked with emotion, "The words mean, *My soul is yours...and my body too. I love you with all my heart.*"

Peter stroked Renata's tear-streaked cheek with the back of his hand. "Minha alma é sua...e meu corpo também. Amo-te com todo meu coração."

"Yes, meu amor. You made me whisper those words to you over and over again, *So that I will never forget*, you said."

Renata fingered the deep-blue sea glass that hung from Peter's neck. "You must be that brave cabin boy I met a lifetime ago." She cupped Peter's face in her hands and searched it with her eyes.

Peter spoke. "And you must be that beautiful princess."

Renata wept. Her voice shook. "You remember."

A single tear rolled from Peter's eye. "Forgive me."

FOR RENATA

"Forgive you, meu amor? Forgive you for saving my life and the life of my daughter? For your kindness? For loving me? You have no need of forgiveness from me. You need only do what you taught me so long ago: Forgive yourself."

61

Renie and Mark fell back several paces and watched as Peter, Renata, and their daughter, Pedra, strolled arm-in-arm on Rose Hip Point.

Like so many things in life, the lighthouse had been modernized and was automated now. It had been since 1989.

"I hope your mother hasn't taken on more than she can handle," Mark said.

Renie shook her head. "Mamãe is a very strong woman. I wouldn't underestimate her. And Pedra and I will help her. We all realize that Pete will never get better. And when the time comes when we aren't able to care for him anymore, I suppose he will return to the Soldiers' Home. But until then: Just look at how happy they are."

Mark breathed in a large dose of salt air and turned to face Renie. "Nervous about your trip?"

"Maybe a little," she said. "It's not every day you get to meet your biological father. But I've always wanted to see Portugal and the Azores, where Mamãe grew up."

"Does Mateus still live in Horta?"

"No. He's an artist, and for more than forty years he's been living very happily in Lisbon with his partner, a retired dentist named Roberto."

Still arm-in-arm, Renata, Peter, and Pedra stopped at the lighthouse to admire three mature lilac bushes in full bloom: one purple, one pink, and one white.

"I'd like to talk to you when you get back. Maybe we could have dinner?" Mark asked.

Renie looked into his eyes and smiled. "I'd like that."

Acknowledgements

Many family and friends have given encouragement for which I will be eternally grateful.

A special thanks to my longtime friend, Paul G. O'Connor, a gifted and award winning writer, for countless hours of inspiration, invaluable suggestions, and great advice.

UQTT